THE STORIES WE KEEP

SHAWNA HOLLY

THREE SPARROWS
PUBLISHING

First edition published 2023.
Three Sparrows Publishing, Boerne, TX

ISBN 979-8-9879662-0-4 (paperback)
ISBN 979-8-9879662-1-1 (ebook)

Cover Design by Esther van Bokhorst-Beentjes, Meraki Cover Design

AUTHOR'S NOTE

This is a story of a mother with depression whose thoughts are often guided by her illness. It is not a story meant to glorify depression, anxiety, intrusive thoughts, or suicidal ideation. Nor is it meant to say that all parents experience the things our protagonist does.

If you are currently experiencing any form of distress or crisis and are located in the U.S., please call or text 988 to reach the national Suicide & Crisis Lifeline.

For those who prefer them, a full list of content warnings can be found on the last page of this book.

PLAYLIST

1. "Intro" by The xx
2. "Lovely (with Khalid)" by Billie Eilish, Khalid
3. "Blur" by MØ
4. "Lonely Day" by System Of A Down
5. "Piece by Piece" by Feeder
6. "Where Is My Mind?" by Pixies
7. "Chlorine" by Twenty One Pilots
8. "Run Away to Mars" by TALK
9. "Line Of Fire" by Junip
10. "Only If You Run" by Julian Plenti
11. "Lose Your Soul" by Dead Man's Bones
12. "Iron" by Woodkid
13. "Lonely Soul" by UNKLE, Richard Ashcroft
14. "Special Death" by Mirah
15. "Open Passageways" by All Them Witches
16. "Burning" by Yeah Yeah Yeahs
17. "Curious/furious" by WILLOW
18. "Grace" by Marcus Mumford
19. "Don't Panic" by Coldplay

1

RAIN

What I wouldn't give to be the type of mom who remembers an umbrella and wears weather-appropriate shoes.

This morning, though, I was lucky to get everyone dressed and out of the house on time—or ten minutes late, which is "on time" enough, anyway. The weather was the least of my concerns.

"Are you ready to see Ms. Maggie and Henry?" I ask Noah while unbuckling my seat belt.

"Yup. Noah like Henry," he answers.

"Good. We have to hurry, though. Can we do that?"

He nods.

"All right, here we go!" I pull the hood of my fleece jacket up over my head, grab the diaper bag from the passenger side, then place it in the driver's seat as I step out of the car and shut the door. I push the button to open Noah's door and it slides back on its rails so slowly that for a moment, I wonder if it's broken.

I unbuckle Noah, place him on my hip, then push the button to close his door while opening mine again to grab the bag. As we begin the journey across the black parking lot river to the entrance of the coffee shop, there are no puddles to dodge. The whole lot is a greasy gazpacho of oily water, fast food trash, and fallen leaves. It covers the top of my running shoes and as I trudge forward, splashes my leggings clear up to the knees.

I step onto the sidewalk, under the cover of the awning perched above the door. Glancing through the glass, I see Maggie sitting with Henry. They're smiling and playing peek-a-boo as they wait for us to arrive.

I yank the hood off my head and set Noah to stand at my feet. Pulling the elastic from my ponytail, I shake out my hair and attempt to smooth it all back into place and re-tie it again. Taking Noah's hand, we move the one step needed to reach the handle. Just as I place my hand upon it, I'm hit right smack on top of the head by a giant, shockingly cold raindrop. Looking up, I see a gap about an inch wide between the back edge of the awning and the building. Another fat drop pelts me right between the eyes.

A frustrated growl escapes my lips as I dab the top of my head and my face with the sleeve of my jacket and take Noah's hand again.

"Are you going in?" someone asks from behind me.

I look over my shoulder to find a short, stocky man in a trench coat and tie, reaching around me for the door. I step to the right with Noah as he opens it for us, then my eyes meet Maggie's as we enter.

Maggie and I met several summers back while she was working at the local library. I had just two kids then—a two-year-old and a newborn. Dozing in and out of consciousness while sitting on the floor and leaning against the wall in the play area, I felt a tap on my shoulder. When I opened my eyes, I saw Maggie standing with a halo around her head—a literal halo cast from the building's fluorescent overhead lights.

That's when she told me I couldn't sleep in the library anymore. Then she offered me her name and phone number and directed me to call if I ever needed a babysitter—or a break.

We kept in touch and while Maggie and I don't see each other every day, or even every month, she's the closest thing I have to a real friend outside of those I left behind in Alabama so many years ago.

Regardless of that, though, there are still many days in which Maggie is a bit too much to bear—she's a person who is deliriously happy all the time. The glass is always half-full with Maggie and I can already sense how this coffee date is going to go. Particularly, that today is not a day in which I feel capable of placating Maggie's optimism, nor energized enough to try hopping onto her "good vibes only" train.

"Look at you!" she says, as we approach the table.

"I know, I know. But we're fine." I set Noah into the empty highchair next to Henry's, then tug off my rain-soaked fleece and Noah's equally soaked hoodie. I rub my upper arms for warmth—wishing I could do the same for my cold, wet feet.

Maggie's already ordered my black coffee as well as pastries and kolaches, so I take a careful sip, measuring just how late we are by how cold the coffee has become. *Still lukewarm, so not terribly late.* "Thanks for the coffee," I tell her.

"Of course. Seems like all I do these days is drink coffee, tea, hot cocoa—anything warm to take the edge off all this rain. Have you ever seen so much rain?" Maggie asks.

"Not here, I haven't. Weeks of it. It's just crazy."

"Are you guys going to the parade in San Antonio this weekend? I mean, if the weather cooperates for it?" Maggie blows on her latte, which is topped with a frothy, milky-white heart.

She, of course, thought to bring her umbrella and appears completely comfortable in a fuzzy, pastel pink sweater. A large, beautiful gold hair pin holds her perfectly un-perfect mom-bun in place and matching gold statement earrings dial up the look.

"I don't think so. I should probably work."

Billie Holiday croons one of my favorite songs in the background. I look down at my mug of coffee and close my eyes—just for a moment—to escape into the song's smooth chorus.

"Jenna, I don't know how you do it—stay home with three kids and work, too." She wipes a crumb from Henry's chin as he swipes the rest of his pastry off the table, sending crimson-red raspberry jam splattering across the impeccably clean black and white penny tile floor.

"Well, I don't always do it gracefully." I tear a kolache into small pieces with my fingers and place them, two at a time, in front of Noah.

"Grace or not, it's impressive. I consider it a good day if I've managed to shower," Maggie says with a chuckle.

"What? You still shower?"

"Girl—" She laughs.

"I didn't get the memo that a shower was a requirement for this coffee date, sorry."

"Stop it." She laughs again, but this time it's that uncomfortable one people give when you've said something that rings true, but they don't want to admit it.

I sweep a loose strand of hair that didn't make it back into my ponytail behind my ear. Why didn't I at least ditch the leggings and opt for real pants?

"Tell me about this new friend of yours. What's her name again?" Maggie asks.

"Bonnie," I say.

"Right. How did you meet her, anyway?" Maggie hands Henry another full-sized pastry—chocolate this time—and I'm tempted to set a timer to see how long before he throws this one on the floor, too.

"I saw her sitting on the park bench by St. Paul's a couple times, always alone. So, one day as I was walking by with Noah, I said hello and asked if she needed help. I assumed she was senile or lost."

"That wasn't the case?" she asks.

"Um, no. That woman hasn't needed saving a day in her life."

Bonnie's sweet, strong, and slightly stubborn by nature. She's not someone who could often, if ever, have been described as a 'damsel in distress.'

Maggie sips her latte with a petite little slurp. "And now, you guys—what—hang out?"

"Noah and I visit her once a week. Her house is gorgeous. She has hundreds of books—and these three giant, antique crystal chandeliers you'd have to see to believe."

"Sounds nice. I wish I had a place like that to escape to once a week. Though it seems a little *Tuesdays with Morrie*-ish to me."

That's not a similarity that's struck me before, but if Bonnie was willing and able to impart some sort of wisdom on how to find tangible happiness in life, I'd certainly listen.

"Well, she isn't sick that I'm aware of, and her stories are definitely way more risqué," I say with a raised eyebrow and a hint of a smirk, which catches me by surprise.

"Hmm—I might need to meet this lady," Maggie says with another slurp.

"No way, get your own old lady bestie!" I pretend to shoo her away and tear more tiny pieces of bread for Noah. He's not interested and shoves them both to the floor, so I hand him a milk cup instead.

Sneaking a peek at the clock on the wall, I can see I've only been at this table for twenty minutes. *God, how can time go so slow?*

"Is it weird that I have a 70-something year old friend?" I'm both trying to fill the time and genuinely interested in her answer.

"I don't think so. I think it's nice."

The bell jingles on the door as another set of moms enter with toddlers. All of them are wearing adorable, brightly patterned rain boots; the moms in plaid and polka dots and the kids in dinosaurs and unicorns. The moms pause in the doorway to shake out their umbrellas, while their kids run to a table on the other side of the room. Both mothers seem so happy and completely put-together—like two additional Maggies, copied and pasted into the coffee shop. As if one wasn't enough.

I look over at Noah's thin hoodie hanging on the back of the chair. A drop of water falls from the sleeve and lands in a tiny puddle on the floor.

What did the other two wear to school today? I can't even remember. I bet the moms sitting across from us remember what their kids are wearing—and have no similar concerns about whether they're sufficiently warm and dry.

"You haven't lived near your family since you moved to Texas for college, right? I imagine it gets lonely," Maggie says.

Lonely isn't quite the word I would use to describe it. *Disconnected* from everyone who knew me in what seems like a whole lifetime ago, maybe. *Wistful* for the Sunday night dinners that were once an annoying standing appointment in my ever-so-important teenage social calendar. Maybe somewhat *envious* for the time Mama and GiGi get to spend together, as they both grow older, and I'm 800 miles away—but certainly not *lonely*. Right?

"I guess Bonnie does remind me a lot of my GiGi." I pull my eyes back to our own table and pick at my scraggly nails while homing in on the doughy scent of fresh-baked bread escaping from the kitchen.

What is it they say? Name something you can see, touch, hear, smell, and taste, right? That's supposed to stop the anxiety spiral.

I can see amazing, caring mothers who have it all figured out. I can touch Noah's wet hoodie and know I've failed—again. I can hear friends having real, meaningful conversations. I can smell breads I used to love to bake. I can taste bitter coffee, which puckers the corners of my mouth and makes me crave the piping hot potion from my pot at home, complete with comfy clothes and no expectation of intelligent dialogue attached.

Wait—I don't think I'm doing this exercise right. *How many more minutes?*

Maggie, taking no notice of my increasing impulse to run right out of this coffee shop, continues taking her sweet time with her latte while filling me in on all the details of her mother-in-law's recent visit and the bake sale fundraiser at her church. Occasionally, she throws in a question about what my kids have been up to lately, to which I give the expected, socially acceptable answers and we move on.

She's trying. She really is. It's not her fault I can't connect with any of it today.

"Well, I hate to be the first to leave," she says, "but we have a dental appointment to get to." She starts packing up her things.

Thank God. I take her cue and begin packing our things, too. "No worries. It was good seeing you guys, though." I give Henry's hand a squeeze.

"Let's do this again soon, okay?"

"For sure. Soon." I stand and give her a hug, then she heads toward the exit with Henry on her hip, popping open an umbrella as she steps outside.

Tossing a cash tip onto the table, I scoop Noah up from his seat, throw the wet hoodie over his head, and beeline for the car.

On the way home, as Noah sings along to his favorite nursery rhymes, I struggle to keep the car between the yellow lines, which are barely visible through the pouring rain. I think of Maggie's sweet, oval face. I can't imagine she ever struggles with her kids, or her life, as I do with mine.

Does she also live with her head in the fog, waiting for a glimpse of the sunshine? I doubt it, and I'll damn sure never ask.

Rocking Noah to sleep, cocooned together under his favorite blanket as the weather rages outside his window, I cling to his warm body and breathe him in.

I'm not much of a cuddler, but this is something of which I will never grow tired. Though I know from experience, he will one day grow plenty tired of being handled like a baby and what will I do then? There are no more children in my future: three is enough—and likely too many. Where, then, will I find my peace? It's not with joining the PTA or coaching a soccer team, I know that. This, this part right here, is where it all lies. All my eggs, in one withering basket, already worn thread-bare from the other two having outgrown the confines of my lap.

Noah lets out a heavy sigh, then his chest begins to rise and fall in a steady rhythm. I stand, lay him in his crib, brush the hair from his face, and stare.

What will I do, sweet Noah? How will I survive it?

A solitary tear rolls down my cheek and lands near his ear, darkening the red fire engine-themed bed sheet. I wipe my face and leave him be.

I emerge from the bedroom and head toward the kitchen in search of coffee. Saturdays are the one day a week when I can sleep-in and somehow, I dozed till after one in the afternoon.

"Good morning," I hear from the recliner in the living room.

Andrew's watching something on his tablet while Ryan and Audrey play peacefully on the computer in my office. Noah must be napping already. How does he get them to do that? How is it that just his presence brings calm to their crazy?

"Please wake me up at 11:00 on Saturdays, if I'm still asleep." I'm embarrassed for having wasted away so much of the day, even if it is my day to rest.

"Sure," he answers. "I figured I would just let you sleep until whenever." He runs his fingers through his hair, not even looking up from the tablet in his hand.

His well-intended reply bothers me, especially as I notice the fresh smell of dryer sheets escaping from under the laundry room door and I'm reminded I haven't done a load of laundry—or cooked a meal—in days.

It's not that I don't know these are things that need to be done. Of course I know, and I detest the guilt I feel at ignoring them, but somehow still can't seem to *do* them. These very basic things come at me like the nemeses in Audrey's video games. I throw up my right arm to deflect one, then the left to deflect another, praying I can somehow make it to safety before I'm buried beneath a pile of responsibilities I can't face.

Placing a bowl of one-minute oats and water into the microwave, I pour my coffee while it cooks. Outside the kitchen window, the rain is still falling, almost silently, creating a curtain through which not much at all can be seen. Heavy, but quiet at the same time. I sit at the table with my buttered oatmeal and black coffee and watch it fall.

This type of rain can be dangerous in these parts of Texas. The ground is so hard and dry, it can't readily accept the sheer volume of water released in the downpour. Flash flooding occurs, animals are lost, cars are swept from the road, and occasionally even small children are carried away in the current. But then, just as soon as it stops, the floodwaters seep into the ground, and the danger is gone.

It's never occurred to me before how much the transition from the dark days to the good is just like that—terrifying and deadly one moment, to checking the mail and washing the mud-covered cars the next.

Within a few hours, the rain dissipates and there isn't a dark cloud in the sky. The sun is shining bright, yet the rain still comes—sideways or at a diagonal. Audrey and Ryan love this kind of rain the most because there's no thunder or lightning and they know they're allowed to splash in it to their hearts' content. Despite my half-hearted objections and the cold, they grab their boots and jackets and they're on their way. They'll need baths when they come in and I'm so *tired*, but I let them go anyway.

I throw together a spaghetti dinner while they're outside and Noah plays upstairs.

"Can you call them in?" I ask Andrew.

"Sure. They're going to need baths."

"Yup." I don't look up from my pot. I am not interested in giving baths.

"Okay, I'll take care of it."

Andrew wrangles them inside and they're covered, head-to-toe, in mud which has now found its way onto his favorite gray sweatpants and bare feet. On my very best days, those are my favorite gray sweatpants too. On those days, I can't take my eyes off him. He looks so much like he did when we first met all those years ago, only somehow even better with age.

He guides them to the bathroom, proclaiming, "Don't touch anything!" about a thousand times along the way. Of course they touch everything, giggling as they go. I sigh, grab a wet towel and wipe clean the walls, the dining chairs, the countertops.

I hear water splash onto the tile floor in the bathroom down the hall.

"Oh, no, let's not splash out of the tub. You're going to make Mama super mad." Andrew's statement is met with giggles and more splashing. "No, really, keep it in the tub, you guys!"

Why does it have to be that they're going to make *me* super mad? I am not the only adult in this house.

Climbing the stairs, I find Noah playing in his room. "Hey, sweetie. Are you hungry? Let's go eat."

He stands, drops the toys from his hands, but hangs on to one red car.

"You want to take that one downstairs? Maybe he's hungry too."

"Yeah, hungry too," he replies.

As we make our way back downstairs and through the living room, Ryan cuts the corner from the hallway to the kitchen, sliding on wet feet.

"Ryan, don't—"

His legs come out from under him, sending him crashing to the floor with a thud. He screams.

I set Noah into the highchair, which he's almost outgrown, and move to Ryan.

"This is why we don't run in the house! Are you okay?"

He's crying and holding the back of his head.

"Let me see." I move his hands and feel a lump already beginning to form.

"What happened?" Andrew asks as he enters the kitchen. The front of his soaked tee-shirt clings to every muscle in such a way that I can see them move when he does.

"He slipped and hit his head. Why were his feet still wet?"

"Because he just got out of the bath."

"That's what a towel is for, Andrew!" I pull an ice pack from the freezer. "Here, sit down and keep this on your head." I hand the ice pack to Ryan. A bead of sweat rolls down my face, in a straight line from temple to jaw.

I should've just done the bath myself. No one can control whether a four-year-old remembers not to run in the house, but what can be controlled is whether they have wet feet when leaving through the bathroom door.

Audrey joins her brothers at the table. "What's for dinner?"

"Spaghetti," I answer, knowing exactly what will come next.

"I don't want spaghetti!" she screams.

Every single time.

My chest tightens and for a moment, I can't breathe. My first instinct is to lose it completely, but when I turn and see her waiting for my reply, I'm reminded it will do no good to give one. We've done this song and dance a million times and the ending is always the same.

Turning back to the stove, I pile pasta onto each of their plates, topping it with plain meat sauce with no trace of vegetables besides the tomatoes with which it's made. Luxuries such as bell peppers, onions, and mushrooms in the sauce left us the day she started solid foods. And crunchy peanut butter. And all ice cream that isn't red or pink.

They eat all they're going to eat and Andrew takes them upstairs to brush teeth and tuck them in. I clear the table of our plates, scrape their leftovers into Tupperware bowls, and attempt to attach a lid to one. It's too full and spaghetti sauce squirts all over my blouse and onto the floor.

"Son of a—" I pull a paper towel from the roll and wipe up the floor. The shirt, like so many in my closet, is a lost cause.

Wetting a clean rag, I move to the table, erasing their tomato-on-wood masterpieces from its top. As my hand runs over the indents made by years of pounding cutlery at the hands of tiny humans, I pause. I am both desperate for a break—an escape—and on the verge of tears for how fast they've grown.

"I'm going to hop in the shower and turn in early too," Andrew says as he returns downstairs, then disappears into our bedroom.

"Okay," I reply to no one, as he shuts the door.

I move to the sink, plunge my hands into the opalescent water, and wash the burned ring of spaghetti sauce from inside the shiny, silver pot—part of a set gifted to us at our wedding, back before dark days and good days, bumped heads, and pasta protests. As I scrub, a tiny, perfect bubble escapes the sink. I watch it float toward the ceiling, hit the can light, and pop.

After finishing in the kitchen and tucking Ryan back into bed twice, I hear the shower turn off and Andrew's bedside lamp click. I give it a while longer, then sneak into bed.

As I drift off to sleep, images of the kids joyfully splashing through the mud fill my head. Suddenly, I'm very aware of how much life resembles the sun-shower: It can be so beautiful and bright, but still, there's rain.

2

MEADOWBROOK

The following Tuesday, Noah and I turn onto the street leading into Meadowbrook Retirement Village. We pass a courtyard with a grandiose limestone fountain at the center of the neighborhood. It's surrounded by vibrant pink, red, and violet blooms that you normally don't see around these parts—most people stick with the likes of the native lantana and rosemary shrubs which grow so well here, year after year.

I turn right onto Willow Lane and pull into Bonnie's driveway.

"Look, Mama! Froggies!"

Bonnie's collection of garden gnomes, flamingos, stone animals, and spinning pinwheels are one of Noah's favorite things about coming here. I swear, Bonnie must buy a new one every week, just to make him happy.

"Yes honey, I see them. They're waiting for you to say hello!" I pull Noah from his seat and make my way to the front door, as he runs over to visit his friends. I ring the bell and Bonnie throws open the door. She's donned a smart pair of black straight-legged pants, matching flats, and a silky white top for today's visit. Her beautiful silver hair is up in a classic chignon and pinned in place with a pearl comb to match her chic, but understated, clip-on earrings.

"Hello, there. I've been waiting for you!" She searches the porch for Noah and spots him as he runs around the corner. He heads straight for Bonnie and gives her a tight hug around the legs. "Hi, there, Noah bug! How are you today?" she says with a tousle of his fine hair with her dusty-rose-painted fingertips and a smile of a carefully matched shade.

"Good!" He turns her loose, heads through the front door, and Bonnie stands aside while motioning for me to enter.

"Morning, Bonnie," I say with a smile as we move inside.

Weekly visits with Bonnie always seem to bring me back to life, and I've yet to determine if the good mood I feel when talking with her is truly my own, or simply another case of camouflaging to fit the environment.

"I have the tea all ready for us in the kitchen," she says.

I follow her across the sitting room with its massive crystal chandelier, pale-gold, camel-back sofa, and two mossy-green velvet armchairs. My eyes land, as they always do, on the collection of oversized oil paintings of rolling hills, sunsets, and wheat fields, which seem right on the verge of jumping out of their frames and onto the matching furniture.

"Have I told you how much I love this room? I could sit in here forever."

"Only every time you visit, but thank you. In the end, though, it's all just stuff," she replies with a shrug.

I motion toward the wall of tall walnut bookshelves, which are home to titles including *The Great Gatsby, Madame Bovary, Gone with the Wind, Wuthering Heights, Jane Eyre,* and on and on. "Well, those are certainly not just *stuff*."

"Now those are prized possessions—some were given to me and others I've worked my whole life to curate. My most cherished belongings are all on that shelf," Bonnie replies. "I know you like to read them while you're here, but you're welcome to borrow them too, if you'd like. For now, let's see about that tea while it's still hot, hmm?"

We pass through the wide archway separating the sitting room from the main living room and kitchen. This more casual living room contains a modern, cream-colored sofa with a chaise on one end and a square wooden coffee table with mismatched, but perfectly coordinated, end tables and lamps. In the center of the room hangs the second of the three chandeliers. A massive, glossy black fireplace with a marble inset is centered on one wall. A portrait of a straight-faced woman with rosy cheeks rests upon its mantel.

The kitchen is small, with black, distressed cabinets. There's no island, but rather, an oblong table and six chairs take up the space in the center. The third chandelier hangs delicately above its weathered wood. The countertops and backsplash are marble, and the giant stove hood is a patinaed copper, like something straight from the pages of a magazine.

Bonnie retrieves the kettle from the stove, pours the hot water into a teapot, and places it onto a potholder on a tray. Also on the tray are various fruit-filled pastries, two white teacups, spoons, sugar, and a tiny porcelain container of milk.

"Here we go," she says.

"Can I help you carry that?" I set the diaper bag down on the floor, out of the way.

"No, but you can get the door, if you don't mind."

I open the door as Bonnie crosses the kitchen, balancing the tray as if she's been hosting tea parties her whole life. She moves gracefully, with total ease and impeccable posture.

We step out onto a flagstone patio with a black wrought iron table and four chairs, all covered with seat cushions in a very-French, black and cream stripe. The entire patio is surrounded by the same colorful flowers in the front yard and an abundance of Bonnie's kitschy lawn ornaments too. Noah bounds out the door and into the yard, surveying the space for new additions.

We take our usual seats at the table as Bonnie pours our tea and picks up a pastry. "Noah, love, Ms. Bonnie has a treat for you. Would you like a cookie?"

Noah runs straight over to her with a wide grin on his tiny little face. That boy has yet to meet a treat he didn't like.

"Thank you." He takes her offering and gallops back out into the yard.

"So, how is everything? Have you called your grandmother this week?"

"Uh—no, but I should. It's been a while."

"Yes, you should. Us old people don't like to feel forgotten, you know."

"I know. It's on my list." Calling GiGi is always on my list. Just like calling Mama and Michelle always is. That doesn't make it an easy thing to do. Mama and GiGi's questions are always the same—How are the kids? How's Andrew? How's work?—and nobody expects a genuine answer to any of it. When they ask how I'm doing, they don't expect me to say, "Oh, you know—barely surviving."

And conversations with Michelle are sparse these days, as they often are between best friends who each have their own family to manage. Although, when we do carve out time for a phone call, it's always like no time has passed at all.

"What about you? How's your daughter?" Bonnie mentioned her daughter, Megan, in our first encounter outside the church, and I now realize she hasn't mentioned her since.

"Hmm?" she asks, looking a bit confused.

"She lives close, right? And you go to the same church?"

She looks up from her plate and lets out a hearty laugh. "Okay, I think I owe you an explanation—and maybe an apology—for that one."

"What do you mean?"

"Megan has lived in Houston for the last twelve years or so."

I'm confused and not sure what to say.

"You see, when you get old, you notice there are generally two kinds of people: those who walk right on by you like you don't exist, and those who are kind enough to ask if you're okay," she explains. "And when the kind ones stop and ask if you're okay, it makes them nervous when you tell them you're alone. They don't quite know how to react. It's like you're a stray puppy and they don't know what to do with you. So, I tell them I'm waiting for Megan."

"Wait, what? You mean, when you said you were waiting for her to walk you into church—" I'm unsure if she's serious or if she's pulling my leg, but one look at her face tells me she's absolutely serious. I let out an over-dramatic gasp. "Ms. Bonnie, you lied to me!"

"Well, it almost worked, didn't it? You were so tempted to go right along with your business." Bonnie takes a sip from her cup with her pinkie finger sticking straight out into the air. She looks at me over the rim and I can't help but to bust out with laughter.

"Well, isn't that somethin'?" I say, after regaining a bit of my composure. "And what about the nice lady from the church who said she was going to call someone for a ride home for you?"

She shrugs. "Yeah, yeah, I heard what she told you about how I *get confused* sometimes." She rolls her eyes and uses air quotes with that phrase.

"What? Have you got that poor woman snowed too?"

"Oh, please. That's her own assumption. I only go along with it to catch a ride when these poor feet are too tired to walk home and I've forgotten my phone. I slip the driver a twenty every time she picks me up. Why do you think she keeps coming to get me? That certainly isn't part of her job description as office manager for Meadowbrook," she says with a wave of her hand and another sip from her cup.

And I lose it. I can't keep it together no matter how hard I try. Tears are flowing down my cheeks.

"Boy, I've heard some doozies while visiting with you, but this—this may just take the cake."

"Oh, honey, that's nothing. We haven't gotten to the *really* good ones yet."

"Lord, help me. I don't know how to take that, Bonnie."

"Hmm, maybe with a mimosa—next time."

"Hello, handsome!" Bonnie says as she opens the door, and her arms, for Noah.

He runs right up to hug her legs, as he always does.

"Treat?" he asks.

"Oh, yes, I've got plenty of treats," she answers with a laugh, while smoothing her camel-colored, pleated skirt.

Sometimes I wonder if I should fancy myself up a bit more for visits with Bonnie—at least try to match her energy out of respect. But even just the thought of it tires me, and she doesn't seem to mind my leggings or jeans and tee-shirts, so here we are.

"Well, I've brought treats too, in case you run short," I say, holding a box of doughnuts up for her to see.

"Wonderful. Well, come in, you two. It's finally cooling off a bit, I think," Bonnie says, looking up to the sky. "I bet in two weeks' time it'll be too cold to sit outside, so how about we enjoy the patio again today?"

"Sounds great to me." I take Noah by the hand as we enter the house.

Moving into the kitchen, I see Bonnie already has the teapot on the tray. I place the box of doughnuts on the counter, and she takes out a beautiful white serving platter with pink and green flowers around the rim. She pulls each doughnut from the box and lays them in a row on the platter, each one leaning on the one behind it. Instantly, they feel more special.

Bonnie pulls a cardigan from the back of a kitchen chair and puts it on over a black top with brown and burgundy flowers. Her nails and lipstick are burgundy today too, and I can't help but wonder how some people can go through so much effort to be so put together, yet make it look completely effortless.

We move outside and busy ourselves with setting the table and pouring tea.

"So, what's new, Jenna? Any exciting adventures since last Tuesday?"

"Not unless you count calling the plumber out twice to fish toys from the toilet as an exciting adventure."

"Oh, my. Noah angel, you didn't do that, did you?"

He grins and snags a doughnut off the table.

"Oh, yes, he did. Don't let him fool you, Bonnie. He has plenty of antics."

"Well, it sounds like he's ready for Halloween, then. Plenty of tricks up his sleeves."

"For sure. At least it offered a bit of excitement to the week, though. Everything else was the same ol' boring routine. Take kids to school, pick up kids from school. Order the groceries, eat all the groceries. Cook the meal they won't eat, put away the meal they didn't eat. It's exhausting."

"Well, that's all very important work. You make *life* happen for those kids and it's not at all easy to do when they're as young as yours are," Bonnie says. "But don't you have girlfriends too? To chat and have fun with, away from the babies and the chores?"

This question takes me by surprise, and I pause to think before answering. I've managed to keep our conversations light-hearted over the past few weeks, despite sensing the dark days returning. I don't want to ruin that now.

"Not really. I mean, I have friends I meet for coffee or for playdates occasionally, but nothing regular."

My mind flits back to two weeks ago at the coffee shop with Maggie. Back to us sharing pastries and kolaches with our boys and to the quick escape I so desperately craved.

"Why is that?" She asks as if it's as easy of a question to answer as asking me what's my favorite color or flavor of ice cream. I know the answer, and don't know if I have the courage to utter the words, but I have a feeling I should try.

"Well, I'm not always a social person." I look down at my cup and stir the tea inside. "There are periods where I enjoy being around other people and periods where I don't. I'm sure that has not gone unnoticed by you over the time we've been coming to visit."

Bonnie nods.

"I don't know how to explain it. Sometimes the motivation is there, sometimes not. It's hard to form real friendships when you disappear as much as I do." I keep stirring my tea, afraid to look up.

"Oh, I see," she answers.

I raise my eyes just enough to see her face and I'm not met at all with the look of confusion or pity or judgment that I thought I would be. *But what is that look?*

"Well, I'm glad you still come to see me, even when you're not feeling your best. I think your other friends would be too. What a shame it is for them to never have the chance to know the full you." She reaches for a glazed doughnut and takes a bite.

"That's sweet, but I wouldn't wish that on anyone. The 'full me' is most content in my leggings and fuzzy socks, with a giant coffee mug in my hand and Netflix on the TV," I say to both lighten the mood and prevent this conversation from going much deeper than it already has.

"Oh, I bet you'd be surprised. We tend to have more in common with each other than we realize."

Maybe, but if that's true, who's brave enough to be the first to let their poker face fall?

We enjoy the rest of our morning, discussing everything from the best way to hard-boil and peel an egg to our favorite books and movies. Then, Noah grows tired and it's time to go.

"You know, if you have one of those little play yard things, you're welcome to set it up in the spare room for him next time," Bonnie says. "So you can stay longer and get a little more of a break. It has to be better than going home to do work or laundry, right?"

"Definitely. I don't know if he'll sleep here, but we can try."

"Okay, and don't worry about bringing snacks next week. I want to make little man some of my famous Belgian waffles."

"Now that sounds like a plan."

The following Tuesday, we show up right on time. I knock at the door and hear a clear order to come in. Opening the door, we're hit with the sweet smell of fresh homemade Belgian waffles...and something else. Pumpkin, maybe?

"Ms. Bonnie, it's us. Gosh, it smells good in here."

"Come on in, y'all. I'm in the kitchen," she answers.

On our way to the kitchen, I see Bonnie has the fireplace going. If this place was magical before, it's downright storybook-inspiring, with a roaring fire in the big, beautiful hearth. The flames appear to dance inside each individual crystal on the chandelier and the firewood pops and crackles under the heat. Of course, as Bonnie predicted last week, the cold weather has crept in on us. It's a bit too cold to enjoy sitting outside today, but seeing that fireplace and smelling that warm, spicy scent, I'm not the least bit disappointed.

"I'm impressed you have a wood-burning fireplace. I can't get a fire to stay lit to save my life." I settle Noah down on the rug and pull a few toys and a snack cup from the diaper bag.

"Well, I've spent my fair share of time around a campfire," she says.

"Noah, don't touch it, okay? Hot," I say, pointing to the metal screen in front of the fireplace.

"Yeah, hot." He's more interested in his toys than the fire.

I make my way to the kitchen. "What can I help you with? And what is that amazing smell...pumpkin?"

"Yes. I got to thinking maybe Noah has never tried Belgian waffles before, and I was afraid he wouldn't eat them. So, I made pumpkin bread, too. Nothing fancy, but it's sweet as cake, so I figured it would be a safe bet."

"Oh, you didn't have to do that. Thank you." The kettle whistles on the stove, so I reach over and turn off the burner.

"Sure. Would you mind grabbing the plates from the cabinet right over your head?" Bonnie pulls the sleeves of her gray cashmere sweater up to her elbows and twists her wrist back and forth to maneuver her rose gold bracelet up a few inches too. Then, she retrieves the loaf of bread from the oven and opens the microwave to remove a giant plate of waffles, wrapped in foil, to keep them warm.

I grab plates for all of us and we work to set the table. When we're finished, it's covered with pumpkin bread, waffles, butter, maple syrup, Greek yogurt, milk for Noah, tea and all the fixins for us, and a bowl of fresh fruit. There's enough food here to feed a crowd...and it's so damn cozy, I almost want to cry.

"Wow, Bonnie, you sure know how to throw a party. This is amazing."

"Well, I won't pretend I'm a gourmet chef. This is one of about three meals I know how to make well." She pulls silverware from a drawer and places a fork and knife next to each of our plates.

I coax Noah from his toys with a bribe of cake and fruit. He climbs into the chair next to mine and we make our plates.

"So, how's work?" Bonnie asks.

"Oh, I haven't worked much lately. The college is on fall break, so there aren't many tasks coming through at the moment." I leave out the part about how I haven't accepted any virtual assistant requests from the instructors for weeks, even prior to the break. As the dark days draw nearer, my ability to commit myself to work diminishes, and I don't want to start something I know I can't finish.

"Well, that's nice. And should leave time for a bit of fun, right? What do you like to do for fun?"

There she goes again with the questions I don't have an answer for.

"I'm a mom of small children. I don't have time for fun."

"Well, what did you *used* to do for fun then?" she asks, not taking the bait.

I take a bite of my food and cut a slice of pumpkin bread into quarters for Noah, trying to buy myself some time. What *did* I used to do for fun?

"Well, I loved to read, but rarely find time for that these days. And I was a great runner. Lots of concerts—music was important to me." I take a sip of my tea. "And where I'm from, in the middle of nowhere in Alabama, we spent a lot of time 'muddin' or 'off-roading' at the lake. Gosh, I haven't done that in years."

"Well, you know, folks around here go muddin' too."

I laugh. "Yes, I know. Actually, when Andrew and I were first dating, that was one of our favorite things to do together. He drove a giant truck with massive tires back then. Muddin' was about the only thing it was good for."

Bonnie smiles and I help Noah with the last of his bread. He rubs his eyes with the back of his hand, which reminds me he woke earlier than usual this morning.

"Is it okay if I set up the play yard and see if he'll sleep here today?"

"Sure, let me show you where." Bonnie stands and beckons for us to follow her down a hallway.

Fifteen minutes later, he's all set up in the spare room and sleeping soundly.

"Well, that was a lot easier than I thought it was going to be," I say, re-entering the living room.

"Good. Grab your cup and pull up a seat." She's already made herself comfortable on the sofa.

I do as she suggests, but rather than choosing a seat, I opt for a cozy spot on the floor in front of the fireplace. We spend the next two hours having conversations about anything and everything, laughing so hard at times, it brings tears to our eyes.

"Bonnie, this is amazing. Thank you so much for the wonderful breakfast and for the company. I swear, it's like therapy coming here."

"I'm so glad to hear that because I enjoy our visits, too. Now, help me clean up this God-awful mess before you go, why don't ya?" She stands, and I follow her into the kitchen.

I've tried a few times to explain to Andrew what makes our visits with Bonnie so special, but I can't seem to find the right words. It seems silly to say Bonnie's home feels like it exists in a whole other world—that when I go there, it's like I'm a million miles away from the every-day. I don't think about what's for dinner or work deadlines, school projects, or fundraisers. All of that sort of melts away, and I'm able to just *be*.

However, as Thanksgiving approaches, frigid temperatures and icy winds have swooped in on us and I can feel its effects already. I know there's so much to be done, but I'm finding it hard to muster the motivation to do any of it. The cold weather makes me tired.

I pick up my phone, and feeling ashamed for what I'm about to do, text Bonnie. "Hi, Bonnie. I don't think we'll make it next week. Lots to do here to get ready for Thanksgiving. I hope you understand." A few minutes pass, then I receive a reply.

"Maybe for a few minutes? I've rounded up those old Thanksgiving recipes I promised you."

I sit on her message for an hour, not knowing what to say. Then she replies again.

"Jenna, if you're truly busy, I understand. But if it's that the cold weather is too much to bear, I do hope you'll come and sit by the fire."

She knows. How is it possible? No one ever knows. At least, not until it's too late and I'm too miserable to do anything about it. Maybe I should go.

I make a split-second decision and text back, "Okay. Should I bring anything?"

"No, love. See you then."

The alarm on my phone wakes me from a restless sleep. Once silenced, I hear the all too familiar sound of water on the window.

I slide my heavy legs to the side, leaving them dangling over the edge of the bed. Staring at my toes hovering inches from the floor as I dread setting them down to start my day, a familiar feeling comes over me. I take a deep breath and stretch my back, allowing the air to fill the deepest parts of my lungs.

Hello, old friend, I think, allowing myself to fully recognize the same feelings of dejection and despair that have come and gone so many times before in my life. More so, as a mother.

When the dark days come, I often ponder how the weight of being a mother is like no other. There's a constant worry and guilt that doesn't fade. And while some thrive on the sounds of a busy house—the stomping feet, the never-ending commotion, screams, giggles, and yells—that is not *me*. There are times it gets to me, viscerally, and I wonder if I should've become a mother at all. In those moments, my thoughts turn into a deep feeling I'm not cut out for this; something that is always followed quickly by a roaring wave of guilt.

I plop back over sideways, so my head is at the foot of the bed and my feet are up toward my pillow. Somehow, I feel if I fall back asleep this way, I'll be more likely to wake up again—and I only need a few more minutes to rest. Just another moment to cover myself in the blanket's warmth; to absorb the silence; to hide from all that I know is to come.

But a few minutes turns into an hour, and I only wake again when the bedroom door flies open, and Ryan runs in and bounces on the bed.

"Mama, do I have school today?"

It's 9:00. Preschool started at 8:30 and Noah and I are supposed to be at Bonnie's by now. I shoot her a quick text, "Sorry, Bonnie, running behind. We'll be there in an hour."

As I draw the drapes and stare through the rain to see the fog hovering over the hilltops where the morning storm has passed, I wonder, is that how it's meant to be? Hunker down until the tempest subsides, then live out the rest of your day—your life—in the fog it leaves behind?

Nobody ever warns you of the exorbitant price you pay upon becoming a mother.

"Good morning! Come on in," Bonnie says as she opens the door. The wind is strong today, and I'm thankful she never keeps us waiting on the porch long.

"Good morning." I remove our wet jackets and hang them on a coat rack near the front door.

"Boy, it just comes and goes, doesn't it?" she asks.

"Hmm?"

"The rain."

"Oh, yes." For a split second, I thought she was referring to something much more dire than the weather.

"Fire's nice and warm, though, and so is the tea."

Noah's off and running toward the kitchen in search of something to eat. I follow him, eager to get my frozen hands on a warm cup. The teapot and cups are already on the table, along with something that looks like Fig Newtons.

"Here you go, love. A cookie for you." Bonnie gives one to Noah, which he happily accepts, before running into the spare bedroom to play. We've amassed quite the stash of toys here over the past few weeks and he knows exactly where to find them.

I pull out a seat at the table and reach for the teapot, pouring for Bonnie first, then for myself. I notice the sound of Sinatra's "Summer Wind" emanating from a phantom speaker I've yet to locate.

"Everything okay?" Bonnie has chosen the seat across from me and is stirring sugar and milk into her tea.

"Uh, yeah." Without looking up from my cup, I reach for a cookie. "We had a rough start this morning, is all."

"Do you want to talk about it?"

"No, it's fine, really. I'm only tired. And this weather is not my favorite."

There's a pensive silence before Bonnie says, "Well, how about those recipes? I made copies of them for you. Most were handed down from my grandmother and mother. I used to make them for Megan when she was little. I never cooked much, but Thanksgiving was always the exception." She stands from her seat and walks over to a drawer beside the pantry.

"Yes, I'd love to see them." My voice is less than enthusiastic, but I'm grateful for the diversion—mostly from my unwanted thoughts.

She brings over a stack of papers and we go through them, one by one. So many of the recipes look familiar to me, as GiGi used to make dishes that were quite similar. Getting to know Bonnie makes me miss GiGi more than I have in a long time. Whenever I'm homesick, which is rare, it's not so much the actual physical location I miss, but her presence. She is the very definition of home.

A short time later, Noah grows sleepy and before I can say it's time to go, Bonnie scoops him up.

"How about I try my hand at putting this guy down and you go raid the bookshelf?"

I want to go home, but I know if we leave, he'll likely fall asleep in the car and there will be no nap at home. Then, soon enough, Audrey and Ryan will be home from school. Most days, one or two of them in the house is manageable, but all three is total chaos and overwhelm. Most days, all three of them is just too much.

"Okay. Any suggestions?" I ask her.

"Hmm...why not try *A Midsummer Night's Dream*?"

I nod my head and walk toward the sitting room, finding the book on the third shelf. Grabbing a throw blanket from the camel-back sofa, I move over to the living room to sit on the end of the sofa closest to the fireplace.

As I read, I'm reminded of how much fun it was to perform this play with friends, and how much simpler things were back then. It also dawns on me how smart Bonnie really is. I know now, through her suggestion of this off-beat chaotic comedy, she can sense I'm entering a downward spiral I'm unable to stop. Could *she* help me stop it? Through food, tea, and *A Midsummer Night's Dream*?

I read a few more pages, then drift off to sleep to the sound and warmth of the crackling fire.

3

NUMB

Audrey's running fever and stayed home from school today. I didn't have the motivation to take Ryan to preschool either, so come noon, we are all four still in pajamas. Toys are strewn everywhere. You can't walk without having to kick them out of your path.

The shrill siren of a toy fire truck, stuck somewhere upside down with its button engaged, cuts through the air just as it has been for the last twenty minutes—with no one but myself seeming to notice. My one hope is it soon runs out of batteries.

"Ryan, can you please get your brother to help you clean up some of this mess?" I beg. "Maybe you can each pick up ten things?"

"Noah, help me clean up!" he screams at his little brother, right in my ear. His breath smells of sour milk. *Lord, that boy needs to brush his teeth.*

I breathe into my cupped hands and do a quick smell check of my own: *Oof, like mother, like son.*

Ryan's plea doesn't work, of course, and we all continue to stare at whatever ridiculous cartoon this is that we've been watching on repeat for three hours straight.

By mid-afternoon, the boys are making trips to the pantry every few minutes and coming back with random snacks shoved in their pockets. I know I should force myself to move from this position and make them something to eat, but sending that message from brain to limbs appears to be a real problem.

My phone vibrates and Maggie's name appears on the screen. I have zero energy for Maggie today, so I send the call to voicemail and re-cover myself with the blanket.

"Mama, are you sick too?" Ryan asks.

"No, honey. I'm just tired today."

"Oh, will you play a game with me, then?"

"Not right now, Ryan. Maybe later."

Without protest, he turns from me and goes right back to crashing cars together with Noah. There's guilt for not pulling myself together enough to sit on the edge of the sofa and play with him, but just as quickly as the feeling comes, it goes.

See? He doesn't need me. They have each other.

It's not until the doorbell rings an hour later that I realize I've dozed off. The boys jump up to run over and see who it is.

"STOP!" I say in my loudest whisper. "You know the rule. You don't go over there if someone rings the bell in the middle of the day. You stay here, with me."

This is really only a rule when it's 2:00 in the afternoon, we're still not dressed, and I've spent the entire day trying to disappear into the sofa. It's for protection of my own dignity, more than anything.

We wait, without a sound. When they hear the truck start up and drive away, they run to the front door and look out the window.

"It's just a package, Mama!" Ryan yells back to me on the sofa. "Can I bring it inside?"

"Yeah, okay."

When I wake again, it's 5:00 in the afternoon. I know now I have to get up and make dinner before they eat everything in sight. Sliding my legs off the sofa, I stand slowly as the blood returns to my feet.

Heading to the kitchen, I open the fridge and stare. I open the pantry and stare. What is there to make that's easy, and that they'll actually eat? I don't feel like bribing them to take tiny bites, and I certainly don't feel like fighting to get them to do it.

I open a can of chicken noodle soup for Audrey and spread frozen nuggets on two plates for the boys. I take a box of mac and cheese from the pantry and just as I'm about to open it, Ryan runs into the kitchen and throws open the refrigerator door.

"Ryan, please get out of the fridge. I'm making dinner."

"But I'm hungry now! I need a snack!"

"Your dinner will be ready in ten minutes. You do not need a snack. Please go find something else to do while I make it." My patience is non-existent.

"But, Mama, I need it!" he says as he shoves his hands into the fridge, reaching for something in the drawer.

"No, Ryan! Get out of the kitchen!" I yell, feeling my heart beginning to race.

It never fails that when they see me cooking, they realize they're starving, and they just can't wait. It won't be long before another one wanders in to do the exact same thing.

Right on cue, Noah appears on a green ride-on dump truck. "Snack! Snack!"

I put my foot on the front of the truck to stop him. "No, Noah. Mama's making dinner. Go play!"

"No! Snack, please!"

"No snacks. Find something else to do!"

Together they cry, scream, and throw epic tantrums; joining forces to break my will.

"Mama, I'm hungry. What's for dinner?" Audrey says as she enters the kitchen, wrapped in a fuzzy blanket.

"Oh, my *God*, you're all crazy! Get *out* of my kitchen!" In my frustration, I shove one of the small plastic plates I'm preparing for the boys, and it flings off the counter. It soars through the air like a Frisbee and at just that precise, serendipitous moment, Ryan crosses the kitchen. The plate nails him right in the temple. Frozen nuggets fly from the plate, seeking cover under kitchen cabinets, the dining table, and who knows where else.

"Oh my God!" Audrey screams, in shock.

Ryan's wails can be heard in the next town over, I'm sure. Rushing over, I check for blood. There isn't any, but there's a nice scrape, and the side of his face is red too. How the hell did that even happen? *What did I do?*

"Honey, are you okay? I didn't mean to hurt you," I say. "I didn't know you were going to walk there, but I shouldn't have done it, anyway. I'm so sorry!" I'm in tears. He's in tears. And the other two don't know what to think.

I make sure he's okay, give them all plenty of snacks, and distract them with a movie on the TV. I grab my phone from the counter and retreat to the one place I can ever find peace and be alone—the car parked in the driveway.

Sitting in this safe haven, which I escape to far too often, I watch sporadic raindrops hit the windshield as my head spins with a thousand questions.

What kind of mother am I? Why can't I just be normal? Who hits their kid in the head *with a plate?* Who screams at them like that? Why is it so impossible to maintain self-control? What is this rage, always on the verge of escape? Ryan's definitely telling his teacher about this, and I will have Child Protective Services knocking on my door within days. What if they take my kids? *Oh, my God.*

For a moment, I'm fear stricken, but then the fear is cast aside with just one thought: They'd be better off with someone else anyway.

It's all just too much. I crumble and sob with my forehead on the steering wheel.

There's a soft knock on the glass and I look up to find Audrey, holding her jacket over her head like a tent. Wiping my face with my sleeve, I open my door a few inches to hear her.

"Mama, I'm going upstairs to play on the computer, okay?"

"Okay, honey. I'll be back inside in a few minutes."

She turns to head back in, and I shut the door and pick up my phone to text Andrew. "Please pick up something for dinner on your way home. I don't feel like cooking tonight."

"Are you okay?" Andrew puts his massive Wagyu burger down on his plate and takes my hand across the restaurant's trendy, live-edge wood tabletop.

"Yeah, I'm fine."

He wants to talk, and all I can think is please, let's not do this tonight. I still haven't recovered from the kitchen episode earlier this week, and he senses it.

"You seem...off. More so than I've seen in the past." He treads carefully.

"It's a funk, that's all. You know this weather gets to me. It'll pass."

"Well, don't get mad, but I have to ask: Have you been taking your medication?" He looks at me with eyes screaming, 'please don't kill me.'

I poke around at my ketchup with a fry, trying to figure out what I can say to let him know I don't want to talk. But if not now, then when? We rarely hire a sitter to get out of the house for a date night, and everything is so chaotic when we're home.

"Yes, I'm taking the meds, but I don't know if they help much."

"Well, do you think you should go back and ask to try something different?"

"I don't know, maybe? I've already tried several meds, essential oils, vitamins. I don't know what else I can do." I take a sip of my soda, avoiding eye contact at all costs. "I'm trying, Andrew, I promise I am."

"I know, but I don't like to see you like this. What can I do to help?" He leans back in his chair and folds his arms across his chest.

I shrug. I don't think there's anything he can do. I could never explain it and even if I could, he lives an entirely different existence. He'll never understand.

We finish our meal, then wander over to the movie theater next door, holding hands and dodging puddles as we go. Each time we hop over one or come to a surface which may be even the slightest bit slippery, he moves his hand to the small of my back in support, like I'm completely fragile and incapable of standing on my own two feet.

A movie was my idea. If he's going to insist on a night out, it's going to at least be one where I'm not expected to talk through the whole thing. I let him choose which one to see, knowing at least then it will be something fast-paced and with little risk of bringing on the tears. After the movie, we head home.

Pulling into the driveway, Andrew turns off the car, grabs my left hand, and uses his other hand to cup my face. He turns it toward his. "I love you, Jenna."

I look down. I want to say I love him too, but the words won't come without a flood of tears. So, I nod my head to show I hear him.

He places his fingers on my chin, tilts my head back up again, and leans in for a kiss. His broad, soft lips touch mine and I respond with a quick peck, then turn my head.

"We should go inside so the sitter can leave," I say.

A simple "Okay," is all he has left to give, which is one word more than me.

***

It's the Friday before Christmas and the kids are all home from school. In my energetic fervor before the dark days came again—back when I was first getting to know Bonnie—I scheduled flu shots for all three kids for today.

"Audrey, are you dressed, honey?" I ask as I enter her bedroom.

"Almost...working on it," she answers.

"Okay, come find me when you're done and we'll do your hair." I head to Ryan's room next.

As I'm walking down the hallway, I call out, "Ryan, how's it coming?"

"Um...good," he says.

Oh, I know that answer. That's the 'I haven't done a thing you asked me to' answer and I don't have time for that this morning. I walk into his room.

"Ryan, what's going on in here?" There are stuffed animals and clothes everywhere. Some are on the stuffed animals, some are half-way on, and some are thrown in piles.

"I was trying to find clothes for my animals, too." He slinks to the floor.

"Ryan, when I tell you it's time to do something, that means now. That doesn't mean play in your room for twenty minutes and still not have it done."

"But I wanted them to be dressed too, Mama!"

"I understand, but now is not the time." I pick up a pair of pants and try to help him put them on.

"No, I can do it myself!" He runs to the other side of the room.

"Can you? Because you should have done it already. You've lost the chance to do it yourself because we're going to be late—come here."

"No, I can do it myself!" he screams, on the verge of tears.

"Okay, fine, put them on then!" I toss the pants in his direction.

"You have to leave. I can do it myself," he cries.

"No Ryan, I'm not going anywhere. Put on the pants, please." I stand and step back, letting him have his space, but also letting him know it's really time to go.

He gets himself dressed and then I realize his shoes are nowhere to be found.

"Do you know where your shoes are?"

"In Audrey's room, I think."

"Okay, go get them, please." I point out the door, toward her room. "And hurry!"

Audrey's still in her room, dressed, but lollygagging about.

"Audrey, what are you doing? I said hair was next. Get your brush and a hair tie and meet me downstairs in one minute." I can feel my heart beating faster and my face growing red.

What is wrong with these two?

I head downstairs to make breakfast so they can eat while I get Noah up and ready to go. Before I'm even in the kitchen, I hear, "Ryan, stop it!" from Audrey's room. Then Ryan laughs.

"Nah-nah-nah-nah-nah-nah!" he teases.

"Ryan, that's MINE!" Audrey screams and then there's more teasing from Ryan.

I continue working on breakfast, hoping they'll sort it out themselves, but it gets worse. They're screaming back and forth at each other and I can hear they're also trading what I assume are kicks, pinches, or slaps. I call up to them every few seconds with demands to knock it off, but I know full-well if I'm not right there in front of them, screaming until I'm blue in the face, they'll never listen.

A loud crash and a shrieking scream fills the air. I run up the stairs and into Audrey's room to see her on the floor, holding her hands over her shin.

"What happened?" I ask, as I check to see how badly she's hurt.

"He pushed me into my bed, and I hit my leg...ow, ow, ow, it hurts!"

I pry her hands back from her leg and see a large welt forming on the bone and a large, bloody gash. She must have hit something sharp on the metal bed frame.

"Ryan, what in the world? I asked you to come in here to get your shoes...that was it! Why couldn't you just do what I asked?"

I try to help Audrey up to take her to the bathroom, but she screams in pain with every movement and refuses to go. "Audrey, we have to get you cleaned up."

"Huh-uh! It hurts!"

Ryan is still running around the room, laughing, teasing, and definitely not looking for his shoes. I reach out and catch him as he runs by. Without thinking through my next move at all, I spank him three times—hard.

Now, they're both crying. They're both shouting words, but I can't make out what they are. Audrey's leg, hands, and the surrounding carpet are a bloody mess and Noah's awake, scared, and screaming from his room.

My vision goes black around the edges and with every passing second, I can see less and less of the scene before me.

I can barely hear them now, as my ears seem to be working in conjunction with my eyes to block out the madness—a last-ditch effort to save my sanity.

I sit and lean against the bed, waiting for it to pass.

But what if it doesn't go away? What if I'm having a stroke? What if I'm left like this forever?

A tranquil, unexplainable feeling of relief comes over me. I squeeze my eyelids tight and just stop trying. I don't want to see. I don't want to hear. I soak up the silence.

As my vision starts to return and my ears begin to allow sound, I know there are tears dying to be shed, but I have none to give.

I am numb to the sight before me. Numb to the sounds. Numb to the feelings of anger, frustration, and guilt that I know are there, somewhere beneath the surface.

I stand and locate Ryan's shoes. I walk over to him and put them on his feet. They're still fighting, but I don't care.

I walk to the bathroom, grab the first-aid kit, and return to Audrey's room to take care of her leg. She's screaming in pain, but I don't care.

I take each of them by the hand and lead them out of the room and down the stairs. They're dragging their feet the whole way, but I don't care.

I guide them to their chairs at the table and put their breakfast plates in front of them. They're whining about what I made, but I don't care.

I do Audrey's hair in a beautiful braid, taking entirely too long to do it, and now we're so late for the doctor appointment, we're never going to make it, but I don't care.

I sit on the sofa in the living room, grab my blanket, and hear Noah still crying in his bedroom...*but I just don't care.*

4

RUN

The holiday came and went in a blur as I slept the days away. When I did tag along for things, I did so as a semi-comatose bystander watching everything happen around me, but unable to feel the joy of any of it. It was like watching a movie from the audience; like everything was happening on a big screen in front of me and none of it was quite within my reach. Looking back at pictures, I am there, but there's no life, no sparkle; only a shell.

As I lie in bed, sweet giggles traverse through the wall as Audrey tickles Noah in the next room. The kids are oblivious to my current state, which confirms my suspicion that they don't need me at all.

My phone buzzes as I receive a text from Andrew. "What would you like me to grab for dinner?" it says.

He doesn't even ask if I need him to pick up dinner anymore. He just assumes. He's given up on me.

"Whatever you want that the kids will actually eat. I'm not hungry," I reply.

I place my phone on the nightstand, pull the covers up to cover my ears, and close my eyes. Noah and I visited Bonnie today, like every Tuesday, and even though I slept most of the time we were there, I'm still so tired.

Bonnie's moved the food and tea to the coffee table for the last couple of weeks, hoping to tempt me to eat or drink something, but I don't eat. Sometimes I read, but I mostly sleep in front of the fire. She's asked me twice since Christmas if I'd like to talk, and both times I've declined, thinking maybe someday she'd ask and the answer would be *yes*. She doesn't ask anymore, though. I think she's giving up on me, too.

The crashing sound of falling blocks emanates from the living room.

"No, Ryan! No knock it down!" Noah cries, and Ryan laughs.

That boy, I swear. Meaner than a two-headed snake.

My phone buzzes again. I slide my arm out from under the covers and check it to see a reply from Andrew. "Okay, be home in a half hour."

That means I need to get out of this bed, change out of my pajamas, and clean the house before he gets home—all impossible tasks, given my current state. It's the darkest it's ever been, the longest I've been numb, and I don't even understand what caused it.

Maybe it was nothing other than that I've been teetering on the edge for so long, all that was needed was one tiny push to send me tumbling over. Now I'm dangling by my fingertips, afraid to look down, but unable to climb back up.

How long can I live like this, hanging in suspended animation? How long before my fingertips grow raw and I no longer have the strength to hold on? What happens then?

My heart pounds in my chest—harder and faster—as it only does when imagining exactly what it would be like to find out.

So many weeks have passed, inflicted with numbness, and I wish I could say I feel guilty about it, but there is no guilt, or pain, happiness, or pleasure. There are no feelings at all.

In the car after picking Audrey up from school on Friday afternoon, they're fighting already. I don't know what they're fighting about, but nothing I say makes them stop, or even pause for a breath, so I let them be.

I back into my parking spot, turn off the car, and stare up to the road. A rifle fires from the ranch next door—after-school target practice for the teenagers, I'm sure. At the sound, a flock of birds takes flight from the oak tree at the end of the drive. Will the birds return once the teens disappear? Or will they head south, as their instincts command them to at this time of year?

I open the door for Audrey and Ryan, remind them to go straight inside and pick a snack, and start unloading the groceries. When I'm finished, I pull Noah from his seat, and we go inside too.

Audrey and Ryan are fighting over the step-stool—again.

"Hey, you can't pick a granola bar like me, copycat!" she screams.

"Yes, I can. And you copied me!" he fires back.

They keep going, fighting over who gets the pink plate and who sits where at the table.

Will they ever stop? *I can't handle the noise.*

I walk to our bedroom and pull a pair of earbuds from my dresser drawer. Then I search my phone for something loud to listen to, hoping it will drown out the noise. Settling on an old angst-filled playlist of my high school years, I crank up the volume and start putting the groceries away.

When I dare to look up from my chore, I see they're still going at it, so I don't look up again. After putting away groceries, I empty and refill the dishwasher, then put a load of laundry into the washing machine. I can't bear the thought of taking away the music and coming back to reality, so I let them play and fight and watch way too much TV while I busy myself with anything I can; the goal being to not pay enough attention to have to intervene.

As the afternoon drags on, I'm forced to turn the volume of the music up more and more to drown out the craziness around me. I've asked them to go outside a dozen times, yet they're still here and without my nagging to keep them in check, the house is a disaster and they're louder than ever. I try to ignore them as I slice an apple for Noah, but with each minute, it becomes increasingly impossible.

"Ryan, give it back!" Audrey yells, reaching for a doll in Ryan's arms.

"No, I had it first!"

There's more screaming and crying and each kid is begging me to make the other one do whatever it is they want, but I keep slicing.

As the noise grows and my ability to ignore it diminishes, I sense the fireball growing in the depths of my chest. Without the energy to let it out, though, I'm afraid I'm going to implode. *How do I make it stop?*

There's a very distinct feeling I'm watching this whole scene from above. I can see myself lost in the middle of the chaos, imagining everything I should feel as the person with my feet on the ground, but can't.

Then an unexpected thought finds its way to the surface—I don't have to be here. I can leave.

I place the knife in the sink and slide the bowl of apple slices to the edge of the counter where Noah can reach it. Then, I pick up my phone and walk out of the house to the silence of my car.

As I sit, staring down the driveway in front of me, my mind travels back to my childhood. Do I remember ever seeing Mama or GiGi struggling in the same way I do? Did they also fight a constant battle in their head about who they actually were versus who they wished they could be? Were they also always reaching for something just beyond their fingertips...a chance to do better, be better? Did they run away to find solace in the comfort of their cars, too? Did they spend weeks wishing they could disappear?

Or were they happy?

I can't remember. There's nothing—no incident in my memory—that makes me think they were like me, and I feel more alone than ever.

My phone buzzes with a text message from Andrew, letting me know he's on his way home.

Thank God, only another half hour.

I'm surprised, but thankful none of the kids have come out to find me yet. I know I should go back inside to make sure they're all okay and to clean the place up before Andrew gets home. I know I should hug them, tell them I love them, and take the time to get each one settled into their own activity, so they'll leave each other alone. I know I should be a good mom.

But I can't.

I'm hot, my palms are sweaty, and my heart is racing. I open the door to get some fresh air.

Good Lord, I can hear them from out here.

I can't go in. I close it again and relish in the return to silence.

What feels like an eternity later, I see it—Andrew's truck coming down the street. I breathe a sigh of relief, knowing he'll be here in a matter of seconds, and he can help.

But how will I explain to him why I'm sitting here in the car alone? Why I've left the kids unattended? Why the house is destroyed, as I'm sure it is? He's going to have questions, and I don't want to answer any of them.

That telling bead of sweat rolls from my temple to jaw, reminding me just how much of a mess I really am, and that I should have gone back in the house before he got here.

Then, in either an obvious sign from above, or a fortuitous twist of fate, I see something else—the the diaper bag, still sitting on the floorboard of the seat next to me. It never made it inside after school and my wallet and keys are in there.

Andrew's home, and like the birds in the old oak tree—*I can leave.*

My heart skips a beat, and a conversation ensues with either the devil or the angel on my shoulders, I can't tell which.

No, I can't leave. Where would I go?

It doesn't matter.

How would I explain it to Andrew and the kids?

You don't have to.

But I'm the one who holds this place together.

No, you're not.

But the kids need me...

No, they don't. He's so much more to them than you'll ever be.

But, I'm their mother.

And they're better off without you.

Andrew's truck turns into the driveway. My window is fleeting.

I press down on the brake pedal and push the ignition button on the dash. The car comes to life, sensing the key in the bag. The radio is still on from before, but I can't make out the song. All I hear is that voice in my head telling me to run.

He's getting closer and I can now see his tall silhouette, framed by the setting sun. I look up into the rear-view mirror, hoping maybe I'll see one of the kids standing in the doorway, and I'll be forced to stop, but there's nobody there.

I shove the shifter into drive and in one swift move—as if it has a mind of its own—my right foot goes from break to pedal and pushes down hard.

Tires bark as they lurch forward from their perfectly ordinary parked position and embark upon the utterly unknown. As they turn, I'm drawn nearer to Andrew's truck, making its way down the long, black-topped drive.

Forcing every ounce of strength I have left in my body to my head, neck, and eyeballs, I fix my gaze on the garbage can at the road.

If I look his way, I'll see the confused look on his gorgeous face. I'll see he's motioning for me to stop. I'll see he's surprised, scared, hurt, and pleading...and I will stop. So I keep going, not once looking back, and turn out of the drive.

I point the car down the one road leading out of this place and as I drive away, the only thought running through my head is I have no idea where I'm going. But then that voice from before chimes in again.

It doesn't matter—but you can't stay here.

I'm not even out of the neighborhood yet, and Andrew's blowing up my phone with three missed phone calls and several frantic text messages.

"What's going on? Where are you going? Are you okay?"

"What happened? Call me."

"Jenna, please pick up your phone."

"You're scaring me. Call me!"

I see the messages. I see the phone calls. And I have no idea what to say to him, so I keep driving.

As I come into town, I land at the intersection with the highway. One ramp will take me to San Antonio, the other, further out into the sticks. It's tempting to just pick a direction and go, but first, I turn the car toward Meadowbrook. I need to see Bonnie.

Andrew's still calling as I pull into Bonnie's driveway. As I exit the car and walk up to her front door, I wonder if she's even home. I don't see any lights on in the windows and hear no sounds coming from inside. I knock anyway, and it's not long before she opens the door.

I'm a bit taken aback as it's the first time I've seen her wearing lounge clothes, or maybe pajamas—wide legged sweatpants and a tee-shirt with a gray cardigan layered over the top. Her hair is down, touching her shoulders, rather than up in its usual chignon. Her lips are a pale gray.

"I'm sorry to stop by without notice. If you're busy or not up for company, I can go."

"I'm fine. I'm a little under the weather, is all. What's up?" She closes her sweater tight around her body. "Here, come in."

I do as she says, but when she tries to lead me toward the tempting warmth of the fireplace, I don't follow.

She notices, stops, and turns to face me. "Jenna, what's wrong?"

"I don't know, but I think I'm going to take a bit of a trip. I wanted to let you know, so you wouldn't be expecting us on Tuesday. I wanted to say goodbye."

"What do you mean 'goodbye'? Where are the babies?" She hurries to the sitting room window and looks out to see if the kids are waiting for me in the car.

"They're fine. They're home with Andrew."

"Well, what's your hurry, then? Why don't you come in and I'll put on a pot?" she asks, gesturing toward the kitchen.

"No, thank you. I can't stay."

Bonnie opens her mouth to say something, but stops. She's looking at me hard, trying to find the right words. Then she says, "Huh. Well, okay, if you're sure."

"I am. I just didn't want you to worry."

Is that why I'm here? Or did I come here, hoping she would change my mind? Maybe, but if so, I should have known it would be a wasted effort. Bonnie's not one for telling people what to do.

She walks toward me and puts her hands on my shoulders. "You don't have to do this, love. We can talk about it, whatever it is."

"No, Bonnie, not this time."

She steps back and stares. Then she returns to me and gives a long, tight hug before pulling away again.

"I don't like to give my opinion on the choices of others, Jenna—you know that—but I don't think this is something you should do. Where will you go? I'm scared for you."

"Well, I have to. I can't stay here." I wipe a tear from my face and wrap my arms around my waist.

Bonnie wipes a tear of her own. "Okay then. You have my number. Call me when you get there." She says it the same way GiGi would say it if I was simply driving myself home after a holiday meal with the family.

"Okay." I turn to leave Bonnie's beautiful home and can't help but to take one last look. I don't know what it is, but something feels different—like I'm coming to the end of a chapter in a book, unsure of what to expect in the next. I take a mental snapshot of it and file it away in my memory—pajama'd Bonnie and all.

I slide back into the driver's side of the car and see I have more missed calls and texts from Andrew. The last one catches my attention.

"Jenna, if I don't hear from you soon, I'm calling the police. I'm worried."

I text him back. "No, don't. I'm fine. But I need a break. I'm sorry. Kiss the kids for me. Love you."

Seconds later, he's calling again. I deny the call, turn on the car, and back out of the driveway. Bonnie's still standing on her front porch, sweater wrapped tight around her waist, watching me go. She gives a little wave as I pull away.

Back at the highway intersection, the only remaining question is, which way do I go? If I go into San Antonio, I can see a movie or walk around the shops, go to a bookstore, or find something to eat, then go home. It's my one last shot to do something, *anything* other than what I've already decided to do.

If I take the other way, I'll find nothing but hills, fields, trees, and the occasional Dairy Queen in a small pass-through town. That's a drive with no destination; a drive that can go on forever. That's the drive I've already chosen.

As I accelerate onto the ramp, the reality of what I've done hits me. I've run away. I've left them behind and I can't go back.

Instantly, as if someone flipped a switch in my brain, I can feel *everything*. All the anger, sadness, guilt, self-loathing, resentment, and pain of the last few weeks that I was numb to before, comes down on me at once.

My eyes fill with tears, and I can no longer see the road in front of me. I pull off to the side of the highway, sob, and pray.

What have I done? Andrew will never forgive me for this and my poor babies—I didn't even tell them goodbye. What will they think when I'm not there to tuck them into bed tonight?

My heart hurts and I don't know how to fix it.

When I wipe away the tears again, a giant power pole in the center median of the highway comes into focus. Like a flashback of a memory that has been lost, I see myself putting the car in drive, pushing the gas pedal to the floor, and heading straight for that pole.

Oh, the relief that would bring.

I merge back onto the highway—eyes glued to that pole. Cars are coming up quick behind me, so I speed up. Closer and closer it comes. My heart is racing and everything inside of me is telling me to do it; to end this...to end it all.

Then, like the vision of my car wrapped around that pole flashed through my head before, I see something else: my kids in black, standing graveside. Ryan's crying silently, Audrey's screaming at the top of her lungs, and Noah's face is straight. He doesn't understand.

I've never experienced the feeling of having a literal knife in my chest, but I imagine the feeling that comes with seeing a vision of your kids at your own funeral must be one and the same.

That alone is why I pass that pole with myself intact, but every one I see is a fresh, terrifying opportunity for escape.

They call to me like a siren calls to a ship, promising beauty and love and rest. I'm counting them as they pass: twelve, thirteen, fourteen. The only thing I see clearly now *are* those poles.

Twenty-seven, twenty-eight, twenty-nine. Time and time again, I'm tempted by the songstress and each time I'm saved by nothing more than that vivid, excruciating image of my kids in black.

I drive for hours with no destination in mind. The occasional text message alert or phone call from Andrew are the only sounds. I don't reply or answer any of them. What words could explain what I have done? There simply are none.

Moving through the dark, my sole primal urge—aside from seeking a quick end by means of a power pole—is to put as many miles as possible between this car and that house.

Around midnight, I pass a highway sign for Sulphur, Louisiana. Somewhere, a few miles back, I crossed the Texas/Louisiana state line.

As I search for an open gas station, my mind finds its way back to Andrew and the kids.

Did they miss me at bedtime? Or did they not even notice I wasn't there?

He stopped texting and calling about a half hour ago. Did he go to sleep? Is he able to sleep, not knowing where I am or if I'm coming home?

Part of me wants to think he's waiting up for me and only trying to give me some space, but the realist in me knows he's sleeping soundly; oblivious or even apathetic that my side of the bed is empty and cold. He'll wake in the morning, make breakfast for the kids, and go about his day.

It's better that way, anyway.

Spotting a twenty-four-hour station on the south side of the highway, I stop, fill up the tank, use the restroom, and grab some snacks and caffeine. I know where I'm going now, and it's going to be a long night.

Back in the car and ready to go, I set the GPS. Destination: Asher, Alabama.

I text Andrew. "I'm going home. Need to see Michelle."

Immediately, I receive a reply. "What? For how long? That's a long drive. Jenna, call me, please!"

Leaving the gas station, I turn on the radio, hoping to bury some of the noise in my head, but as I flip through the stations, it all seems so insufferable and pointless. I turn it back off, thankful for the return to silence.

For an hour, I watch the mile markers pass by—the same way I watched those poles—and the minutes on the clock change almost to the cadence of their passing.

In the darkness, it's easy to imagine every sign, tree, and car I pass is the same sign, tree, and car...over and over again, like I'm stuck in The Twilight Zone or some kind of sick, impervious time warp. The thought of this is panic-inducing. I turn the radio back on, allowing each new song to serve as a reminder that time is real and I'm not spinning my tires in place.

An hour later, the moon goes missing, hiding behind a ceiling of dense, fast-moving clouds. It's pitch black and that anxious feeling I'm going through the motions of driving the car, but not really going anywhere, strikes again.

I press further down on the gas pedal, climbing to eighty, then ninety, then one hundred miles per hour; trying my best to outrun the never-ending darkness and the disquiet that comes with it.

Another hour passes. I'm out of coffee and my eyelids are growing heavy. I've been awake for about twenty-one hours and I'm starting to feel it. I consider pulling off to the side of the road to rest, but instead, roll down the front windows, hoping the frigid wind will bring me back to life.

As I make my way down the highway, I cycle between feeling like I'm caught up in some sort of alternate reality and none of this is real—and sobbing because I know it is. It's so tempting to stop, call Andrew, beg him for forgiveness, and turn the car around.

I can't imagine what he must have thought, watching me barrel past him in the driveway with my gaze fixed on the road, not daring to glance his way. Or when he walked inside and discovered I had left without the kids.

No, even with a massive part of my being craving nothing more than to turn around and head back home with my heart in my hands, the rest of me knows I can't go back. I've come too far, and yet, I still have so far to go. If I turn back now, if I try to go back to that house, I'll never make it. Even if I make it through the drive, I won't last. I have to find a new beginning—one that doesn't preemptively start with fate's decision that I should wind up dead.

I stop for gas one more time, grab more snacks and coffee, and press on for the final leg of the trip. Just as the sun climbs up from the horizon, illuminating bulbous pastel clouds, I pass the Asher city limit sign.

Feeling both terrified and relieved, I turn onto Main Street, then find my way to the old residential neighborhood behind the tiny shops and restaurants. A few more turns, then I pull into the driveway of that familiar, single-story bungalow that has been my second home for as long as I can remember.

I park behind Michelle's black Ford Explorer and stare at its colorful Alabama license plate. Peeling my death-grip from the steering wheel, I stretch my fingers, and release a much-needed sigh of relief.

Dear God, I've made it. And by some miracle, or sheer luck, I'm still alive.

5

ASHER

It's too early to knock on the door, so I leave the car running for heat, turn up the radio to keep me awake, and let my mind wander back to all the memories Michelle and I have made here over the years.

Her family moved to Asher—and to this house—when we were in the sixth grade. She was the new kid in class, and I was the quiet one without a lot of friends. As soon as one of us worked up the courage to talk to the other, we knew we were sisters for life.

We were inseparable. If she got a job at Blockbuster, so did I. If I went to summer camp, she went too. If she tried out for track, I did it right there with her. That's how I discovered I had a talent for running, and that talent put me through college without a mountain of debt.

We dated the same boys, though obviously not at the same time. We even dated a pair of brothers once, which we thought was the coolest thing ever—"Hey, if we marry them both, we'll have the same last name and be real sisters!" Those relationships didn't last through the summer, but I remember getting my first kiss out of it, right over there on Michelle's front porch steps.

When it came time for college, my scholarship offer took me to Texas and Michelle's didn't. We cried like we would never see each other again and I remember that heartache being worse than any breakup I'd experienced in my young life. But I went home on school breaks and she visited a few times. We both started dating college boys, and the pain got a little easier to bear. We spent several nights a week talking on the phone way too late, then dragging our butts out of bed for early morning classes, but we never once considered not making that call.

Then, Michelle met Thomas. Theirs was a whirlwind romance. They were engaged in four months, married in six. Their whole family (and the whole town, for that matter) thought they were nuts, but somehow, they knew it was right.

They stayed together in an apartment on campus when they were first married and, amid all the newlywed excitement, we didn't talk as much as before. After graduation, they returned to Asher. As a combined graduation and wedding present, Michelle's parents gave her the home she grew up in, packed up their things, and moved to Florida in search of bluer skies and sandy shores.

Once Michelle and Thomas were married and settled into their new life in Asher, our long, late-night conversations were right back on track. That's when I told her all about the redneck Texan by the name of Andrew, who I met shortly after graduation, who drove a jacked-up truck, and who kept asking me out. She was the one who said, "Well, what are you waiting for? He sounds pretty dreamy to me." Michelle always had a soft spot for the ones who were a little rough around the edges.

She was the reason I found love, because as with so many other times in my life, she nudged me just enough to convince me to go for something I found terrifying. And of course, she was right—with his kind heart, towering height, sky-blue eyes, and that subtle Texas drawl, he was oh-so-dreamy.

From the corner of my eye, I see the curtains in the living room window open. It's a quarter after seven and Michelle must be up with the kids.

What will she think of me when she finds out what I did? When I tell her all my darkest secrets, which I've never been brave enough to admit in a single one of our calls? Will she yell, tell me how stupid I've been, and send my ass back to Texas? She probably should, but hopefully we can put off that conversation until after I've gotten some rest. I'm so tired that it's hard to focus my eyes, let alone my thoughts. I pick up the diaper bag, take a deep breath, and get out of the car.

The anticipation of admitting to her what I've done brings on the tears before I even reach the front steps. I knock on the door, but there's no answer. I wait, then knock again, then wait some more.

Standing here waiting to confess—waiting to be judged—is agonizing. The weight of the diaper bag is too much for my sleepless emotional self to bear. My knees give way and I collapse, in what I imagine to be slow motion, to the hard concrete porch.

I cross my legs and text Michelle, "Open the door." Then I lean forward, allowing the bag in my lap to bear the weight of my tired body and soul, as warm tears cascade down my cheeks in the cold morning air.

A moment later, the front door swings open. I wipe my face and look up to see her, standing there in pink pajamas and a satin sleep bonnet.

"Jenna! Girl, what are you *doing* here?"

I try to stand, but it takes more effort than expected, and I don't quite make it all the way onto my feet. Michelle reaches down, places her hands under my arms, and pulls me up. I open my mouth to say something, but the words don't come.

I can't imagine what she's thinking, staring at this mess that has heaved itself upon her doorstep without warning, but her only move is to wrap her arms around my shivering shoulders to offer a hug.

She pulls back to get a good look at me—no doubt trying to judge the severity of my emotional state— then picks up my bag and pulls me inside.

"How long were you out there? I heard the knock, but thought it was the damn delivery man. He's the only one who ever knocks this early. You must be freezing!"

"It wasn't long. I'm okay." I take a seat on the sofa.

"Do you want some coffee to warm you up? Or tea?"

"No, thank you. All I need right now is a bed, if that's okay. I drove all night and I'm pretty tired."

"Yeah, of course. Do you need your bags so you can change?" She moves toward the front door.

"There are no bags, Shelly." I stare at the floor beneath my feet.

"Oh." She pauses, processing the weight of those five words. "Well, let me get you some of my pj's then—be right back." She disappears for a few minutes, then pokes her head into the boys' room to check on them before returning to the living room with a set of clothes. "I can't guarantee they'll stay this quiet forever. Hopefully, you can sleep."

"Pretty sure I could sleep through anything right now." I take the pajamas from her hands and stand. "Thank you."

"Yeah, sure, but...are you okay? Are the kids okay?"

"They're fine. They're with Andrew." My words spew forward in a way that lets her know I'm exhausted, and not at all in the mood for a talk.

"Okay. Go get some rest." She nods toward the hallway with the spare bedroom in the back of the house. "Oh, and Thomas is out of town for a couple of weeks, so it's just us. We shouldn't be bothered by anyone else."

I nod and grab a throw blanket from the sofa before walking back to the spare room. It was converted from an old porch at some point in its history and is always drafty.

As I enter through the narrow doorway, I realize nothing here has changed since Michelle and Thomas first moved in. The same lavender quilt her Nan made for her is draped across the end of the bed. The same white lace curtains cover the too-small, divided light window and the same brass chandelier hangs precariously from the low ceiling. If there's one thing I can always count on from Michelle, it's consistency.

I change into the provided flannel pajama pants and gray long-sleeved tee, spread the quilt up over the bed, and add the extra blanket from the living room on top. Then, I turn on the floor fan for white noise and slide under the warm, thick covers. Before laying my head on the pillow, I send a text message to Andrew. "Made it to Michelle's. Going to get some rest. Love you."

Then I click off the vintage hobnail table lamp and sleep.

———

I awaken to the thundering sound of four little feet stampeding into the kitchen.

"Shh, Auntie Jenna's trying to sleep."

"Sorry, Mama," Jasper says.

I roll over and look at the time on my phone: 6:27. It must be dinnertime for the boys. Come to think of it, I haven't eaten a proper meal in over twenty-four hours myself. I should join them, say hello, and put some sustenance in my rumbling belly.

"Mama, this one has ketchup on it. It's not mine."

"Uh oh. Alex, does yours have ketchup?" Michelle's voice sounds a little frantic.

"Yup."

"Okay, so they got our order wrong and put ketchup on both burgers. Jaz, can you maybe try it with ketchup?"

"No, I don't like it!" Jasper's scream is both a whine and a demand, all in one.

"Well, that's all I have, unless you want peanut butter and jelly for dinner," Michelle answers.

"Aw, I really want a burger."

"I understand, but mine has ketchup on it, too. So, unless you're willing to try your burger, I don't know what else to tell you."

"Okay, I guess I'll try it." His answer is followed by a moment of silence.

"Well, what do you think? Has it grown on you yet?"

There must have been some sort of head shake or disapproving face, because the next thing I hear is an amused laugh from Michelle.

"Okay, okay, I'll make you a sandwich then. At least you tried it. Yay, for you!"

She's calm. She's laughing and having fun. She's not angry the restaurant messed up her order, and she's not frustrated with Jasper for refusing his burger. At least she's not showing it, if she is.

My brain spins off and recreates that scene in my kitchen, with my own kids. The ending to my story doesn't look anything like what I overheard here though—not outside of the good days, anyway. How does she do it?

On second thought, maybe I'm not hungry after all.

I force myself to focus on the humming sound of the fan and drift off once again.

◆

This time when I wake, the house is silent, and the room is pitch black. It's 2:45 in the morning. I have been sleeping for...nineteen hours. How is that possible?

There are several missed calls and text messages from Andrew, full of more requests for me to call him back and more questions about when I'm coming home. I can't think about that right now, so I lay the phone upside down on the nightstand because somehow, upside down means those questions don't exist.

I turn on the lamp and see a basket sitting on the nightstand. Inside it is a phone charger, a bottle of water, a banana, a granola bar, some trail mix, a Hershey's bar, and a new toothbrush and travel-sized tube of toothpaste.

She really is the sweetest, and she really does think of everything.

I don't feel hungry now, but I eat anyway. Then, thankful for the ability to brush my teeth, I stand and tiptoe to the door. I lift it up by the door handle as I open it, knowing it squeaks if you don't, then cross through the kitchen and living room to find my way to the bathroom in the main hall.

As I flip on the bathroom light, I'm startled by my own ghostly reflection. It's the first time I've seen myself in a mirror since arriving here, and the image before me is staggering.

My skin and lips are even more pale than usual, probably from dehydration. My eyes are red from all the crying and also black from the smudged mascara. A bird's nest of tangles sits atop my head with neglected, dark roots at least two inches long.

I look and feel like a mangled zombie, and it's impossible to look away. For once, the outside somewhat matches the inside, and it's sadly cathartic.

I grab the countertop with both hands to steady myself and look down, away from my miserable face in the mirror.

"I shouldn't be here." The words are barely audible, but they're there, hanging out in space and daring me to grab my keys and run again, this time back to Texas where I belong.

My thoughts turn to my babies, and what story Andrew has told them to explain why I'm away. The last thing I want is for them to realize I've abandoned them or to think I don't love them, but as much as it hurts, I can't go back. I don't *know how* to be their mom, and no mom is better than an awful mom, I'm sure.

I wipe away the tears and stare again at the haggard reflection in the mirror. Seeing myself, in this pure state of madness and overwhelm, confirms what I already knew: I did what had to be done. Now, it's time to accept it and push on—to whatever may come next.

I use the toilet, brush my teeth, and wash my face with the hand soap sitting on the counter. Then I tiptoe back across the house to my room. Lifting on the door as I close it without a sound, I resume my half-alive position in the bed.

Lying here in the dark, waiting for the sleep to carry me away, crystal-clear visions of myself with Audrey as a newborn baby flash through my head.

I was so happy. I was convinced my whole life was changed. Convinced every care and worry I ever held was suffocated out of existence the moment she was laid in my arms. Looking into her innocent glistening eyes, listening to her sweet gentle breaths, she became my whole world. In that world, so miraculous and bright and full of hope, there was no room for anything but love.

Oh, poor, naive me. If only I knew then what I know now. But what? What would I have done differently? Knowing full-well that's an impossible question with a non-existent answer, I force-stop the thought process and focus again on the humming of the fan, until the sleep rescues me once more.

6

MICHELLE

It's 6:13. I know they'll be up soon, and as much as I want to stay in bed all day again today, I also know I have to find the fortitude to get up and walk out of this room.

But what do I tell her? How much do I tell her? Michelle and I have hidden nothing from each other before—except this. I've never once shared with her how overwhelming motherhood is for me; how quickly I lose my patience and become a monster even I can't control. I've never talked to her before about the white-hot rage that seems to be ever-bubbling beneath the surface or how sometimes I have vivid, detailed daydreams of what life would be like if I'd never had kids at all. And there are no words to explain to her how drastically it all changes when the dark days slip away—how it's like I'm living a different life when they disappear, and the good days come. She's going to think I'm crazy, and she'll probably be right.

I hear footsteps in the hall, then the TV in the living room comes on and I make out the sound of cartoons. The boys are up. I wait for Michelle.

Soon, I hear her in the kitchen, pouring cereal and calling the boys to the table. I slide my feet to the floor, stand, and throw the covers up to the top of the bed. Then I open the door and step into the kitchen.

"Auntie Jenna!" the boys scream, jump out of their seats, and run to shower me with hugs.

"Hey, guys! Look how big you've grown...oh, my goodness!" I squeeze them back and kiss them both on their cheeks. "Did y'all sleep well?"

"Yeah! We're having cereal for breakfast. Want some?" Alex asks.

"Sure. Cereal sounds great."

"Back to your seats, y'all. We have to hurry, or we'll be late." Michelle pours milk into their bowls and beckons for them to come back to the table.

"We have other options, if you don't want cereal." She points to the fridge. "We usually do a quick breakfast before church, then I make bacon, eggs, and all that good stuff after we get back."

"No, cereal is fine. I will take some coffee, though." I stand, head over to the Keurig, and choose the darkest roast she has. Then I return to the table with mug-in-hand.

"Did you sleep okay in there? I know it can get cold." Michelle takes her seat at the table.

"Yeah, I slept fine. The extra blanket helps." I pour my breakfast into a white bowl with a turquoise rim. Michelle's bowl is a pottery piece in a rusty red color with giant yellow sunflowers painted onto it. The boys' are navy blue with bugs painted on one and robots on the other. Nothing in this kitchen matches, and that's partly why I love it so much.

I look up from my bowl and sneak a quick peek across the table. She watches my every move, waiting. I know she's dying to know why I'm here and I don't blame her. I would be too, but I'm at a loss. I don't know what to say or where to start.

Done with the small-talk and wasted time, she reaches over and puts her hand on mine. The stark contrast of our skin colors serves as an instant reminder of how different we are: She's a normal, emotionally-regulated mother and I, most certainly, am not.

"Okay, so what's going on? Why are you here alone?" she asks.

Well, there it is…literally on the table.

I don't answer right away. I'm hoping my silence will force her to move on to another subject and I can come back to this one once I have a plan or some answers. But she doesn't give up. She waits.

"I ran away," I mumble. I don't know any other way of saying it, besides just saying it.

She pauses for a moment, then says, "What do you mean you ran away?" Pulling her hand from mine, she looks at me with a straight, careful expression, trying not to scare me off.

"I mean, I ran away. I couldn't take the madness anymore. Then, I realized I didn't have to! So I went to sit in the quiet of the car to re-center, like I always do. But this time, the diaper bag was there, and my keys and wallet were inside it…and…I turned the car on, hit the gas, and left." My words tumble out in a jumbled-up mess that would have been indecipherable to most people, and there are so many details missing, but they're there, waiting to be received.

"*What*?" Her voice is surprised, loud, and a couple of octaves higher than normal. "You left the kids—alone?"

"No, of course I didn't leave them alone, Michelle. Andrew was pulling into the driveway. They were fine." I put my spoon down on the table and grab the coffee mug. I take a rather large gulp to fill the awkward silence and the scorching hot liquid burns my tongue. Her reaction is what I expected it to be, but it hurts more than I imagined it would. How did I ever think she could understand? She's not like me.

"Wow." She's looking at me, but not really looking at me. Her dark eyes are focused on the bridge of my nose and her stare is blank and faraway.

"I'm sorry, I shouldn't have come here, I guess." I stand and turn back toward my room.

"No, Jenna, sit down."

I stop, afraid to sit back at that table and afraid of what she'll say next, but I do as she says.

"You mean to tell me—" She places her elbows on the table and leans forward, finishing her sentence with a whisper. "—that you actually did it?"

"What?"

"I mean, I've threatened to pack my bags and run away a thousand times, but I would never have the courage to actually do it!" She stares at me in what appears to be genuine wonder.

"*Courage?* That's what you think it took? More like total insanity!"

With that, her expression changes, and her raucous laughter fills the tiny kitchen.

"Y'all done?" Michelle asks, for what must be the twelfth time.

"Yeah, all done," Alex answers.

"Good. Go play video games or watch TV in your room for a bit while Auntie Jenna and I talk. We're not going to church today."

They both hop down from the table and take off running to their room.

"So, what happened? I want the whole story." She stands to fetch another cup of coffee.

"That would take a while and I'm not even sure I know what the whole story is."

"Well, I don't have anywhere else to be. And we don't play hooky from church all that often, so we won't see those boys again until lunch. They're going to milk it for all they can."

I take a moment to think. Where do I start?

"Well, I don't know. Sometimes it's all too much. I mean, I love my kids of course, but some days are better than others." I stab at the cereal in my bowl. I barely ate two bites before we got into all this, and now it's just a soppy mess.

"Uh-huh, I get that," Michelle says.

Those words light an angry spark inside of me. No, she doesn't *get that.*

"Do you? I mean, I'm not talking about having a bad day, Michelle. I'm talking zero patience, uncontrollable rage, a tongue that holds nothing back, and way too often wishing I'd never even become a mother at all—stuff you'd never dare tell anyone about." I lean forward over the table to make sure she catches the next part. "I contemplated running my car into a power pole for the first fifty miles of the trip out here."

Her jaw drops and for a moment, she appears at a loss for words. Finally, I have her attention.

"Wow, I had no idea."

"Yeah, well, no one does." I sit back in my seat and take a sip from my cup.

"So, when did it all start? Or has it always been this way? I mean, I know you dealt with a bit of depression in college, but I thought you seemed to handle that okay."

"Oh, that was nothing compared to all this. This—this is on a whole other level. I can't even explain what makes it so different and I feel guilty about it every damn day...because what the hell do I have to be depressed about? I have an amazing husband, three beautiful children, a comfortable home, a car to drive, food to eat, we don't struggle for money, we're healthy. I am an immensely privileged, middle-class white woman who should have nothing in the world to be sad about." I look off to my left and out of the kitchen window, begging the tears not to come now.

"You've got that right," she quips.

I know Michelle's family has struggled for generations, as Black people born and raised in the south. Even if I've never lived it and can never truly understand it, I still know, which makes me feel even more childish and stupid for being here now.

"But you also understand that you're human, right? And humans feel things," she says.

I nod.

"So, if it wasn't college, when did it start then?"

I pause to think. "I'm not sure. Sometime after Audrey was born. Maybe when she was about three months old? I thought it was the hormones."

"But it never went away? All these years later, and it's never gone away? God, Jenna, that's awful."

I can see she feels sorry for me, but I don't want her to feel sorry for me. I want her to help me fix it.

"Oh, it goes away—and then it comes back. My life is an emotional roller coaster of ups and downs that never ends. I'll go weeks feeling horrible, barely able to get myself out of bed. Then, over time, I start to feel better."

I think my eye contact is a bit much for her. She looks away to give herself a break, but I can't help it. I want to know if she understands. I need to know if she can relate to anything I'm saying. I need to know I'm not alone.

"I notice little things like appreciating the sunshine when I'm running errands, or I catch myself enjoying a bit of small talk with the cashier at the grocery store. That's when I know the dark days are fading away. After that, I get to be normal for a few weeks and everything is great, but it always comes crashing back down again."

"Have you talked to your doctor at all? Maybe it's a chemical or hormonal imbalance or something?"

"Of course, I have. And I've tried the meds, but they don't help. Nothing does. I'm at a loss here, Michelle. I'm beginning to think I'm just bat-shit crazy."

She stands, walks over to the cupboards, and starts pulling out ingredients. "No, you're not crazy. I'm no professional, but back up to wherever you think could have been the beginning. We're gonna talk it out...and make cinnamon rolls, because we need something to do with our hands, yeah?"

"Yeah." I stand and fetch her mama's recipe book from the shelf in the corner. Those cinnamon rolls were famous in this town for decades. If Michelle wants to make them, I'm not about to stand in her way.

We measure, pour, mix, knead, roll, and bake...taking our time along the way. Then we make the frosting with her mama's secret ingredient—a few tablespoons of bourbon. While we're doing it all, we talk. I tell her stories I've never dared to even tell Andrew. I tell her feelings I've never admitted to myself before...and the whole time, I'm watching for understanding to come upon her. I don't have the courage to ask her outright if she's ever felt any of this. I'm terrified of her answer.

"Hey, have you ever put bacon on top of these after they're frosted?" I ask.

"Um...no, but—" A devious smile appears on her face. "Don't you dare tell Mama."

"Never." I turn toward the fridge and pull the bacon out of the drawer. We fry it up, chop it up, and toss it on top of the cooling rolls.

"Oh my God, they're almost too pretty to eat, but Lord, if I'm not going to devour at least three." Michelle pulls plates from the cabinet, and I grab the milk from the refrigerator. The smell in this house is unbelievable—enough to even bring two video-game-entranced little boys out from their hiding place.

"Mama, what did you make? I smell bacon!" Jasper appears from the hallway, skips to the table, and hops into a seat.

"Mmm, cinnamon rolls!" Alex says, before he's even turned the corner. He runs up to the table too, but stops short when he sees Jasper sitting in his chair. "Jaz, you're in my seat."

"Nuh-uh, I got here first."

"But this is where I sit. Your seat is over there." Alex's face contorts in that particular way all five-year-old faces do right before they're about to lose it.

"Hey, we worked hard on these rolls and we want to enjoy them in peace, okay?" Michelle takes a knee in front of Alex, so she can look him in the eye. "Baby, I know you want your regular seat, but Jasper got there first, so it's only fair."

Alex opens his mouth, and I can hear the whining and crying and see the impending epic meltdown coming before it even happens.

"But that means it's your turn to get the special seat next to Auntie Jenna." She smiles with a scrunched-up nose and squeezes his shoulders with over-exaggerated excitement.

"Yay! I like sitting with Auntie Jenna!" Alex runs over and gives me a light punch in the arm before climbing into the chair next to me.

Another picture-perfect example of patience and grace from Michelle. Like before, I compare it with how I would have handled the same situation with my own kids, and it makes me want to cry.

After they've finished their cinnamon rolls and milk, the boys run for their coats, then dash out the back door to play in the yard. I round up the dishes and carry them over to the sink. "So, how do you do that?"

"Do what?"

"Keep your calm like that, know what to say, mother them with such...kindness?" I'm scrubbing plates and waiting for some tiny morsel of wisdom to come loose and change my whole world.

But Michelle looks at me, confused.

"The chair thing. I would not have achieved the same outcome you did, at least not that peacefully."

"Oh, that was textbook—straight out of a role-playing exercise we did in a parenting class I took when Jasper was two." She brings over more dishes. "And nobody should ever allow us in the same kitchen together. That was a terrible idea. Look at this mess!"

"You took a parenting class? And learned something useful?" I'm surprised, as Michelle's never been the type to take a 'how-to' class in anything, much less something as presumably innate as parenting.

"Well, yeah. I was talking with a friend one day about some problems I'd been having with Jasper, and she suggested we go together. It was free, so I thought, why not? Turned out to be a great class. I still have the book, if you want to give it a look."

I'm not all that interested in learning how to parent my kids from a book, but if it helped her, then maybe it can help me too. "Yeah, sure. I'll try literally anything at this point."

Michelle crosses the kitchen, stopping mid-way. "Jenna, what is it that brings on the need to go sit in your car for peace? What happens before that?" She throws her towel up over her shoulder and turns to look at me.

"Usually I'm trying to accomplish something. Getting us all in the house after school, getting everyone ready for bed or to go somewhere, or even trying to do homework with Audrey or cook dinner. There's three of them and one of me—and they're so loud—and always fighting!" I stop what I'm doing and meet Michelle's gaze. There's a sparkle there, which I interpret as a tiny gleam of hope. "Why?" I ask, desperate for any insight she has to offer.

"Be right back." She turns and jogs out of the kitchen and to her bedroom. When she returns, there's a book in her hands. "Here. This is the book. Read it."

"Um, okay?"

"Jen, what if most of your problem stems from literally not knowing how to effectively parent your kids? And don't take that the wrong way!" She puts her hands on her hips to let me know she's serious. "Look, we aren't born knowing how to do this. We have to learn how to do it well, like with anything else, and there's no shame in that. Imagine if you learned how to communicate with your kids—to get them to listen, understand, cooperate—without all the yelling and drama. I bet you'd spend a lot less time in your car and that's a start, right?"

"Well, yeah. I don't think it would fix everything, but man, if I could do what you do with Jasper and Alex with Audrey and Ryan? What a difference that would make."

"Read the book. And there's a website on the back where you can check for classes in your area. I think this can help you."

"I'll read it. Thank you." She gives me a little side hug, trying to not make a big deal out of it, for my own comfort's sake. Then, she leaves to go check on the boys outside.

I look down at the cover of the book, then flip it over to the back.

"I don't know who you are, lady—" I say, looking at the photo of the tanned, golden-blonde author on the back cover. "—but it would be great if you could, you know, change my life. No pressure though." I roll my eyes at the thought of it, then toss the book through the bedroom doorway and onto the bed.

One can only hope.

7

NIRVANA

Before turning to head back into the kitchen, I see my phone, still plugged into the charger on the nightstand. I haven't checked it in hours. I'm sure there are messages from Andrew, and while I'm feeling better after having a bit of face time with Michelle, I'm nowhere near ready to answer all his questions. I consider turning around and leaving the phone right where it lies, but I can't do it. So, I take the four torturous steps to reach the table and pick it up.

As expected, there are several text messages from Andrew. He's given up on calling already. Surprisingly, though, there's also one from Bonnie.

"Oh, no. I never let her know when I got here."

"Who?" Michelle's back in the kitchen and must think I'm talking to her.

"Bonnie, the lady I told you about before. She texted."

I open the message and read it with Bonnie's raspy voice in my head.

"Hi, love. Checking in to make sure you're okay. Will I see you and sweet Noah for our visit on Tuesday? Let me know, so I can make something extra special."

Will she see us on Tuesday? That would mean leaving tomorrow, and I don't think that's going to happen.

My fingers move quickly across the screen. "Hi, Bonnie. I'm in Alabama visiting a friend. I don't think we'll make it this week. Sorry."

"Hey, where are your clothes? I'll throw them into the wash with mine," Michelle asks as she enters the room.

"Over on the chair. I need to run to Walmart once they're done. I need to pick up some toiletries and a few other things."

"Like more underwear? 'Cause I'm not providing those." She laughs as she picks up my dirty clothes and tosses them into the laundry basket on her hip.

"Yeah, yeah, among other things."

It feels so good to have Michelle around again. I would give anything to find a friend like her back home, but it seems so impossible to do. This friendship took decades to get to where it's at. I can't comprehend how people our age find new people to do that with, when we're so much older and life is incessantly busy—and I don't have the patience to wait that long to get to the good stuff. No, I don't need a new friend back home. I need Michelle.

"I don't suppose there's any chance you guys would ever reconsider moving to Texas, is there?" It's not the first time I've asked her this since I moved away.

She sits beside me on the bed. "We've talked about it."

"You have?"

"A few months back, Thomas heard rumors at work that several people were going to be laid off or transferred to other locations out of state. Texas was one of them."

I pull my leg up onto the bed and turn my body toward hers, excited to hear more. "And? Why didn't you tell me this before?"

"Because it didn't work out. But we talked about it and decided that if the opportunity comes up again, we'll go for it."

"*What?* I never thought I'd ever hear you say those words." I hug her around the neck, as my brain spins with visions of life and motherhood with Michelle right there with me. What a complete game-changer that would be.

"Believe it or not, Thomas is not as much of a homebody as you think he is. He's ready to try someplace new. We wouldn't be in San Antonio, though. His company's Texas location is in Austin."

"I don't care. I'll take it!"

"Well, we'll see what happens," she says with a laugh. "Now, are you gonna go commando so I can wash those two-day undies or keep *ridin' em* out until you pick up some more?"

"I think I'll hold on to my breeches, if that's okay with you." I crawl up to the top of the bed and under the covers. "And I'm going to take a nap."

"Fine, but you know 'breeches' are pants, right?" she says over her shoulder as she leaves the room.

"Oh, whatever. Hey, shut the door!"

"Ugh!" she doubles back and shuts the door.

Just like old times.

———◇———

When I wake from my nap, I hear clothes tumbling in the dryer. I check my phone and see another message from Bonnie.

"Okay, love. Call if you want to talk. I worry about you. Hugs."

It's getting late and the afternoon sun is casting playful, intricate shadows through the lace curtains and onto the ceiling.

I wonder what Andrew and the kids are up to? They're probably playing outside or at the park. He's so much better about getting them out of the house than I am. Do they miss me at all, or have they already gotten used to me not being there? Do they ask when I'm coming home? Do they miss my bedtime snuggles?

The guilt rolls in like a dark, gray fog, as I realize bedtime is the only time I ever offer them snuggles. As the tears threaten to escape, I climb out from under the covers and check on the laundry.

The clothes are mostly dry, so I take mine out and walk to the bathroom for a quick shower. Then, smelling like strawberries from the kids' shampoo, I wander out to look for Michelle. I find her playing a board game with the boys in their room, and the guilt comes again, as I struggle to remember the last time I sat down to play a game with *my* kids.

"Hey, I'm going to the store. Want me to pick up anything?" I zip my hoodie over my freshly laundered shirt.

"Yeah. Does frozen pizza sound okay for dinner?" She takes her turn with the game and moves her tiny red man forward a few spaces.

"Always. Anything else?"

"Wine—lots of wine. And maybe some fruit and milk."

"Okay, I'll be back soon. Call me if you think of anything else."

On the way to the store, I notice all the ways Asher has changed since I lived here, and all the ways it's still exactly the same. There are still only three stop lights. The corner store hasn't changed at all, and judging by the number of cars and people out front, is still a pretty happening place to be on the weekend. The shops on Main Street are all still open, though I only recognize a few of the business names on the doors now.

I continue down Main Street, come out of the historic district, and enter the newer part of town. Here there's a Waffle House, a Hardee's, a CVS Pharmacy, and about everything else you could ever need, including Walmart. I pull into a parking space near the front, grab my wallet, and move inside.

I make my way to the clothing section first and pick up a couple of packs of underwear, two extra bras, a pair of jeans, one pair of black leggings, and four comfy tops in my size. Next, I move to the health and beauty department for a brush, shampoo, conditioner, face wash, moisturizer, and deodorant. Do I need makeup? I don't plan to go anywhere I'd need it, but it feels weird to be without it. I push the cart over a few aisles more and throw in the bare basics: powder, mascara, blush, and lip gloss.

Next, I need to find my way to the grocery side of the store, which seems like a continent away. I take a deep breath and set off for the furthest aisle in the back to find the milk. After what feels like forever, I make it, and grab a gallon to put in the cart. The wine aisle is next. I choose a few bottles with cute labels and add those to the cart as well. Next comes the pizza and fruit, and boy, I think I might make it out of here unseen.

I put the last of the items in the cart and head toward the checkout. Of course, there's only one lane open and a line stretching to Birmingham. I consider pretending to shop in the clothing section until the line is shorter, but decide against it. I've got to get out of here. If Mama or GiGi walk in, I'll never be able to explain why I'm here, or why I haven't let them know.

My heart is racing, and I feel myself growing warm. I've got to stand in that line—and I really should have asked Michelle to make this trip!

I push the cart to the end of the line and do a quick scan around me to see if I recognize anyone nearby. I think I'm in the clear but realize I'm wrong when I spot the cashier. I look over at the other lanes, hoping maybe another one will open, but no such luck. And there's no way I am standing in a self-checkout line. That's a guaranteed invitation for attention, given that I can never get through them without needing some sort of assistance.

My only hope is that maybe she won't remember me.

I join the line, and as it moves, make my way up to the conveyor belt. Placing my items on it, I make every effort to avoid eye contact. Then, I hear a big gasp followed by, "Jenna Lewis! Wow, is it great to see you!" She addresses me by my maiden name, as people tend to do in this town.

"Hi, Paula. How are you?" The person in front of me goes on their way and I unload the rest of my cart.

"Doing great. Amanda's moved away to college, but she still talks about you sometimes. You were her favorite babysitter ever, you know," she says with a smile.

"Aw, thanks, that's sweet. She's a great kid—well, young lady now, I guess." I push my items closer to her, hoping she'll get the hint and speed this thing up.

"Well, as are you. Boy, I can't wait to tell your mama I saw you here. What brings you to town, anyway?" She scans a couple of items at a pace I think Ryan could beat in his sleep.

"I'm visiting a friend, but I haven't told Mama I'm here yet. I'm hoping it will be a surprise." I give her that look—the one that hopefully says, "Please keep your trap shut, lady."

"Oh, how fun! She's going to *lose* her mind." Her voice is loud and so full of faux-southern drawl, it's making my head hurt already. She continues, "What a great *surprise* that will be."

Oh, yes, a great surprise. I smile and nod.

She swipes the last item on the belt and my card is in and out of the reader before she can even tell me the total. Stuffing the last couple of bags into the cart, I say a quick, "It was great seeing you. Bye!" and move toward the exit.

"Bye, hon. Don't you be a stranger, now. Come back and see me soon!" As she yells across the two-dozen people standing between us, I have a sinking feeling every single one of them has turned to watch me run out the front doors.

I haul ass across the parking lot and throw my bags into the back of the van. I shove the cart into the return, hurry back to the car, and plop myself into the safety and relative privacy of the driver's seat. My breath is fast, like I've just snuck out of a high school boyfriend's bedroom window, and my thoughts are similar too.

"Oh, I am so busted. So, so busted." I tap my head twice on the steering wheel, start the car, and head home.

"Michelle, that was a really bad idea!" I proclaim, carrying the bags in through the front door.

"Why? What happened?" She rushes over to take some of the bags from my hands.

"Paula Coats is what happened! You didn't tell me she works at Walmart and, of course, there was only one lane open, and she was in it."

"Oh, yeah. I guess I didn't think about that. Do you think she'll tell your mama you're here?" She pulls a bottle of wine from a bag and starts searching the kitchen drawers for a corkscrew.

"I'm sure she will. That lady tells everyone everything. My mom is going to kill me."

"Well, you were eventually gonna go see her anyway, right?" Michelle asks.

"I don't know! You're my safe haven here, Michelle. You don't judge. You listen and help. As you know, that is not my mom or GiGi. I'm not ready to answer to them yet. I was kind of hoping I wouldn't have to do it at all." I collapse onto a seat at the table and put my head in my hands. "How do you tell your mom and grandma you've run away from your family? I can't explain it all to them. They'll never understand."

Michelle slides a glass of red wine in front of me and continues putting away the groceries. "Well, you don't have to tell them today. I say we drink and talk some more, because that's what we do best."

"Cheers to that." I raise my glass, take a swig, then slouch down in my seat, wishing I could fade deep down into its floral fabric.

We spend the next four hours making and eating dinner, giving the kids baths, putting them to bed, talking, and doing a whole lot of drinking. As we're sitting on the living room floor playing a game of Uno and still trying to dissect my problems, I pluck up the nerve to ask her the big question.

"So, can you relate to any of this? I mean, it seems like a crazy question, but have you ever dealt with depression or this kind of—anger?"

She thinks for a moment, then chooses her words carefully. "Yes, I've been depressed before, but never to the extent you have. I think I was just stuck in a rut." She places a blue five on top of my blue two and takes another drink from her glass. "I didn't have many friends here at the time, and Jasper and I were going through the same motions every single day. It was monotonous and boring and gave me too much time to think."

"So, what did you do?" I take my turn, then try to make eye contact, but she doesn't look up.

"I started to notice the little things that made me happy, and I did more of that," she answers.

"Like what?" The game is moving fast and I'm not ready for it to be over yet. I need some answers before this conversation gets lost in the shuffle.

"Well, like Nirvana."

"What in the world?" I laugh louder than I mean to. The wine is making me light-headed, I think.

"Yeah, one day I was driving in the car, skimming radio stations and I heard a sliver of 'Come as You Are' on the classic rock station. I started to flip right by it, like I always did, but then I thought, 'Why should I?' I cranked it up, rolled down the windows, and sang as loud as I could."

"And that made you feel better?"

"Hell yeah, it did! And from that day on, I've never censored what I listen to around the kids again. Nirvana, Outkast, Missy—whoever—now they just sing right along with me." At that, she picks up her phone, finds a playlist, and the opening chords of "Come As You Are" blast through the speakers in the living room.

"Shh, you're going to wake them up!"

"Nah, they're used to it. They'll sleep through anything." She dances around the living room, flipping her head back and forth, but it doesn't quite lend the effect she's going for with her short, tight curls. I can't help but to laugh.

"See? This is what you need. You need to dance!" She pulls me up from the floor, and hesitantly, I join her.

Then she stops. "Hey, it's only 10:00. I bet I can still get a sitter. Let's go to The Tavern!"

"Oh, that sounds like a bad idea." I shake my head from side to side in disapproval. "Is it even open on Sundays?"

"Sure, it is. And why is it a bad idea? Paula Coats has probably blown your cover by now anyway, right? You might as well get out and have some fun while you can." She laughs as she texts someone on her phone. A few seconds later, she receives a reply.

"Girl, we've got a sitter! She'll be here in fifteen minutes, so go put some makeup on that face. We're going out." She jumps up and runs to her bathroom.

"Michelle, I don't even have any shoes besides my sneakers. I'm gonna need some boots!"

"Go get 'em, girl. You know where they are. Fourteen minutes and counting!" she yells from the bathroom.

"Good Lord, this is insane." I mutter as I move toward her room.

"Nah, this is just fun," she says.

"Well, same damn thing!"

Michelle cackles in response, and I search her closet for boots.

The babysitter arrives right on time and we're out the door in a flash.

"Are you sure she didn't mind coming so late, on such short notice?" I ask, looking back to the front door from the sidewalk.

"Yes, I'm sure. She's a college kid. She comes home on the weekends and never turns down a chance to babysit for me. And Lord knows she doesn't have much of a social life. She reminds me of you, actually." Michelle nudges me with her elbow.

I roll my eyes and wrap my arms around myself in attempt to generate warmth, but it's not working. "Well, what are we doing standing here, then? Can we walk already?"

"Walk? No way, I'm not walking. I Uber-ed it." Michelle checks the app on her phone for an update. "He's less than a minute out."

"Uber? I didn't know Asher has Uber. This little town is coming up in the world."

"Well, it's one guy, so don't get too excited."

"We could walk, you know. It's only about a half mile." I look down the street again, desperate to either find shelter in a car or start moving my body.

"He's coming, I swear. Look, I bet that's him down at the light." Michelle points up to the next intersection and I see a silver hatchback cross through it when the light turns green.

A few seconds later, the car stops, and Michelle opens the back door. "Hey, Josh. How's it going tonight? Busy?"

"Meh," he answers. "To The Tavern?"

"To The Tavern!" Michelle answers back with a laugh.

"It's under new ownership, you know." Josh pulls the car out of park and turns us around to head back the way he came.

"Really? Who this time?" Michelle asks.

"Nicole McComb. Her daddy bought it for her about a month ago." He rolls through a yellow light at the intersection.

"*Nikki McComb*?" Michelle and I voice in unison.

"Yup. Which means the only thing you'll find on the jukebox these days is country music from the 90's. She's hired all her old cheer buddies as waitresses, too."

"Oh, good grief, Michelle. Is there anywhere else we can go?" Nikki McComb was not one of our favorite people in high school.

"No, not really. Thomas and I will sometimes go to the movie theater and have dinner and drinks there, but the last showing is around 9:00. We've missed it."

Josh turns the car left onto Main Street, drives a few blocks more, and stops in front of The Tavern. The building still looks the same as it always has, only the cedar shingles on the front are more weathered and a couple of letters are blinking in the neon "Open" sign. I look at Michelle with a "are we really going to do this" face.

"Oh, come on. We never hid from her before, and we certainly aren't going to do it when it's the only place in town to get a drink. A honky-tonk isn't my first choice either, but we take what we can get." She grabs me by the arm and pulls me across the bench seat and out of the car. "Thanks, Josh. See you back here at 1:30?"

"I'll be here. Y'all don't get yourselves into too much trouble." He laughs, puts the car in drive, and pulls away.

8

TYLER

Michelle opens the door and shoves me inside.

As we enter, the sound of Garth Brooks fills my ears and smoke stings my eyes. I find a table in the far corner, where there's not much light, and slide into the booth. "I thought you can't smoke in public places here anymore?"

"There's a smoking area out back, but it finds its way in, especially later in the night when people are feelin' pretty good. This isn't San Antonio, you know. What do you want to drink?"

"I think I need something strong for this. Jack and Coke, please."

"Be right back." Michelle turns and makes her way to the bar, and I pull out my phone to pass the time.

The minutes drag by and I grow increasingly anxious for her to return. As I scan the bar for Michelle, I spot an all-too-familiar, chiseled face.

"Oh my God," I say out loud, even though no one can hear me.

He lights up with a surprised smile as he pulls his massive frame up from the bar stool and crosses the smoke-filled room.

Oh no. God, what is he doing here?

"Well, look who it is." He flashes those big, beautiful white teeth, scoots into the booth next to me, and plants a soft, warm kiss on the highest point of my left cheek.

My heart skips a beat—then another.

"Tyler," I say, lost in his presence already. "What are you doing here? You're still in Florida, right?"

"Yup, but I come back sometimes on the weekends to see my mom and this weekend is Paige's birthday, so here I am."

"Well, lucky me." I smile as he places his arm around my shoulder, and I lean into him the same wonderful way I always have. "So, how old is your baby sister, then?"

"She is twenty-seven, if you can believe it." He takes a sip from his glass—bourbon, I'm sure.

"Wow, that makes me feel old."

"You? That makes me feel old, not you." He touches the tip of my nose. "You are as gorgeous and young as ever. I swear you never change." He tucks a loose strand of hair behind my ears, then trails his fingers down the back of my neck, sending a shiver down my spine.

"Well, thank you, but that couldn't be farther from the truth. But, for old time's sake—" I raise my empty hand as if I'm holding a glass, "—Cheers to our youth."

"Cheers—to the good old days." He smiles and pretends to clank his glass with mine. "But where's your drink? You can't toast without a glass."

I look toward the bar for Michelle just as she appears with two cocktails in-hand and a stern look on her face.

"Tyler. I didn't expect to see you here," she says in that same cool voice she's always used with him.

"Why hello, Shelly. I should have known if I found our Jenna alone in a booth, you'd be close by."

"Yup, always. You know that." Michelle waves for him to stand. "May I have my seat back, please?"

"Sure thing, darlin'." He stands and moves to the other side of the table.

"Actually, I need to run to the ladies' room. You coming?" She pulls me up before I can answer.

Tyler looks at me and grins. "I'll be here, saving the table for you."

I smile back, but barely, as Michelle pulls me across the dance floor and towards the bathroom. As soon as we make it inside, she flips herself around to look at me.

"This *cannot* happen." Her voice is harsh and protective.

"What are you talking about? Nothing is going to happen. I'm married, for crying out loud." I check my makeup in the mirror and desperately wish I would've worn more.

"You know it's never mattered if you were with someone else; not with him. He is your kryptonite, Jenna."

He really is.

"Okay, so I promise I'll be good."

"That doesn't work. I've heard it a thousand times. What is it about him, anyway? He's such an *ass*." She scrunches up her nose in repulsed disapproval.

"No, he's not. He comes off that way, but I promise you he's not. And he's one of my best friends. We've been friends for almost as long as you and I have, you know."

"Yeah, I know. That doesn't mean I understand it." She shuts herself into a stall to do her business, and I take the one next to her.

"I'll be fine. It's not like we're going to be here all that long, anyway. But *God*, it's good to see him."

I hear a huge, exasperated sigh from the next stall over, then a flush, a quick rinse at the sink, and a slamming bathroom door—and she's gone.

As I approach the table, I see Michelle lean towards Tyler and say something with a serious face. She spots me, says something final, and scoots in toward the wall while motioning for me to take the seat next to her. No doubt, she's been warning him to keep his distance.

I sit down next to her and reach for my drink. Tyler reaches to push it toward me. Our fingers touch, and the hair on my arm stands on end.

I can't explain it, but somehow, even after all these years, the spark is still there. It's a weird relationship we've shared since high school. We've been through so much together, would give anything to see the other one happy, and there's not a single thing we can't talk about. There's so much honesty and pure love between us—and a completely unhealthy dose of chemistry, too.

Our friendship has not been an easy one for the significant others in our lives to accept over the years. More than one relationship has ended because the innocents involved swore there was something romantic going on between us and it's hard to say if they were wrong or right. It got better after moving to Texas, but still, when we saw each other those few times a year, we fell right back into our old, comfortable ways. We made mistakes, relationships suffered, but we never gave up on each other. Our friendship always came first—until I met Andrew.

"So, did you see Nikki at the bar?" I ask Michelle, hoping to break the ice between the two of them.

"Oh, I saw her. She was working down at the other end, though, so I didn't get the pleasure of leaving her a tip." She stirs her cocktail with the tiny straw and giggles.

"Well, I say we go check out the jukebox. See if we can find anything good." I stand and wait for Michelle to join me. "Be right back," I say to Tyler.

"Sure, babe. Play a song for me." He says this without even making eye contact, as he picks up his phone and starts scrolling. It's not a flirtatious gesture. It's a genuine request for a song he'll enjoy. And somehow, that connection—the fact I know him well enough to do that—gets to me even more than any intentional flirtation ever could.

There's a line for the jukebox, but a lull at the bar, so I leave Michelle to hold our place and go for a backup round of drinks. As I walk up, Nikki spots me and saunters her Daisy Dukes down to my end of the bar.

"Well, I heard you were in town. I guess the rumors were true," she says with one hand on her hip.

"Yup, but only for a few days. Just long enough to shake things up a bit around here, you know. I like what you've done with the place," I say, trying to keep things civil, despite her inherent cattiness.

"Yeah, it's a lot of fun. But I suppose you want a drink?" Surprisingly, she doesn't seem in the mood for chit-chat. She's probably anxious to get back to her higher-tipping customers of the bearded variety.

"Yeah. A Jack and Coke, bourbon on ice, and vodka tonic, please." I slide my card across the bar. "And you can open a tab."

"Ah, I know that trio. So, you've found Tyler, have you?" She smiles a mischievous, knowing grin. "And where is your handsome husband, anyway?" Placing one hand over her brows as if shading the sun, she searches the bar for Andrew.

"I don't know, Nikki. Where's yours?" I ask, knowing full-well she's divorced. "The drinks, please?"

"Okay, okay. Only trying to make small talk, sheesh." She mixes the drinks and places them in front of me. I grab all three and take them back to the table without another word.

"Ah, yes. Thank you, J-Lew." Tyler pushes his empty glass to the side and reaches for the full one. Then he grabs my hand and pulls me into the booth. Our knees touch beneath the table and it's hard to ignore. "You haven't told me why *you're* here, you know. Or why you're alone."

"Well, that's a long story."

"And I've got all night. So do you, I think." He takes a sip of his bourbon as the ice clanks in his glass.

The smell of that sweet whiskey on his breath brings on a rush of fiery, intense memories I'm not prepared to relive at this moment. I've got to get away. "I still haven't picked my songs. We'll talk later, okay?"

I stand, take one look at his curious face, and turn without waiting for his reply. I find Michelle at the jukebox, choosing her songs.

"Boy, your white girl cheeks are *tellin'* on you, you know," she says, still trying to make clear her disapproval.

"Are you done here?"

She pivots, looks at me and says, "Yeah, I'm done." She squeezes my hand, then heads back to the table—her way of letting me know she's through badgering about Tyler. We've done this so many times before, and there were often morning-afters when Michelle could have said, "I told you so," but she never did.

Only able to scrounge up two quarters from my wallet, I choose two songs from the jukebox. Then I return to the table to find Michelle and Tyler laughing hard. She's always been such a mother hen, but the two of them have their moments too. I smile and take my seat next to him. Michelle doesn't even bat an eye.

"And then, I have the good sense to turn and run out of that place, but when I look over my shoulder, you two are gone!" She's laughing so hard, she's having a difficult time putting her sentences together.

"Yeah, because this one froze up like a deer in headlights—" he says, poking me in the ribs. "—and couldn't even move her feet. So, I picked her up and shoved her under the risers!"

"And that was the day I learned how Michelle truly felt about me. You didn't even come back. You left me behind!" I say to her.

"Hell no, I didn't go back. Breaking into the gym wasn't even my idea. I wasn't about to go down for it. That was all on you." Her laughter is so full of life and energy, and I envy every second of it.

"Uh-huh," I tease.

"Hey, I never said I was a ride-or-die kind of chick, okay? No false advertising here."

We laugh and continue to tell stories, making several trips back to the bar in the meantime. What seems like hours later, Michelle jumps up.

"This is my song! I played this one! Jenna, come dance with me. Let's go!" She pulls me up before I can argue and the next thing I know, we're on the dance floor doing the Cotton Eye Joe.

"Seriously, Michelle? This song makes me feel so old."

"But you sure haven't forgotten how to do it, have you?"

"Never!" I laugh and look over at Tyler. He's grinning and shaking his head at the two of us out on the dance floor, so I wave for him to come join us. He mouths a polite, "No, thank you," and holds his hand up like he's trying to stop traffic. I can't help but to laugh out loud and when the song is over, we return to the table, out of breath.

"Well, you two have still got it, that's for sure." Tyler says, as we rejoin him.

I bump him with my shoulder. "Hey, at least we're having fun. I haven't had actual fun in a long time." I look into my glass and suddenly feel very guilty about everything: the fact I'm three states away from my kids, that my husband doesn't know when I'm coming back, that I'm in a bar with Tyler (of all people), and that I'm drinking entirely too much Jack and Coke and having a great time doing it.

But it's not the time or place to let the darkness come, so I jump up from the booth. "Do they still sell cigarettes here?"

"Oh, boy. You're *gone* if you're asking for smokes," Michelle laughs. "But yes, I think so."

I walk up to the bar and nudge my way between a couple of smelly old men in flannel shirts. Waving to Nikki, I catch her attention and she holds up her pointer finger, asking me to wait. Finally, she comes my way.

"What can I get for ya? You guys sure are burning through my whiskey pretty quick. I might have to ask you to switch up your drinks soon." She reaches for a new glass.

"I only came for cigarettes. What'cha got back there?"

⁂

I grab the pack and lighter off the bar top and start walking back. Before I get there, though, a distinctive guitar riff emerges from the speakers, and I look to Tyler. It takes him two seconds to recognize Neal McCoy's "The Shake" and he is up and out of his seat. He grabs the items from my hand, throws them onto the table, and pulls me toward the dance floor.

"You're coming with me."

I look over my shoulder at Michelle with a shrug that says, "Well, I can't say no." She shakes her head, laughs, and waves me on. I have her blessing and I am not about to let it go to waste.

We dance like a couple of love-sick teenagers, and I soak up every minute of it. I forgot I even know how to dance like this. He pulls me close at all the right moments—my chest squeezed tight into his—so close, I can smell the scent of detergent on his pearl-snap shirt. Then he pushes me away, spins me 'round until I'm dizzy, and reals me back in to match his step, side-by-side.

At the song's end, he pulls me close once more and uses the proximity of my ear to his lips to his advantage. "That was your doing, huh?" His breath tickles my neck and sends shivers down my spine.

"Well, of course. Just for you."

Then the next song begins, and a crooked smile appears on his beautiful, full lips. "And this one too?"

"Sure enough, cowboy." I wrap my arms around his neck, and we lose ourselves in the sweet words of Andy Griggs. This song, and its "You Won't Ever Be Lonely" promise, has always served as our vow to each other that no matter what happens in life—as relationships come and go and as we ride the roller coaster up, down, and back up again—neither of us will ever be alone.

All I see is the blur of the neon lights spinning around me. All I feel is the hurried heartbeat within my chest. All I hear is this song. When it becomes too much and the dizziness takes hold, I rest my head on his shoulder, entrusting him with my every move. Where he leads, I follow, and he never steers me wrong.

The song ends and the dance floor clears, but we're still here, lost in time. I raise my head and he places his hands on either side of my face. Then, he tucks my chin in toward my chest and gives a long, soft kiss on my forehead.

"Why don't you go grab those smokes and we can walk out back?" he asks, still holding my face in his hands.

"Okay." At this point, I'm willing to rob the bank next door if he asks me to.

I walk to the table and see Michelle isn't there. I scan the room and find her at the bar, talking with a friend. She's laughing and having a good time, so I grab the cigarettes and return to Tyler. We walk down the narrow, dark hallway toward the exit sign at the back of the bar and step out into the cold night air. It feels so good on my warm, damp skin.

He opens the pack, places a cigarette between my lips, and flips the lighter to ignite the flame. I lean forward and let it take hold. As he lights one for himself, he sits on the curb and gestures for me to take the spot next to him, so I do. Starting to feel the chill of the air, I snuggle in close for warmth—and to get one more hit of that irresistible scent escaping from his pores. A sudden wave of memories flashes through my mind: The two of us in a world all our own, skin-to-skin, enveloped in that scent, and exploring wherever we desired.

"Jenna, why are you here?"

I'm pulled from my daydream as he breaks the silence. I sit quietly, unable to speak or look him in the eye.

"Talk to me. You know you can."

"I ran away," is once again all I can muster for an answer to that question.

"From what? What do you mean?"

"I got in my car, put it in drive, and ran away." The tears come and Tyler wipes them away with the back of his finger, then wraps his arm around me.

"So, you...left him?" His words come out slowly, like he's afraid to speak them.

"No, not really. I'm not sure exactly what I've done." I'm trying hard not to break down and he knows it.

He pulls me up from the curb and back down to sit in between his legs, his butt still on the curb and mine on the street. I pull my feet up into a seated fetal position, my knees closed together. His knees close in tight on either side of mine and his arms wrap around my torso and legs. He's putting me in a safe space, hoping I'll talk.

And I do. I tell him everything. I tell him about the mood swings, the anger, how horrible of a mother I am, and the constant inner battle to be better. The guilt. The resentment. The longing to do anything to make it all stop. I give him the abridged version of my unbearable torment and he listens, squeezing me tighter when I need it most.

I lose track of time and don't realize how long I've been talking, how many cigarettes we've burned through, or how long it's been since he last said a word, until my phone buzzes and I see a message from Michelle.

"Josh is here. Where are you?"

"Out back with Tyler. You go on. I'll find my way home."

"What???"

"I'll be okay. Leave the front door unlocked, please," I answer.

"Don't do anything stupid. Love you."

I put my phone away without responding to that last one.

"Everything okay?" Tyler asks.

"Yeah, Michelle's leaving. I'm sorry to have dumped all this on you."

He pulls me up from the curb as he stands, then turns me around to look at him. "I'm glad you did. I understand now."

"What do you mean?"

"I mean, as much as I was hoping this all meant I was finally going to get my chance, this isn't it."

There's a hint of a smirk and I know he's trying to make light of the situation with a joke, but there's truth to it, too. Suddenly I feel the guilt once again—for leading him on tonight and for all the times I've done it in the past. I'm also angry for all the times he's done the exact same thing to me, and angry at the universe for never allowing our paths to be in sync. Then, of course, I feel guilty for feeling that way when I'm married to Andrew. The feelings are too much. The drinks and cigarettes were too much. I pull away.

He pulls me in again. "Listen, you are not a bad person. You are not crazy. You are a wife and mother who loves your family so much, you let it tear you apart."

"Ugh," I say, in true disbelief.

"You let those adorable kids of yours take, and take, and take until you don't recognize yourself anymore. Then you—and I think Andrew too—are the ones to pay for it when you've run out of yourself to give."

I don't buy it. My mind is whirling with thoughts of all the horrible things I've said and done to those poor babies, and that can't be anybody's fault but my own. I am a monster. There's no denying that.

"You may not believe me now, but I want you to promise me something."

"What?"

"Whenever you're feeling inadequate, angry, or alone...you call me. Or Michelle. Or GiGi or your mom. You call someone—anyone—who can help you remember who you are. Call the ones who make you laugh, who you can share old stories with, who can remind you that you know how to dance. And for *God's sake*, go on a date with your husband."

We both laugh as the tension lifts with his words. He pulls me to his solid, broad chest and holds me tight. *God, he's so warm.*

"Thank you, Tyler."

Another kiss on the forehead is his only reply.

"We'd better go." I turn toward the door.

"Want a ride home?" he asks, still holding my hand as we walk.

I think about that for a second. "No, I think I need to walk. Clear my head, maybe work off some of that Jack before trying to sleep."

"You sure?" He opens the door for me, and I enter back into the bar first.

"Yeah, it's only a few blocks. I'll be fine. And it's *Asher*."

We cross through the bar and exit out the front door. On the sidewalk, he cups my cheek and looks at me one more time. There are so many words in that head of his. I can see them floating behind his eyes.

"You're stronger than you remember." He leans in and whispers into my ear, "Love you, J-Lew."

Then, he turns and walks away.

———◇———

As Tyler rounds the corner toward the parking lot, I realize I never paid my tab. I open the door and walk back up to the bar.

"We've already served last call," Nikki says when she sees me waiting.

"I just need to close out my tab."

"Give me a sec." She takes a credit card and receipt to a burly, bald man at the other end of the bar—or to the red-head sitting on his lap, I'm not sure which. "How are you getting home tonight, Carl? You guys need me to call you a ride?"

"We're good, Nikki. Thanks." He shoves the receipt in his pocket and the two of them stand and stumble out the front door.

"And I suppose, since Michelle left without you, you've got a ride somewhere with Tyler?" She places my bill and credit card on the bar top in front of me. She's fishing.

"No. I'll be walking, but thanks for your concern," I answer, letting her know the intent of her question is not lost on me.

"Y'all really should let it happen already," she says, wiping down the bar. "I mean, clearly, things aren't all unicorns and rainbows with you and—what's your husband's name? Anyway, you and him. Otherwise, he'd be here, and you wouldn't be making out with your old high school boyfriend on the dance floor."

"He's not an old boyfriend, and we weren't making out. And you'd think, after all these years, you would have learned to mind your own business." I sign the receipt, slashing through the tip line with gusto, to catch her attention.

"Well, you sure weren't trying to be discreet. If you don't want people to talk, you should be a little more careful." She smiles a teasing, hateful smile and stabs the receipt onto the check spindle.

"Hmm, you mean like you were with Justin? Yeah, maybe I should have taken notes." I turn to leave. Everybody in this town knows Nikki's affair with the junior high wrestling coach is what pushed her high school sweetheart of a husband right out her front door. "Been fun, as always, Nikki. See ya' around."

"You don't know nothin' about me and Justin, bitch!" she screams after me as I reach for the door.

"Classy as always, I see." I exit the bar and hear an angry growl from Nikki as I let the door slam behind me.

As I step back out into the night air, I realize just how fast my heart is pounding. She's mad, and that makes me nervous. You never know just what Nikki McComb will do when she's mad.

9

COUNTY

I tuck my wallet under my arm, zip my jacket to the top, and hide my hands in the pockets to keep them warm. As I walk along the sidewalk, I'm shaking—and not only from the cold. I truly dislike confrontation, but there's something about that woman that has always gotten under my skin.

I feel the cold sobering me up a bit, but I still wish I hadn't drank so much. I can't even remember how many cocktails there were, as I lost count somewhere around midnight. It's been years since I've drank like that, mainly because kids wake up at the same time every morning, regardless of how much fun their parents enjoyed the night before. The thought of the kids brings tears to my eyes again. *God, can't I go one day without the tears?*

Realizing how much I miss them, despite knowing they're so much better off with Andrew, the tears come faster and my vision blurs. I miss the uneven concrete on the sidewalk, clip it with the toe of my boot, and stumble forward onto the hard, cold ground.

It takes a few seconds to comprehend what's happened and the burning sensation in my knees and palms seems to cut deep into the core of my being. It's a pain that is from so much more than a late-night meeting with unforgiving pavement on a moonlit street.

I don't have the ability to pick myself up from my landing place, so I stay and cry. I've hit that part of my drunken escapade where the fun has ended and all the emotions it was keeping at bay come sweeping back in like a monsoon tidal wave on an unsuspecting beach.

I should have gone home with Michelle. At least then, she would have been there when this part hit. I lift my head and look down the sidewalk. I still have so much further to go before I even make the turn off Main Street, and I know I'm never going to make it.

Suddenly, blue and red lights flash across the wall of the building next to me. A sheriff's car pulls up to the curb and stops.

I pick myself up off the ground and dry the tears. A uniformed man emerges from the car, comes around its front, and steps onto the sidewalk to meet me.

"You okay, ma'am?" he asks.

"Yes, I'm fine. I just tripped on the sidewalk is all."

"Where are you headed?"

"I'm walking home—well, to my friend's—from The Tavern. It's just around the corner, a few more blocks." I point down the road.

He steps closer and now I can more clearly see his face and the name tape on his chest.

"JD? Oh my God, you're the sheriff?" A loud bullhorn of a laugh escapes, and I quickly cover my mouth with both hands to shut myself up. He is not amused.

Being the youngest of five children—and the only boy—JD spent most of the first eight years of his life unwillingly covered in his sisters' makeup and pungent perfume. They would hold him down to help him try on new shades. He was known as Pino around our neighborhood for the longest time, which was of course short for Pinocchio—partly because his sisters acted as if he was their wooden doll on a string, and also because of the colorful cheeks he so often sported, thanks to the cherry red lipstick they preferred for his blush.

Then, he grew up. His sisters continued to give him hell, of course, but their power over him lessened as he became one of the most talented running backs Asher High has ever seen. That small town fame and a dimpled smile won him the hearts of many girls in Asher—those who didn't grow up in our neighborhood, witnessing the daily humiliation inflicted upon him by his sisters, anyway.

JD folds his arms across his chest. "Yes, I'm the sheriff. And I got a call about an impaired subject causing trouble on this street. That wouldn't be you, would it, Jenna?"

"Oh, please. You mean you got a call from Nikki. There sure isn't anyone else out this late who would phone that in."

"I'm going to need you to submit to a field sobriety test, ma'am." He steps closer.

"No, JD. I'm only trying to get home. I didn't drive anywhere. I'm walking." I realize my voice is growing louder, and it's not helping my case any. "Look, it's like ten minutes from here. Can I just go?"

"No, ma'am. You'll need to submit to the test, or I'll have to take you in for the night." His hands move to his hips and he widens his stance, wanting me to fully understand the weight of his importance.

"Will you stop with the 'ma'am'? We've known each other since we were both in diapers! And I'm not going anywhere or taking any test. I'm going home."

He steps closer. "Please place your belongings on the sidewalk."

"Are you serious? JD, this is crazy!" I can't quite wrap my head around what is happening. It feels as if it's all a cruel joke, but I do as he says.

"No, what's crazy is you stumbling your drunk ass down the sidewalk in the middle of the night, refusing a sobriety test, and choosing to sleep in my cell instead." He pulls my hands behind my back and snaps the cold handcuffs onto my wrists. "You should have taken the test, Jenna."

"Lord, that Nikki. If I ever—"

"I'd stop right there, if I were you," he says, walking me to the car.

His words are running together, growing softer and softer until I can't even hear them anymore. I know he's still talking, but it's as if his sentences are disappearing into the night air before ever reaching my ears.

I slide into the back seat and flinch with the slamming of the door. JD collects my things from the sidewalk, then enters the car. He puts us in motion and flips a sharp U-turn in the middle of the street.

That swiftness of the change in direction snaps me back into reality. "I'm going to have to report that illegal U-turn, you know."

"Got any more jokes, or are you done?" He looks at me through the rear-view mirror.

"Oh, I'm done. I am so done."

In this moment, it's crystal clear why I wasn't all that upset to leave this town in the first place.

"Hope you have someone to call," JD says as he leads me to a phone in the corner. I pick it up and dial Michelle's number.

"Hello?" she answers with a groggy voice.

I hear a series of beeps and a robotic voice telling me to wait...wait...wait, while she accepts the call. A few seconds later, Michelle once again says, "Hello?"

"Hey, it's me."

"Jenna? What the hell are you doing at the jail? Are you okay?"

"Yes, I'm fine. Nikki thought it would be nice for JD and I to have a little reunion. He picked me up on Main Street when I was walking home. Who the hell elected him sheriff, anyway? This town has lost its mind."

"*What?*" She laughs. "That's hilarious! Uh, I mean, that's crazy."

"Yeah. Anyway, he won't let me out until I've 'slept it off' for at least eight hours so can you come pick me up after 10:30 tomorrow?"

"Yeah. But how do I explain to the boys that we have to go bust Auntie Jenna out of the slamma'?" She laughs again, thoroughly entertained by her own joke.

"Haha, you're *so* funny." I hear an automated voice on the phone tell me I have one more minute for the call. "I've got to go. See you in the morning."

"All right, but Jenna—"

"Yeah?"

"Don't drop the soap!"

"Ugh, Michelle!" I hear her laughing even louder as I slam the phone back onto its cradle.

JD takes me by the elbow and leads me through a heavy, locked door and down a row of individual jail cells. They're all empty, but he puts me in the one at the very end, anyway.

"Sleep tight." He shuts the cell door and walks back down the aisle.

I hear the heavy door shut and the electronic lock engage. I lie down on the thin mattress and a few minutes later, the lights dim so they're barely bright enough to see my hand in front of my face. The buzzing sound they were making before is gone and it's dead silent in this cell.

I can't sleep with silence. Too many thoughts come with the silence.

For hours, I lie awake, and they come at me incessantly, like a charging army attempting to gain ground. I'm weaponless and forced to retreat further and further until I can no longer stand against them.

The whiskey isn't doing me any favors either. The room spins and stops. Spins and stops. And just when the merry-go-round of the spinning room, deafening silence, and crushing darkness become too much—when I'm on the verge of screaming at the top of my lungs just to hear a sound—the lights come on.

It must be morning. Finally, with the lights on to calm the spinning, and their buzzing giving my brain some place to focus, I close my eyes and sleep.

The heavy door slams shut, startling me awake. Footsteps grow louder as they approach, but I have no interest in standing to see who it is.

"Breakfast," JD says as he opens the cell door and sets a tray on the small stainless-steel tabletop hanging, cantilevered from the wall. "My shift ends at 11:00. Deputy Schmidt will take my place and see you out if you're still here." Then he turns, shuts the cell door, and makes his way back down the aisle and through the exit.

I roll over to get a look at the contents of the tray: an apple, a box of cereal sitting inside of an empty paper bowl, a muffin, two small containers of milk, and a plastic spoon.

My stomach twists into knots at the sight of food. I feel like it's about to turn itself inside out, shoving anything left in there right up and back out. For a second, I consider moving closer to the toilet, but I settle for turning back onto my left side and breathing through the nausea instead.

My head pounds to the rhythm of my heartbeat and as thankful as I am for the buzzing sound of the lights, they are torture on my eyes. I turn onto my back, drape my arm over my face, and bury my head in the bend of my elbow.

Why am I even here? How did a simple run for drinks turn into all this? And what the hell time is it? I remember seeing a clock in the aisle, but I'm afraid to move from this spot to look for it—afraid my head and guts would not-so-politely object to the disturbance. So, I continue focusing on the buzzing of the lights and the cadence of my breath.

I hear the lock disengage and the door open. Footsteps approach, and the cell door opens.

"They're here to pick you up." JD motions for me to stand.

I do as he requests, walk through the cell door, and down the aisle in a type of walk of shame I've never experienced before—not even with Tyler.

We stop at a plexiglass window where I sign for my belongings, which are handed to me in a plastic bag. I remove them and turn to JD, waiting to be shown out.

He looks as if he's on the verge of saying something, as if he regrets bringing me here after all. He opens his mouth to speak, but I cut him off with a glare and a quick shake of my head. I don't care to hear what he has to say.

He motions toward a door a few feet away and I walk toward it. JD waves a badge in front of a sensor, then pushes the door open. As I step into the waiting room, all the air in my lungs is forced out all at once.

"GiGi? Aunt Kitty?" *Oh, dear God. No wonder JD's sorry.*

"Yes child, GiGi." She stands from her seat, tucks her purse under her arm, and stalks over to JD. Tilting her head back, she stares into his eyes. The top of her gray head barely comes to his armpit. "John David," she begins.

"Ma'am?"

She pushes her long, thick, wavy hair over her left shoulder. "I did not ask you to speak, son."

JD slouches and I smile a bit on the inside, even though I'm terrified of what will happen once she turns her attention to me next.

"John David, I am so disappointed in you. You know full-well my granddaughter didn't do anything to warrant being locked up in here like some common thief!" Her countenance is stern, showing little emotion, but her voice is everything to the contrary.

He looks over at me again with that face that tells me he's sorry.

"Don't you look at her," GiGi snaps.

His head spins back 'round to GiGi and his hands are behind his back like a child who's been caught stealing from the corner store.

"I'm not sure what this is all about, but with the way news travels in this town, I'm sure it won't be long until we find out. I hope for your sake it was worth it," she says.

GiGi steps away from him and grabs me by the arm. Then she turns to Aunt Kitty. "Come on Kitty, let's go."

Aunt Kitty jumps out of her chair to follow us. GiGi pauses with one hand on the door and calls back over her shoulder. "I'll see you in church on Sunday, John David. I expect you'll be escorting your grandmother?" She looks his way but doesn't wait for a reply. "Good. We share a pew."

—◆—

GiGi and I exit the building and Aunt Kitty's chuckling before we even step off the sidewalk, but quiets with a quick "Shh," from GiGi. We continue on with our dramatic exit until we reach the car, open the doors, and climb inside. Then, it all comes out. We're laughing so hard we're crying, and my head feels like it's about to explode, but it's so incredibly worth it.

"GiGi, how in the world? How did you know I was here?" I ask from the back seat once I've caught my breath.

"Well, that's something we need to discuss, isn't it? But not here." She starts the car, pulls out of the parking lot, and heads back into town. She turns on the radio and we ride without speaking, but my head is spinning with all the things I'm expecting her to say once she does speak again. A scolding from GiGi is not for the faint of heart and I imagine I've got one for the record books coming my way today.

A few minutes later, she turns into the Waffle House parking lot and while I'm glad for the stillness of the parked car after all the bumps, curves, and turns on the way here, my stomach contents violently lurch into the bottom of my throat at the idea of food.

"Oh, I don't know if I can eat this right now, GiGi." I place a hand over my unpredictable belly and shudder a bit at the thought.

"Nonsense. This is exactly what you need." GiGi opens her door and I reluctantly follow her and Aunt Kitty inside.

GiGi chooses a table and she and Aunt Kitty sit on the same side, leaving me alone on the other, to face them like a firing squad. The server comes to take our order and I attempt to request plain wheat toast and water, but GiGi isn't having it.

She stacks my menu and hers and hands them over to the server. "No, she'll have the All-Star Special—eggs over easy—with bacon *and* sausage. Scattered, smothered, covered on those hashbrowns. And coffee—you might as well bring the pot. I'll take the biscuit and gravy with a side of bacon."

"Okay, and for you, ma'am?" the server asks Aunt Kitty.

"I'll have what she's having." Aunt Kitty points to me.

"You know you're not supposed to eat that crap, Kitty. You're going to drop dead by tomorrow if you do," GiGi says.

"Yeah, well, I'll die happy then, won't I?"

GiGi rolls her eyes, hands the server Aunt Kitty's menu, then shoos her away from our table. Then, she looks me in the eyes for the first time since I walked through the door at the jailhouse. She takes a bottle of aspirin from her purse, dumps two into her palm, and pushes them across the table. I accept and swallow them both, even without any water.

"To answer your question, I knew you were in Asher because Bonnie told me so," she says, with her crimson red nail-polished hands folded together in front of her on the table.

"Bonnie! But how?"

"Yes, Bonnie. She found me on Facebook and sent a message telling me who she was and that you left rather suddenly. She said you weren't in the best frame of mind when she last saw you and she was worried about you."

"Facebook? I didn't even know Bonnie does that." I have shared stories of my childhood and relationship with GiGi many times with Bonnie, but it never occurred to me that she would be the one to blow my cover.

"Well, everybody *does that*, honey. Anyway, she said you were in Alabama staying with a friend and I know the only friend you have left around here is Michelle, so we went to her house this morning. Imagine my surprise when I show up and she's putting her kids in the car to go bail you out of jail."

"She ratted me out? Figures," I answer, as the server returns with three mugs and a pot of coffee.

"Well, it took some convincing, but yes." GiGi fills her mug and mine, then passes the pot over to Aunt Kitty. She fills her cup half-way, then tops it off with about twelve little tubs of creamer and an absurd amount of sugar. GiGi and I sip ours black.

"I don't know how you can drink that nasty stuff, Kitty," GiGi says to her.

"Hey, you worry about yourself, okay? I'll take my coffee how I take it."

The two of them have always boggled my brain. They've been best friends since they were five years old and as far as I know, GiGi has always bossed Aunt Kitty around like this and she's always fired right back, but never even attempted to put an end to it. They thrive off the bickering, I think, and remind me of a slightly cruder version of Michelle and myself.

"What'd John David lock you up for, anyhow? Michelle didn't get to that part," GiGi says.

"Then how did you know I wasn't a 'common thief', as you put it?"

"Well, because I know my granddaughter and I know John David. You don't have to be a genius to figure out something's not quite right with that whole situation."

"That's a lot of faith to put in me, GiGi."

"Well, am I wrong, or what? What did you do?" She throws her hands up in the air, gesturing for me to tell her already. GiGi often talks with her hands, sometimes so well she doesn't need any words at all—and she credits the acquisition of this talent on the influence of her Italian mother.

"No, you're not wrong, of course. I got into an argument with Nikki McComb when I left the bar. She knew I was walking myself home and called JD, out of spite. He asked me to take a field sobriety test, which I declined, so he brought me in."

"Well, why didn't you take the test?" Aunt Kitty chimes in.

"Because it was JD! I figured he was messing with me and would let me go. I wouldn't have passed that test anyway, clearly."

"So, do you have a court date or owe a fine, or what?" GiGi asks.

"No, I don't think so. I don't think he even officially booked me in. There was no paperwork, photos, fingerprints, or anything like that. They do that stuff when you're officially booked, right? That's not only in movies? Hell, I don't know—I've never been arrested before!"

GiGi and Aunt Kitty both laugh, and several heads turn our direction.

"Well, you'd think there would have been some of that, if you were charged," GiGi replies.

"I wonder why he didn't just take you home?" Aunt Kitty asks, as she pours herself another half-cup of coffee.

"Well, I may have tripped and fell on the sidewalk—" I look to GiGi, a little afraid to go on. "—And sat there crying like a baby for a few minutes before he flipped the blue lights on."

"*Lord*, Jenna—" GiGi says.

I wince. Uh-oh, here it comes.

"Why on God's green earth would you come back to Asher to have your mid-life crisis, anyway?" she asks. "You shoulda' known better. Everyone and their dog is going to know all your business before you leave here."

"My—my what?" I ask, a bit taken aback by her abruptness and choice of words—though I'm not sure why. GiGi isn't one for beating-around-the-bush.

"Okay, maybe not *mid-life*, but certainly a crisis, right?"

"Well, I guess so. I didn't really think about where I was going. I started driving and before I knew it, I was half-way here, so I kept on." I take a big drink of my coffee, hoping it can fuel my will to live throughout the rest of this conversation. "I never intended to put you out or make a scene. I just needed to see Michelle."

Our food arrives right on time and with it, I breathe a discreet sigh of relief. The server presents GiGi with a tiny plate with one biscuit, gravy, and two pieces of bacon. Then she sets all four of my plates in front of me, returns to the counter to re-stock her tray with Aunt Kitty's, and squeezes those onto the table too.

"Geez, you two. You'd think we were feedin' an army here," GiGi says once it's all laid out on the table.

"Well, you ordered it," I reply with as much of a laugh as my pounding head will allow.

"You gotta soak up that booze somehow. Speaking of, you need a shower. You smell like a whiskey bottle—and an ashtray."

"Oh, thanks, GiGi. And double thanks for bringing me out in public then." I take a big bite of bacon and man, was she right—the salty greasiness of it perfectly hits the spot.

"It's not the first time they've seen the likes of you in this Waffle House, I can tell you that," Aunt Kitty says as she breaks the yolk of her eggs and mixes them in with her hash browns.

I know what Aunt Kitty means by those words: that there have been other drunkards and hung-over souls within these walls before.

But how many sad, lonely, depressed, anxiety-ridden women have sat in this booth before me? Did they find their way out to the other side? Or are they still fighting, alone and hopeless? Or worse yet, have they given up and given in to their version of a tragic car-meets-power-pole daydream?

Staring at my plate, I poke the food around with my fork, lost in my own thoughts.

"Are you going to eat that or just maim it?" GiGi asks.

I take a bite, but don't answer or look up this time.

"You know you're going to be okay, right?" She cuts a bite off her biscuit.

I shrug my shoulders.

"Honey, finish up so we can get out of here and you can get some rest. We've got a long row to hoe before we can get you back home." She finishes her coffee and pours another cup.

"GiGi, I don't even know where to start."

"Of course you don't. But the first thing you're going to do is call your husband and tell him when you'll be home. Pick a day and stick to it. He deserves that, at least."

"I don't know if I can do that. I don't know if I can go back."

"You'll go back. You didn't leave because you're unhappy in your marriage, I don't believe—right?"

"No, it's not that."

"Well then, what's your other option? You will have to go back."

"I just—I need to figure a lot of things out first."

"Yes, you do. And while you're figuring it out, you need to let your husband know you haven't up and left him for good."

"But what if I have? What if I can't find my way back to them at all? There's just so much I don't understand; that I'm afraid of. If I go back there—" I lower my head and giant tears roll down my cheeks as I recall how hard I had to fight to resist ending it all on the way here.

"You have to have faith, child. Faith in yourself and faith in all of us—that we can help you find your way back home."

I know she's right about calling Andrew, but the rest of it seems impossible. This is why I ran to Michelle rather than her when I first arrived in Asher. Michelle's an enabler. She'll do anything and give you anything. She likes to lecture until she runs out of words, but she'll never try to force you to do something you're not ready for. She lets you come to your next move on your own. GiGi's expectations are always much higher. She doesn't believe in wallowing or putting off the hard work. If something needs to be done, you do it.

I was not ready for that when I showed up in Asher at daybreak three days ago, and I'm not so sure I'm ready for it now, but I guess we're going to find out.

10

PERSPECTIVE

We finish our meal in relative silence, with the conversation contained to the occasional, "Mm, this is good," or "Pass the pot," when our cups run low.

GiGi was right, of course. The heavy, grease-soaked meal was exactly what I needed to calm my queasy stomach and thankfully, the ride home is much less carnivalesque than the unpleasant ride to the restaurant.

We reach GiGi's neighborhood and, similar to downtown Asher, it seems not much here has changed since it served as the magnificent, picture-perfect backdrop to my seemingly uneventful childhood.

I've always loved how it feels coming back here. It's a feeling of truly being home—knowing the location of every crack in the sidewalk large enough to send you flying over your handlebars, which neighbors' yards have the best pecan trees (and which neighbors won't care when you snag a few for a snack), and which hilltops make for the best stargazing with your best friend on a warm summer night. It's memories of neighborhood picnics on the Fourth of July and trick-or-treating, even when you were way too old to be trick-or-treating, but you did it anyway.

It's a kind of place and childhood that doesn't seem to exist anymore, but every time I come here, I think maybe it could. It's nostalgia and wistfulness, inspiration and encouragement, and sadness and despair, all coexisting on every narrow, tree-lined street—or maybe only within the hearts of those old enough to remember their magic in decades gone-by.

GiGi pulls into the driveway and parks on the left of Aunt Kitty's pristine, baby blue 1962 Cadillac Coupe Deville. That car is only one piece of Aunt Kitty's eccentric personality. Everything from her name to her brightly colored jewelry, dramatic makeup, and platinum blonde pixie cut lets you know exactly what you're in for when striking up a friendship or conversation with her. She's spunky, fun, and fierce, but a big ol' softy at heart. I've often wondered if she's crafted herself as this caricature for the sole intent of providing the confidence boost she must so often need to face off with GiGi, day in and day out.

Aunt Kitty and Uncle Charlie bought the Caddy, brand new, right before she was due to have their first baby. One of my favorite photos in Aunt Kitty's house is a small black and white image of Uncle Charlie and a very pregnant Aunt Kitty standing in front of that car, dangling the keys in front of them, beaming with pride.

They were riding the high of all the firsts: first true love, first home to call their own, first shiny new car, first baby. They were staring the future right in the face, with complete abandon. Of course, all that changed a few weeks later when Aunt Kitty gave birth to a beautiful, sleeping baby girl. How cruel fate can be, even to those who least deserve it.

As we step out of the car, I see a mother with two young girls playing in the driveway across the street. They've got sidewalk chalk and bubbles and are making the most of the welcome break in the cold January weather. The mother looks over at us and gives a friendly wave with her right hand, holding a travel mug of something in the other.

I'm reminded of similar times in my childhood when we sat in this driveway, playing while the grown-ups sipped their coffee, sweet tea, or whiskey and discussed the latest in the neighborhood drama or politics. Reagan and Bush were names I knew well, even if I didn't know who they actually were.

But the striking difference between us back then, and this mom across the street now, is she's all alone. These days, we're *all* all alone.

GiGi walks around me to get to the back of the car and pops the trunk, interrupting my thoughts. Then she removes several Walmart bags and the diaper bag and hands them to me. I look inside and see all my things from Michelle's, plus a couple of Hershey's bars she snuck in there too.

"Thank you, GiGi."

"Sure. Run upstairs and wash off that stink. Then drink some water and take a nap."

"Yes, ma'am." I turn toward the house and walk up to the front door, finding it unlocked, as I knew I would.

Stepping inside, I feel as if I've entered a 1990's time capsule of mauve, hunter green, and brass. It's shocking how much of this is once again en vogue. Leave it to GiGi to never go out of style.

I grab a water bottle from the fridge, then turn to walk upstairs. As I climb to the second story, faces of the past greet me from the stairwell walls. Grandpa Philip is there, as well as Uncle Bo, my great-aunts and great-uncles, cousins and second cousins, and of course a young version of my mother too. So many of these beloved faces no longer exist in our world. How sad it must be for GiGi to meet them every time she travels up or down these creaky stairs.

I reach the landing and follow the hallway to the left. The second door on the right is my usual resting place, with the bathroom located across the hall. I open the bedroom door and toss the bags onto the pink floral-print bedspread. The curtains are pulled back, flooding the room with the mid-day sunshine, so I cross over to the window and pull them closed.

I dig through the bags and find Michelle has included the flannel pajama pants and long sleeve tee-shirt she let me borrow at her place. I grab those, a pair of underwear, and toiletries and carry them across the hall.

As I shower, I envision every bit of that steaming hot water is soaking right down into my bones. I'm so tired and for a second, I close my eyes, but images of Audrey, Ryan, and Noah flash before my closed lids and I can't take it. So, I open them once again, turn off the water, and step out into the cold.

Moments later, I'm enveloped in the warm comfort of GiGi's bedspread, surrounded by generations of works of art, trophies, and prize ribbons.

Here, under this blanket, I don't need the white noise of a fan to calm my thoughts. Here, I'm free from the torture of my mind. Here, I'm not broken, awful, or unworthy. Here, I'm just...home.

As I come down the stairs, I can see the darkness through the living room windows. The entire house is lit by lamplight, giving it that cozy, homey feeling I loved so much as a child. It's one of my favorite things about visiting GiGi. I turn the corner into the kitchen and see by the clock on the microwave that it's 8:30 at night.

"Mornin', sunshine!" GiGi calls from the laundry room at the back of the kitchen.

I cross the room and she wraps her sturdy, strong arms around my shoulders and gives a great, big hug. I still feel so small in her embrace, even though I surpassed her in height such a long time ago.

"What smells so good, GiGi?"

"Oh, that's a five-cheese, bacon mac-and-cheese I've got in the oven." She picks up a laundry basket full of clean towels and enters back into the kitchen.

"I knew there was a reason I enjoy coming here so much." I take the basket from her arms and carry it over to the table where we each take a seat and set to folding the towels.

"Oh, so it's the mac-and-cheese? Okay, this fall I'll be sure to send you a picture of the mac-and-cheese with a full account of how creamy and amazing it is, so maybe you'll actually bring my great-grandbabies home to see me for Thanksgiving, okay? Or maybe I'll make one of those ooey-gooey moving picture thingies with the cheese stretching to high-heaven and send it to you that way." Her hands are moving quickly, somehow folding towels and pantomiming her words at the same time.

"Do you mean a 'gif', GiGi?" I say with a laugh.

"Yeah, that." A timer sounds and she stands, places two potholders on her hands, and removes the bubbling casserole dish from the oven. She sets it down on top of the stove, removes her potholders, then does a swift one-eighty to face me. "What would you say to a Bloody Mary? I imagine it feels like breakfast-time to you after that long nap, right? And maybe you could use a bit of the hair-of-the-dog?"

"Well, I wasn't drinking vodka, but yeah, that sounds amazing."

"Good. We'll consider it the veggies for our well-balanced meal." GiGi moves to the bar in the formal dining room and returns with a bottle of vodka. Then, she pulls an open bottle of Bloody Mary mix from the refrigerator. She sets to making the drinks, complete with celery sticks, green olives, black pepper, and a dash of Tabasco, sets them on the table, and returns to her seat.

"Here we go. Cheers." She holds up her glass and I do the same.

"What are we toasting to, though?" I ask.

"To fresh starts," she replies.

We clank our glasses together and I take a big swig of the thick, tomato-red liquid. The warmth of the vodka, tanginess of the mix, and spiciness of the Tabasco hits my taste buds all at once, and at full-force, numbing my throat a little as it makes its way down.

"Geez, GiGi, you sure don't mix a boring drink, do ya'?" I cough to force the devil-drink the rest of the way down.

"Well, what would be the fun in that?" GiGi's throaty laughter bursts forward so abruptly, it makes me wonder if maybe she's already sipped one or two of these before I came downstairs.

We finish folding the laundry, making small talk as we go. Then, after loading it all back into the basket, GiGi walks over to the cabinet and pulls out two bowls which she piles full of the still piping-hot, velvety smooth mac-and-cheese. She brings the bowls back to the table and we dig in.

I'm not sure if the awkwardness is mutual or only felt on my end, but sitting here eating and not talking about how I ended up here in the first place is killing me. Maybe this is what she's counting on, though. That I'll be the first to bring it up, if she waits me out.

"So, you haven't asked me why I'm here." My voice breaks the silence between us.

"Oh, I know why you're here."

"You do?"

"Well, of course I do. I gleaned enough from Bonnie and Michelle to put two-and-two together. And do you think you're the first to ever be in your position? Hardly." She takes a bacon-loaded bite, then dabs the corner of her mouth clean with her napkin.

"How much did Bonnie tell you?"

"Enough for me to know you should thank your lucky stars you found yourself a friend like her," she replies.

"Yeah, I know." I take another sip of my drink, puckering a bit at its strength. "I honestly don't know what I would have done without her these past few months. Her home is—well, it's hard to describe—it's a safe place. It sure makes me miss you, though."

"Well then pick up the damn phone, will ya'?" GiGi says, tossing her arms into the air—fork still in hand—flinging a few noodles behind her head.

"Yes, ma'am," I laugh, and take another bite as she inspects her fork, probably wondering where her bite has gone.

"Jenna, you're nothing special, you know," GiGi says a few seconds later.

"Thanks, GiGi."

"You know what I mean. Women—mothers—have gone through what you're going through since the beginning of time. It's only natural."

"Well, why the hell doesn't anybody ever talk about it then?"

"That's a great question. In my day, it was taboo. You kept it to yourself and if your husband was awake enough to see it, he either handed you the bottle or took it away—whichever was necessary. Then you pulled yourself together and went about your day. But in this day and age, there's no reason not to talk about it. I don't understand why you girls put so much pressure on yourselves and then refuse to acknowledge its repercussions. And why the hell do y'all feel you need to do everything on your own? We never did. Do you ever recall a time when there weren't three or four of us adults around helping with you kids?"

"No, not often. But it's different when you don't live near family, I guess."

"Yes, that's true, but is Aunt Kitty family? Or Donna and Jean? I know you remember them."

"Oh, yes, I remember them all right. Smoked like a couple of freight trains, they did."

"But they were here, right? And so were their kids. We did it all together. When one needed a break, we took up the slack. We were a community. Where's your community?"

"I don't know. Bonnie's it, I guess."

"Yeah, because she's old-school and she gets it. But she's not enough. You need to put your pride aside and ask for help sometimes. You need to find your sisters."

I remember the poor mom across the street this afternoon and I know GiGi's right.

"Do you think it's that easy? I mean, is that all there is to it? Finding friends?"

"Hell, no, it's not, but it's a big part of it." She takes another cheesy bite, then continues, "You probably need to find yourself a shrink, too."

"GiGi! Nobody calls them that anymore." I laugh.

"Well, forgive me. But you need to find someone you can talk to—who can offer you more than a fun night in a bar that gets you thrown in jail. Or more than Bloody Marys and mac-and-cheese, for that matter."

"Well, I think the Bloody Marys and mac-and-cheese are pretty fantastic."

"Good. Have another. You have a phone call to make."

"You awake?" I text to Andrew.

"Yeah," he replies.

I take a deep breath and pull my legs up to cross them under me on the bed. I'm thankful for the liquid courage of those two drinks, but still can't help but feel it's nowhere near enough. Pushing the button to make the call, my heart pounds hard in my chest.

"Hello?" he answers in his smooth baritone voice.

"Hi."

Silence.

"Are you there?" I ask.

"Yes, I'm here. It's good to hear your voice."

"Yours too." I didn't think through what I was going to say before I called. I was afraid if I thought about it too much, I'd lose the nerve to do it. Now, I'm wishing I would have devised a plan. "How are the kids?"

"They're fine. They miss you, though."

"I miss them too...and you."

Silence.

"Andrew, I'm really sorry."

More silence.

"Andrew?"

"Yeah, I'm here."

"Are you going to talk to me?"

Another pause.

"Jenna, I'm not sure yet how I feel about what you've done—" His voice trails off and leaves me in silence once again. "—But I understand it, on some level."

My heart sinks and the floodgates open.

"I'm—I'm so sorry. I'm sorry I'm not the mother I should be or the wife I should be—I'm just sorry, Andrew. I don't know if I can be fixed. I want to fix it though. I'm going to try." My head pounds. The pressure built up inside is too much.

"Just come home, Jenna. We need to work this out together," he says.

"I don't know if I can."

"What do you mean? You're not staying in Asher—right?" His voice sounds frantic and a little angry.

"I don't know how to be their mother, Andrew. I'm so horrible to them. I don't want them to hate me."

"And you think abandoning them will keep them from hating you?" Now he's definitely angry.

"I don't know! I don't know anything at this point. I need some time."

I hear GiGi clear her throat in the hallway. She's eavesdropping and making herself known, so I'll stick to the original plan of giving him a date. I squeeze my eyelids tight and scream on the inside. I don't want to lie to him. I don't want to make a promise I can't keep. But I guess I'm going to have to do just that.

"Sunday. I'll try my best to be home on Sunday."

"Okay. The kids will be happy to hear that. Don't let them down, Jenna. Come home."

The silence is on my end this time.

"Jenna?"

"Yeah, I hear you. I'll try, Andrew, I promise."

I hear GiGi's feet shuffle back down the hallway and her bedroom door close. Satisfied with what she's heard, she's taken herself to bed.

11

GLORIA

The next morning, GiGi's knocking on the bedroom door before dawn. She opens it and says, "Time to get up. We've got walkin' to do."

"Walking? Since when do you walk?" I wasn't expecting an early morning wake-up call, and I barely slept. My brain opted to pour over the potential scenarios of what will happen once Andrew discovers my colossal, unhinged lie instead. I'm tired.

"I go with friends a few times a week. So, get moving or we're going to be late." She turns and leaves the room.

I groan and roll myself off the bed. I dig through my bags for a tee-shirt, my extra pair of yoga pants, and sneakers. I pull the shirt on over the long-sleeved tee I slept in, then finish dressing and make a quick stop in the bathroom.

As I come down the stairs and enter the kitchen, GiGi tosses me a banana. "Here, eat this. And take these." She hands me a pair of purple gloves and matching earmuffs. She then pulls two bottles of water from the fridge, and we head out the door.

The frigid January wind whips around the corner of the house the moment I step onto the porch. I wrap my arms around myself and plead, "GiGi, seriously? It's cold out here."

"What? Have you lost your grit? You used to run cross country in worse weather than this. And a lot earlier in the morning, too."

"I was seventeen! I didn't have any sense," I say, as I climb into the passenger seat of GiGi's car.

We drive until we reach the city park and I see Aunt Kitty's Cadillac parked next to a small, red pickup truck. "Who do you walk with, anyway?"

"Kitty and another lady from church, Gloria. Sometimes Kitty brings her niece, Krista, too." She parks and we both exit the car and walk up the trail to where the others are sitting at a picnic table.

"Gloria, this is my granddaughter, Jenna. She's visiting for the week."

"Oh, yes. Kitty's told me all about you," Gloria says, with an odd look in my direction.

"It's nice to meet you," I reply, cautiously. I'm not sure if that look on her face is always there or if it's a gesture of disapproval meant only for me.

"And this is my niece, Krista. I think you two met a few times as kids, but you know, that's been a while," Aunt Kitty says.

"Hi," Krista says, as she reaches out to shake my hand.

She's a little taller than I am, but similarly built. She's younger than me and probably has never birthed a child, given how flat her stomach is in those leggings—or maybe she's just worked a lot harder than I have at making it that way.

"Well, let's get moving. It's cold out here," Gloria grunts.

"See? Cold." I whisper to GiGi as we head east on the trail.

We walk for a while with Aunt Kitty telling me all about Krista and Krista never getting a word in to tell me about herself. Then

GiGi starts in with discussing my high school days, college accomplishments, and all the details of my beautiful wedding—all of which leads her to gushing over her great-grandbabies.

"But you left them, right?" Gloria chimes in for the first time since our awkward introduction.

"Wha—what?" I'm not entirely sure I heard her correctly.

"You have these beautiful angel-babies at home and a loving husband who you're responsible for taking care of and you left them. Why don't you tell us about that?" Gloria is still walking. The rest of us have stopped.

"Gloria!" GiGi proclaims, shocked.

Gloria looks over her shoulder, realizes she's left us behind, and turns to face us with her hands on her hips. "Well, didn't she?" she asks GiGi.

I interrupt before GiGi has a chance to respond. "I, uh...that's not exactly what happened, but—"

"But what?" Gloria asks, not giving up.

"Well, I wasn't—wasn't in a good place."

"Oh, please. You're married with small children. Of course, you weren't in a good place. None of us ever are. But that doesn't mean you *leave*." She starts walking again and GiGi and Aunt Kitty rush to catch up.

Krista looks at me with her mouth gaping wide. I jog to catch up with everyone else and she follows suit.

"Look, I don't know what Aunt Kitty's told you, but there's a lot to this story and I don't particularly feel like discussing it with strangers."

"No, no, of course you don't. That's the shame talking, you know," Gloria says.

"Gloria, really!" GiGi halts and I can see the fury growing in her face.

Aunt Kitty's looking at me mouthing, "I'm sorry, I'm sorry," over and over again.

"Look, I have a lot of feelings about what I've done, but shame isn't one of them. At first, maybe, but I know now that I did what I thought was best for my family. I thought they were better off without me."

That's something I haven't even told GiGi, and the emotion it brings up is too much. I wipe my eye with my sleeve.

"Well, maybe you were right."

Gloria cranks her speed up another notch, and I'm almost at a jog to keep up. Aunt Kitty tries to hold GiGi at a distance by pulling her back, and Krista is still right by my side.

"I've tried to be respectful, but how dare you judge me? You don't even know me!"

"Oh, I don't have to know you. I've seen enough deadbeat mothers in my life to know what one looks like when it's standing right in front of my face."

The fire in my chest is back, stronger than I've ever felt it before, and I stop, frozen in place. GiGi opens her mouth, points her finger, and starts toward Gloria, but stops again when she hears me speak.

"You horrible, horrible old *hag*!" I scream at her back as she's walking ahead of us.

She stops and turns to face me. "Tell me...tell me I'm wrong."

"You are wrong. You have no idea what you're talking about! I love my family. I would give anything for them and if that means leaving, so I don't ruin their lives, that's what I'll do!" I'm sobbing, screaming at the top of my lungs at this old lady who I don't even know. "I know I'm not perfect, but I do the best I can. I'm learning. I'm figuring it out. I am a good mom!"

My words are high-pitched and desperate and as I look at Gloria's face, a small, crooked smile appears there.

How dare she do nothing but stand there and smile at me when my whole heart is exposed, on display for the world to see? How dare she taunt me with that—*that face*? I clench my fists tight. I've never wanted to tackle somebody to the ground as badly as I want to tackle this old lady right now.

"You a runner?" Krista asks.

"Yeah," I mutter through clenched jaws.

"Let's go." Krista takes off at a full sprint.

I pivot on my toes and all the anger and confusion and disbelief inside of me explodes like a starter's gun and I'm right on her heels, seeing nothing but the neon pink streak of her shoes in the gray morning light.

What is *wrong* with her? Who could attack a total stranger like that? And what in the world did Aunt Kitty *tell* her? Is that how she feels about me, too? No, it can't be. Aunt Kitty is my Aunt Kitty—she could never.

I can barely see through the tears, but I follow those pink streaks, refusing to slow my pace.

Several minutes later, my chest is on fire, but I keep going. Then, when I don't think I can make another stride and slow down, Krista kicks it into high gear and, in some superhuman way, moves even faster than before. But I won't let her get away.

I dig deep and force myself to regain my position behind her, matching her pace once more. Our feet are in sync, pounding the pavement in a fast and furious rhythm.

As my lungs burn, I feel a sharp pang in my rib cage, letting me know my breathing needs control. I focus on our footfalls. Breathe in—step step—breathe out—step step. Breathe in—step step—breathe out—step step.

After a few minutes of this, I'm finally able to speak. "Good Lord, you are fast!" I call to her from behind.

"Do you want to stop?" she asks.

"No, but maybe we could find a decent pace?"

For the first time, she slows, and I pull up into a position beside her.

"You're pretty quick yourself," she says, breathing much easier than I am.

Breathe in—step step—breathe out—step step.

As we run, side-by-side, I can't help but feel a connection with this stranger next to me. Our breathing is in-sync, our stride is in-sync, and I'm reminded of how amazing it was to do this same exact thing with Michelle all those years ago.

I run without speaking another word. I run without thinking another thought. And I am free.

———◆———

We turn a curve around an enormous oak tree. In the distance, I see three figures sitting at the picnic table.

Why is she still here? Couldn't she at least have the decency to leave?

I slow to a jog and then a walk. Krista takes my lead and does the same. In a few minutes, I'm walking in circles on the path, both trying to bring my breath back down to normal and buying myself time before I must face that wretched woman again.

"Do you know her?" I ask Krista with a nod in their direction.

"No, not really. Not outside of walking with her here. But what a witch!"

"Yeah, that's one word for her. Well, let's get on with it then." I turn toward them and start the walk back.

Krista follows a step or two behind me and as we approach, I look no one in the eye. I walk right past them as I head straight for the car.

"Jenna—" I hear GiGi say.

I ignore her and keep walking.

"Jenna!" she says again, and again I ignore her.

Then, I hear another voice—*her voice.*

"I know you're a good mom!" Gloria yells after me.

I stop and turn around. "What?"

"I know you're a good mom—and a good person," she says again.

"No, you don't. You don't know me at all. So, whatever they said that makes you want to apologize, don't bother." I turn and start to walk away again.

"Jenna, I do know you. I was you. I spent four months locked up in 1972 because I was you."

This time when I halt, I don't know what to do. I don't want to face her. I don't want to hear her story. I don't want her pity or empathy or kindness. I want her to go away so I can pretend I've never looked upon her horrid face.

But then I feel a hand on my elbow. "Come, child," GiGi says to me, as she pulls me back toward the table.

I know I don't have any other option. When GiGi says come, you come. I walk with her, looking at the ground, and take a seat on one side of the table.

"Jenna, I know you're angry with me," Gloria says, as she sits opposite of me. "But I've been where you are. And what I needed then, more than anything in the world, was for someone to force me to believe in myself. Because all I believed at that point in my life was that the right mix of painkillers and alcohol would put me out of my misery...but it didn't. I tried, but it didn't."

I look her in the face and see glossy eyes, which appear softer than they were before.

"I couldn't believe in myself. I couldn't believe I was worthy of my own children, that I was good enough for them, that I could make my husband happy, or that I could be kind or show or receive love. I was numb and empty inside. I considered slitting my own throat, just so I could *feel* something before I died. But I didn't have the courage for that, despite also not having the courage to live." She pauses, waiting for me to respond.

"And?" I whisper under my breath.

"Well, the neighbor found me passed out in the lounger on the back patio. At first, she thought I was napping, but something told her to take a closer look. I wasn't breathing. She called for help, and it saved me. Only, I didn't want to be saved."

She pauses again and Aunt Kitty steps closer to hand her a tissue she's pulled from her pocket.

"When they released me from the hospital, my husband drove me straight to a facility. I never got to see my kids or say goodbye. I disappeared for four months of their lives." She dries her eyes with the tissue before continuing. "That ugly building is where I learned my worth. It's where I learned my kids did need me. That they did love me, and I loved them. It's where I learned to feel again."

"How?" I ask.

"Lots and lots of therapy. Alcoholics Anonymous. And the right mix of mood stabilizers, which some of my AA buddies didn't approve of, but I had decided to live—and that was a big part of what I needed to do it."

"So why couldn't you just tell me this? Instead of going through all...that?" I gesture toward the running trail to reference the verbal assault that took place there minutes before.

"Because I know first-hand, well-meaning people can tell you repeatedly that you're a good person, a good mom, and you have value and strength and courage and love. But unless you come to that conclusion on your own, you'll never believe it."

"Why did you think I would?"

"I didn't. And if someone would have done to me back then what I did to you now, it wouldn't have worked. I was too far gone. But you? There's hope for you yet. You stood up for yourself, which tells me, deep down, you still have faith in yourself."

Gloria dabs her face again, reaches across the table to take both of my hands in hers, then says, "Jenna, can you ever forgive me? I didn't mean it. I know you're a good mom and I hope one day soon, you'll truly know it too."

I nod my head.

"Atta' girl," GiGi says.

"Did you know about this? Did you set me up for it?" I ask her.

"Are you kidding? I was about to give you the signal to take her from the left while I came in from the right."

There's laughter, then Gloria turns to Krista. "And that run...Wow, I don't think I've ever seen two grown women run like that. Maybe that was much needed as well?" She aims the question at me.

I'm not ready to make nice with Gloria yet, so I don't answer. But she's right. *God, that run felt good.*

On the way home, Gloria's words are still tumbling through my head along with GiGi's, Andrew's, Tyler's, and Michelle's too. I try to pull the most important pieces and file them away in my brain, but they're all running together and it's driving me crazy.

"Do you think we can stop somewhere for a notebook or journal on the way back?" I ask GiGi as she drives.

"Sure. There's a cute little bookstore on Main Street with tons of them, but it doesn't open for another couple of hours. Walmart's open though."

"Walmart's fine." I can't wait a couple of hours. I need to get this whirlwind of words onto paper before I lose my mind trying to mentally card-catalog them all away.

A few minutes later, we pull into the parking lot. A quick trip in and out later, I've got a brand new, canvas-covered journal and writing pen in my hands and we can't get home fast enough.

We pull into the driveway and I am out of the car and into the house in a flash, without so much as a word to GiGi. I know she didn't have anything to do with Gloria's little stunt, but I'm still not in the mood for chit-chat, nonetheless. And I know Gloria meant well, but I'm still angry at her, too. I need to write.

I head upstairs to my room and shut the door. Sitting on the bed, I force open the plastic wrapping on the journal and tear apart the cardboard packaging on the pen. I think of Michelle and begin writing anything and everything that comes to my mind.

"We aren't born knowing how to do this. We have to learn how to do it well."

"Read the book...take the class."

"Notice the little things that make you happy—and do more of that."

Nirvana.

"This is what you need. You need to dance!"

"Don't drop the soap."

That laugh...

I write "Michelle" at the top in cursive writing. As I think further on the conversations and experiences we've shared since I came here, I doodle in the margins of the page, filling it with lots of hearts and bad sketches of Hershey's bars, cowboy boots, wine bottles, pizza slices, music notes, books, and bacon-covered cinnamon rolls. I stare at it for a few minutes, making no more marks at all, then close my eyes, thank God for Michelle, and turn the page.

Pearl snaps.

That scent.

Those eyes.

"You are not a bad person. You are not crazy."

"You love your family so much, you let it tear you apart."

"…you've run out of yourself to give."

"Call someone—anyone—who can help you remember who you are."

"For God's sake, go on a date with your husband."

"You're stronger than you remember."

At the top of this page, I write "Tyler." I fill the white space with more music notes and cowboy boots, a whiskey glass with a square ice cube, neon beer signs, and a pack of cigarettes. I think about Tyler—and our friendship and history together—and give thanks for him, too. Then I turn the page again.

"You're married with small children. Of course, you weren't in a good place. None of us ever are."

"Shame."

"Deadbeat mother."

That face.

"I know you're a good mom!"

"There's hope for you yet…"

"You stood up for yourself. Deep down, you still have faith."

On this page, I write "Gloria" in my best Gothic-style letters, color them in with the black pen, and consider making nothing but black scribbles all over the white space of the page.

But then I remember her story, her despair, and her desperate attempt to make it all end. And I choose, instead, to fill it with various forms of beautiful flowers—my best attempt at showing her recovery, rebirth, and ultimate redemption and deliverance from her own cruel mind.

I take a moment to think about all she must have gone through and as I do, I can feel those feelings too…right here, right now. They're not new to me. I've felt them all before. But, I think, if Gloria can lay them to rest, maybe there's hope I can too.

12

AUNT KITTY

The next morning, GiGi knocks on the door again. This time I'm waiting for her, dressed and ready to go.

We grab our bananas and waters from the kitchen, head to the car, and make our way to the park. As we pull into the parking lot, I see the same two cars as yesterday: Aunt Kitty's and Gloria's.

"You gonna be able to face her without wanting to punch her lights out?" GiGi asks as she parks the car.

"Well, wanting to and actually doing it are two different things, so I think I'll be all right." Although, the knot forming in the pit of my stomach indicates otherwise.

We walk over to the picnic table and I'm happy to see Krista has come with Kitty again today.

"Morning, ladies. You ready?" GiGi asks the group.

"Of course we're ready...been waiting here for fifteen minutes for you," Aunt Kitty answers.

"Not my problem you insist on arriving early everywhere you go," GiGi replies.

We start walking and after five minutes or so, Krista says to me, "You wanna?" with a pleading look on her face.

"Yes, I wanna."

"See ya'll in a bit," Krista calls back to the others as we take off in a jog.

"Thank you," she says, once we've gone beyond earshot. "I love spending time with Aunt Kitty, but man, all of them together can drive you a bit batty. Plus, that just seemed like it was going to be super awkward."

"How often do you come with Kitty?"

"A couple of times a week. She has no kids of her own, you know, which means no grandkids either. And with Uncle Charlie gone, she gets lonely, I think."

"Yeah," I reply, thinking of that old photo of Aunt Kitty and Uncle Charlie in front of the shiny new Caddy—so happy and so in love.

We've picked up the pace a little and are running side-by-side.

"Does she ever talk to you about what happened? With her baby?" I ask between breaths.

"No, not really. I mean, she has, but only once or twice that I can remember. I think it messed her up pretty bad."

"Yeah, I bet."

We finish our run, cool off, and sit at the picnic table, waiting for the others to return.

"Man, I have really missed running without a treadmill or a stroller," I say, before taking a sip from my water bottle.

Krista laughs. "Well, when do you leave? Maybe we can get in a run each morning before then?"

"I'm not sure yet. And yes, please, let's do it."

The others return and pretend to stretch, though mostly they gossip about what so-and-so was wearing in church on Sunday or whose grandkid has gotten themselves into trouble again this week. We say our goodbyes and head back to the cars. To my surprise, Aunt Kitty tosses her keys to Krista. Then, she walks ahead of me to GiGi's car, opens the passenger door and climbs inside. I take the seat in the back. Krista hops into the driver's seat of Kitty's car and drives away.

"Where to today, Kitty?" GiGi asks.

"Let's do Hardee's this morning. Sound good, Jenna?"

"Yeah, that's fine by me, but what's the point in exercising only to eat fast food after?"

"Well, you're missing the point, dear. We don't walk for the exercise," GiGi answers.

"And we really, really like to eat," says Kitty.

As we pull up to the Hardee's drive through, the scent of bacon hangs in the air and makes my empty stomach growl with anticipation.

As a child, Saturday morning breakfasts here with GiGi and Mama were a part of our regular routine. Even as an adult, eating here provides a sweet sense of nostalgia that warms me from the inside—the kind that only comes from reliving something truly special, even if you didn't realize it at the time.

There's no line, as it seems all of Asher is still asleep this early in the morning, including the drive-through employee.

"Welcome to Hardee's. What can I get for you today?" a sleepy, slow voice mumbles through the speaker box.

GiGi turns to me. "Buttermilk biscuits with sausage gravy and black coffee?"

"Yes, ma'am."

"I'll have two orders of biscuits and gravy and a breakfast platter with bacon, please. Coffee for all, and lots of sugar and creamer." GiGi turns to Aunt Kitty with a disgusted look on her face. Aunt Kitty scrunches her nose and sticks out her tongue in reply.

"So, do y'all do this every day after you walk? Pick up food and go home to eat it?"

"Yup," GiGi replies.

"Hmm...sounds nice."

Minutes later, we're back in GiGi's living room. She's clicked on the lamp and the fireplace and we're digging through the Hardee's bags to find our food. The curtains are still closed tight and if we hadn't recently come in from outside, it would be easy to believe the sun has yet to rise.

GiGi's taken her favorite spot in the armchair, Aunt Kitty's seated on the end of the sofa, and I'm cross-legged on the floor with my back to the fire.

The coffee table is our dining table this morning and the arrangement is so cozy and wonderful, it's almost painful.

Why can't I have this back home? Why can't I find my own Kitty to eat junk food with after a walk spent gossiping and talking about nothing important at all? Someone so comfortable and familiar to me, we don't even have to ask what comes next. We simply climb into the car and go.

I need my Texas Michelle.

Could Maggie be her? No, I don't think so. Maggie's too put-together. She has it all figured out. I need someone shattered and glued back together, like me—someone who gets it. But where do you find a person like that? I can't walk around town holding a "Broken Mother Seeking Broken Mother Friend" sign to find her.

Why isn't there a safe place for people like me to go to for comfort and rest when they're feeling at their worst? Or for coffee and conversation when they're feeling fine? Someplace like Bonnie's, but for everyone. Someplace where friends like Michelle can pick you up from the ground and bring you inside into the warmth when you need it most.

"You okay?" GiGi asks as I stare at my food, lost in thought.

"Yeah. I have a lot on my mind, I guess."

"Like what?"

"I don't know. I guess I just wish I could have someone to do this kind of stuff with."

"Well, why can't you?" GiGi asks.

"Because it's hard to find real friendship like this." I gesture to the two of them. "You guys have known each other for decades. Michelle and I have too."

"Well, you have to start somewhere," GiGi says with a mouth full of biscuit.

"Yeah, I know."

"And it's not always pretty, you know," adds Aunt Kitty. "We've been through some pretty rough times and we haven't always liked each other. Actually, there was a solid chunk of time when I hated this old bat and never wanted to see her again." She throws a crumpled-up napkin toward GiGi and it pelts her right in the face.

When it hits, GiGi's cuts her eyes to Aunt Kitty, squinting as if she's annoyed. But her head doesn't move and two seconds later she's back to looking down at her food and loading her fork for another bite. She doesn't say a word.

"Really?" I ask.

"Yes," Aunt Kitty replies. Then she's silent and looking at GiGi as if she's asking for help or permission to go on.

"Well, go on and tell her. It's your story, not mine," GiGi says to her.

Aunt Kitty looks down at her coffee as if she doesn't know what to say or where to begin.

"Well, you know I lost a child, right?"

"Yes, ma'am. I do."

More silence. GiGi hands Aunt Kitty a napkin and she folds it up into a tiny square to hold tight in her palm. Then, she uses it to dab her eyes, drying them of the tears that have come, even before she's begun.

———⧫———

"Losing a child, even one who has never taken a breath on this earth, is the most torturous thing that could ever happen to a person. It's not supposed to happen. You prepare yourself for losing your spouse, because you know from the get-go you have a fifty-fifty shot at having to deal with that in your life. But a child? Nobody ever prepares themselves for that.

"When she was born, and there was no crying, or movement, or hint of pink in her precious little face, my whole world stopped, frozen in time. We didn't have the technology you have today. There was no way to know or prepare. No warning. She was active and moving around hours before. Then I felt cramps and started bleeding and we thought, 'This is it!' Charlie put my suitcase in the Caddy and we drove to the hospital. He was telling jokes during the contractions to give me something else to focus on and running red lights all along the way. We were happy and excited and so ready to meet our baby.

"But then, everything stopped. I couldn't breathe. I couldn't speak. They wanted me to hold her, to say goodbye, to name her...but I couldn't. Charlie did, though. He held her and hugged her enough for the both of us. And he named her Grace. But when it came time to leave and we were required to fill out paperwork to record her name, I couldn't do it. And they wouldn't let Charlie do it alone. So, she was Baby Girl Mitchell."

Tears are falling for all of us now.

"When they told me it was time to go home, I said I wasn't leaving without my baby. I wanted my baby. I ached and cried and screamed in agony for her and all I remember is the nurse telling me I needed to calm down...that I was upsetting the other mothers on the floor. I yelled at her, 'I don't give a damn about the other mothers! They can all go to hell!' and that's when they shoved a loaded needle right into my behind.

"I screamed at the pain of it, and from pure anger. Then the room started to spin. I lost my balance and went to sit on the bed, but the nurse guided me into a wheelchair instead. Leaving the hospital with an empty womb and empty arms was the hardest thing I've ever done. Even with the tranquilizer keeping me calm on the outside, I was still raging on the inside. I wanted to destroy everything they wheeled me past on the way out, but my hands and feet couldn't move enough to do it. All I could do was cry.

"Charlie carried me over the threshold—the same way he did a year earlier, after our honeymoon—and up the stairs and into bed. I begged him over and over again, every day for weeks to give me the bottle of painkillers from the hospital and a glass of water so I could put myself out of my misery. So I could be with her. He never got frustrated or upset with me through that, not once. He simply kissed me on the forehead and sang. Charlie's voice was like an angel, solemn and deep. It was the only thing that could keep me calm enough to fall asleep.

"I spent weeks in that bed, taking pain pill after pain pill, even when I didn't need them anymore. I took tranquilizers to keep the anger at bay and to help with the sleep. When they wore off, I pulled wallpaper from the walls, shoved chair legs through windows, ripped pillows open with my bare hands. I was lost in a world without a sense of time. It all still felt like it had happened *today*. I relived the anguish of seeing her pale blue face thousands of times in my mind and there was no way to stop it. I was killing myself slowly, not with pills or a knife, but by driving myself out of my mind and body with grief."

GiGi sniffs and takes a deep, shaky breath. Her chin quivers as she reaches out to take Aunt Kitty's hand.

"But then, I remember waking one morning to a commotion downstairs. I could hear Charlie's voice, speaking calmly, and a woman's voice responding to him. Her voice was not so calm." She looks at GiGi and smiles.

"I heard him say, 'It's the only way, Laurel. She needs more help than I can give.' Then I heard your grandmother say, 'I'll be damned if you're going to lock her away. I'll kill you first, Charlie Mitchell.' And I thought, lock me away? What does she mean? And a minute later, she was in my room. She was taking my clothes and belongings out of the suitcase he packed and putting them all away. I asked her to tell me what was going on and she said, 'Nothing at all for you to worry about, ya' loon. Close your eyes and take a nap, why don't ya'?' And then, she sang until I did."

I look to Aunt Kitty, wondering if she has more she wants to say, but she's looking at GiGi with tears streaming down her cheeks and clutching her hand so hard her fingers are white.

GiGi, sensing Aunt Kitty's reached a point she's unable to go on, says, "Yeah, well, my voice wasn't as angelic as Charlie's and you let me know it, too." Then she blows her nose delicately into her napkin.

Aunt Kitty laughs a little then turns GiGi loose so she can blow her own nose. "Your pig-headed grandmother saved my life and I hated her for it. I didn't want to live. I didn't want to walk this earth without my baby, but she made me do it anyway. The first thing she did was take the pills away. She said to me, 'Kitty, you've got to learn to live with the grief on your own, without these.' And she dumped them all down the toilet."

"We went through a lot of pillows in those first few weeks," GiGi says.

"I still don't know why you kept buying more," Aunt Kitty replies.

GiGi thinks on this for a few seconds before responding. "It was my way of showing I wasn't giving up. That you could tear apart all the pillows you wanted to, and I would only bring more."

"Well, even so, it took a few months before I could even get out of bed on my own. She came over every morning at eight-thirty to dress me and make me at least sit up in bed to eat a little something. Then, eventually, she was making me sit in the chair next to the bed for breakfast. Then, a few weeks later still, she was practically dragging me down the stairs to the kitchen table."

"Then one day," GiGi interrupts, "I showed up, and she was already dressed. She did it all on her own." She looks at Aunt Kitty. "That was the first day I thought, 'She's going to be okay.'"

"And it still took a long time before I felt like I was living a somewhat normal existence again. I was out of bed, but the sofa became my new resting place. On the days when the weather was nice, she would convince me to go sit on the porch swing with her outside, but it never lasted long. Too many kids playing up and down the street. I couldn't take it. I hid in the house, afraid to go to the grocery store or anywhere else. I didn't want to see those beautiful kids, or adorable toddlers. Heaven forbid, should I come across a newborn baby. I didn't cook or clean. You did it all," she nods toward GiGi. "And I'm pretty sure you saved my marriage at one point too, even if you won't admit to it."

"I've told you so many times that day was all in your imagination, Kitty. It didn't happen."

"Well, then that was one hell of a vivid dream or hallucination then, because I remember being in bed and hearing you shout at Charlie downstairs." She turns her head to talk directly to me. "She said, 'Charlie, you will stop seeing that woman.' Then he said, 'We're friends, Laurel. We play golf at the same club and sometimes have lunch together after. There's nothing going on, I swear.' And here's the good part…he should've kept his mouth shut, but he went on to say, 'And besides, last I checked, there were two names on our marriage certificate and yours isn't one of them.' Then there was a loud slap and your grandma said, 'You wanted your wife back, and by nothing but God's own hand, you're getting her. Don't you go wasting that miracle now.' Then the front door slammed, and she was gone.

"I waited a while, but eventually made my way downstairs and found him sitting with a beer at the kitchen table. I said, 'Charlie, is everything okay?' He stood, put his hands on both of my shoulders, gave me a hard, long look, and said, 'Yeah, honey, I think so.' He hugged me then and for the first time in nearly a year, I hugged him back. And things got much better after that."

"I was pregnant with your mama about eighteen-months after Kitty lost her baby," GiGi says. "I was terrified to tell her, but when I worked up the courage to do it, she smiled and gave me the biggest hug. As I grew fatter and lazier, she never left my side. She was in the waiting room at the hospital the whole time and was the first person to hold Catherine after we did. She baked the cake for her first birthday party…and her second…and her third. She was as much a mother to her as I was. And she cried as hard as I did the day she married and left home."

"Hey, let's not relive that agony, too," Aunt Kitty quips. "I think I've experienced enough for one day."

We've run out of Hardee's napkins to blow into, so GiGi stands, walks down the hallway, and returns with a box of tissue.

"Jenna, if there's one thing I have learned from all of this, it's not to take people for granted. I was never blessed with another baby, but every child I see somehow becomes my child. I am a mother with no one to call my own, so they all become my own. You have three children who need you and I hope you never forget that. Don't take them for granted. Don't take yourself and how much they need you for granted. And if you're lucky enough to have a stubborn old broad in your corner who can pull you back from the depths of hell—and help you live again—don't take her for granted either." She turns and smiles at GiGi, who takes her hand and gives it a squeeze.

"Okay, enough of that. You ready for me to take you home so you can freshen up?" GiGi asks Aunt Kitty.

"Yup. I'm ready."

"All right. Here, let me help you up."

"I got it, I got it. What do you think I am? An old lady or some-thin'?"

"Well, you're not the belle of the ball anymore, I can tell you that," GiGi says.

GiGi throws open the living room curtains, and the sunshine pours in for the first time today. In the light, I can see every line and age spot on each of their faces, arms, and hands. I can see how they use each other as guides to get around furniture and for stability to get down the front porch steps. In the light, I can see why they bicker and fight. They do it because it's what brought Aunt Kitty back to life. They do it to survive. They do it out of love.

After they've left, I go upstairs and take a shower. Then, I wrap the towel around my wet hair and return to my room. Pulling the journal from the nightstand and flipping to a fresh page, I wonder, where do I even start?

I put the pen to the paper and draw a border made of flowers. Then, I draw a scroll for the banner and write "Kitty" inside of it.

Loss...grief.

Anguish...hopelessness.

Friendship...love.

Revival.

Strength...courage.

"Don't take them for granted."

"Don't take yourself for granted."

"They need you."

Thinking through all of this and writing the words on paper makes me experience Aunt Kitty's story all over again. *What an amazing woman.*

I draw in the white spaces of her page. I draw a rudimentary version of a car to represent Aunt Kitty's Caddy, a baby rattle with a bow around the handle, a syringe with a long needle on the end, and three intertwined hearts with the initials "C", "K", and "G" written inside of them. The heart with the "G" is in the center and has big, radiant angel wings. Then there's a pill bottle, pillow feathers floating around the edges of the page, and a suitcase. Finally, I draw storm clouds with a tiny sun trying to poke out from above and the words "love" and "sisterhood" in block letters at the top.

I hear GiGi's car pull into the driveway and place the journal back in its drawer. Then I pick up my phone and send a quick text message to Michelle.

"I love you. Thank you for being YOU."

After that, I text Bonnie.

"Hi, Bonnie. I hope you're doing well. Things are coming together, I think. Thank you for everything."

And Maggie.

"Hi, Maggie. Just sending a note to say how thankful I am for your friendship. Hugs."

And finally, Mama.

"Hi, Mama. I don't know if GiGi's already told you, but I'm in town. It's a long story. Please don't be mad I haven't come by yet. I love you."

It doesn't take long for Mama to reply.

"Jenna, of course I know you're in town. I figured when you were ready to see me, you'd let me know. Love you too, sweetheart."

I hear GiGi in the kitchen downstairs and decide I'll reply to Mama later. I put on my socks and head down. When I arrive, I see her sitting at the kitchen table having a second cup of coffee and staring out the kitchen window and across the front yard.

"You okay?" she asks after I've taken a seat.

"Yeah, I'm okay. I had no clue about Aunt Kitty, though. I mean, I knew, but I didn't know all that. Or that you were such a big part of it." I pour myself a cup. "And I think it is your story too, you know."

"Huh?" she asks before taking a sip.

"You told her to tell me the story because it was her story and not yours. I think it is your story, too."

"Well, maybe a little. But you'll never understand what that woman went through if you weren't there to see it first-hand. She was eighty-pounds when I started visiting her every day—wasting away from a broken heart. And every pound she put back on and every inch she came closer to saving her own life, she fought for, with a strength that came from I don't know where. She is a warrior."

The kitchen is quiet for a moment as we both ponder her words.

"And what's sad about it—" she continues, "—is that when people look at her today, they only see an old lady. Her story has been long forgotten by those who were around at the time to see it, and those who never knew her back then don't know anything about it at all. But people don't remember she was an awarded schoolteacher either or that I was a critical care nurse. Growing old is, well, interesting. And lonely at times. If I didn't have Kitty—"

Her voice trails off and I think of all the times I watched out the living room window for GiGi to return after her shift at the hospital. She's right, I haven't thought about that in years.

We spent a lot of time here with GiGi when I was little, and she was my favorite person in the world. Her coming home was the highlight of my day. Dad was non-existent most of the time and Mama was all business. "Did you finish your homework? Did you read tonight? Did you pack your lunch? Clean your room?" She was always so full of questions.

GiGi was the fun one. We baked cookies, played Monopoly, worked in the garden, and screamed letters at Wheel of Fortune on the TV. Those are the memories fresh in my mind—not the ones of her saving lives when she wasn't here doing those fun things with me.

"Jenna, I know Michelle is your Kitty. But I think you know now, you need to find your Michelle back home, too. And not only because it would be nice to have a good friend. It's critical. Do you understand? Life isn't always easy. And I know everything has always come so easy to you in the past, but you're getting to the hard stuff. You need your Kitty and you're going to have to put yourself out there to find her."

I nod my head. "Yes, ma'am. I see that now."

"Good. Also, we're leaving for church at 4:30, so make sure you're ready."

"Eh—do I have to go?"

"Oh, relax. It's only a volunteer night with the women's ministry, packing food to take to the shelter. Those women like to get in and get out quick, so they can head to Marilyn's to drink wine and scream at each other over bunco after." She takes another sip. "Your mama will be there volunteering, too."

"All right, all right. But, GiGi—"

"Hmm?"

"Don't you ever take a day off? Stay home in your pj's and do nothing?"

"Child, if I did that, I'd be dead already."

13

MOXIE

As GiGi drives us to the Asher First United Methodist Church, I watch the town roll by from the passenger side. The weather has turned colder again, and the sky is gray and overcast. Every few seconds, she clicks on the wipers to clear up a few drops of rain, then clicks them off again when it's dry.

Nat King Cole's "When I Fall in Love" serenades us from the speakers on the dash and GiGi hums along to her favorite lines.

Our recent kitchen conversation has me wondering what else GiGi has seen or been through in her seventy-five years on this earth. Aunt Kitty was fortunate enough to have Uncle Charlie with her until a few years ago, but GiGi lost Grandpa Philip when Mama was a teenager. She was in her mid-thirties, like me. What was that like? How did she survive?

The thought of it brings a sinking feeling in my gut, as I can't help but think about how it would feel to forever lose Andrew from my life.

We pull into the parking lot and GiGi parks next to a familiar blue Volkswagen with a "Schnoodle Mom" bumper sticker on the window. Mama's already here.

"Do you think she's mad at me for not going to see her first?" I ask, pointing to Mama's car.

She pulls the keys from the dash and tosses them into her purse. "Only one way to find out."

I meet GiGi around the back of the car, loop my arm through hers, and we walk to the side door of the church, which opens into the fellowship hall. As soon as we enter, I spot Mama standing at the back of the room, hugging a friend hello.

She sees us and puts one finger up to pause the conversation, then makes her way over to us in a hurry. She meets me with a long, tight hug then pinches the back of my arm, digging in hard with her pointed nails.

"Ow, Mama!" I say, rubbing my throbbing arm.

"Well, that's what you get!"

"So, you *are* mad, then?"

"Only that you didn't come see me first. Or call when you needed to talk. Or ask me to visit. Or...well, yeah, I'm upset." She places her hands on her hips and looks at me with a scowl. Then she shifts and crosses her arms in front of her body.

She's not mad. She's hurt...and worried.

"I'm sorry. I wasn't trying to hurt your feelings."

She starts to reply but is interrupted when a woman in a gray pantsuit clears her throat.

"Ladies, can I get your attention, please?" The chattering contin-ues and she calls for quiet a couple more times before, finally, all eyes are on her.

"Okay, thank y'all for coming. We've never done this before, but I think we can figure it out, right? The food is on the tables in the back and the bags are here, in this box. When we run out of food to pack, we'll bring more from the kitchen. We've been asked to pack until it's gone, which seems easy enough, so let's get to it."

As soon as she moves, the eager women rush forward to grab bags from the box, as if afraid that if they don't get there first, they'll miss out—like a game of middle-aged or geriatric Musical Chairs. I step back and out of the way. GiGi and Mama are ahead of me, unapologetically throwing elbows to weasel their way through.

The crowd clears from the box of bags and, like a hungry swarm of bees, descends upon the closest table. I take a handful of bags and wait.

Mama and GiGi are still fighting their way through. Mama places four cans of tuna and two applesauce cups into her bag, then squawks, "Where's the peanut butter? Don't we have some around here?"

"On the next table," GiGi yells back, poking her head above the crowd in an attempt to be heard, and stuffing her bag with crackers and canned chicken.

"Anyone seen the vegetables?" someone calls from a couple of tables over.

"There's corn on this table here, Lola. And green beans on that one to your left," a raspy, deep voice replies.

"Ow, my foot!" comes a cry from somewhere in the middle of the room.

"Sorry, Marilyn, I didn't see you there!"

Total chaos. No traffic pattern. No rhyme or reason as to how the food is laid out. No guidance for how many of each item to include.

It's loud and unorganized and sending my anxiety through the roof. *All this, just to get to bunco?*

"GiGi, what is going on here?"

"What do you mean?" she replies as she struggles to push her way up to the canned beans.

"I mean, who's in charge? *Gray Pantsuit*?" I point toward the woman who waved the green flag on this Indy 500 and see her nodding at the crowd in misguided approval.

"Uh—I don't know. I guess so. What do you have in your bag so far?" She looks over her shoulder, trying to see what I've got that she may have missed.

"Nothing, because this is craziness! We're going to be here all night—and somebody's going to get trampled—probably poor Marilyn."

"What's wrong?" Mama says, returning with her peanut butter, and brushing a dislodged tendril of hair out of her eyes. Her face is still all scrunched up between the eyebrows like it always is when she's upset with me.

"Do you know who's in charge here? Was there no plan?" I ask her.

"No, I don't know." She stuffs more cans into her bag.

"Well, this is a mess."

"And?" Mama's still not looking at me as she continues to cram items into her bag.

"And what?"

"Do you have a better idea?" she asks.

"Oh, no—not my circus; not my monkeys."

"Hmm," is Mama's answer.

"Hmm, *what*, Mama?"

"I didn't say anything," she replies.

"You don't have to say anything, but I still know when you have something to say."

She stops what she's doing and turns to me. "Jenna, you were class president, National Honor Society president, cross country captain, and manager at Blockbuster at seventeen. If you're unhappy with something, fix it!" She glances at me with eyebrows raised and expectation in her expression.

"All I'm saying is they should've realized you can't throw fifty people into a room and expect to get something done without a plan. Who even invited all these people? Way too many people!"

"Hmm," she repeats.

"*What*, Mama?"

She turns to face me again. "The Jenna I raised took charge and fixed things. She knew no other way. Whenever she walked into a bad situation, she did her damndest to make it better and was smarter than most at doing so. Seems to me you've lost the ability, or the courage, or—something."

"She's lost her moxie." GiGi says as she appears out of thin air, behind Mama.

"I have not lost my moxie. This is just—"

Mama has said her piece, so she turns her back to me and continues filling her bag. GiGi tucks hers under her arm and gives me two quick hand claps to say "Chop, chop," before getting back to it.

"Ugh!" I step out of the crowd and take a hard look at the insanity before me. We really will be here all night if something isn't done and given that Mama's frustration with me isn't going away any-time soon, this isn't where I want to spend the rest of my evening.

I spot a chair against the wall and climb on top. "Excuse me. Can I get your attention, please? Hello?" The hectic hive of women buzzing about before me seems to pause, in unison, as they hear an unfamiliar voice and turn to see who it is.

"Hi. Uh—I know many of you, but not all. Hi, Ms. Sanderson." I give a little wave back to my old Sunday School teacher, who's swinging her arms through the air, trying to catch my attention. "My name is Jenna, and I'm here with Laurel and Catherine. I'd like to take a few minutes to move some of this stuff around and make it easier for us, if that's okay?"

Blank stares.

"Okay, so, if you could please place whatever bags you've packed on the floor in front of the tables and maybe, I don't know, go get a cup of coffee or something? Meet back here in fifteen minutes?" I wait for replies but get none, so I step down from the chair. The confused women move toward the kitchen, at the prompting of the women who I do know.

Once they've cleared out, I get to work. "GiGi, can you find all the proteins and put them on the first table?"

"Sure thing, boss." GiGi gives a salute and starts gathering items.

"Mama, can you grab all the fruit and put it on the next table? I'll get the veggies." She doesn't answer me or even look my way, but sets to collecting the fruit.

We work to sort items, empty the filled bags, place all items where they belong, and gather the empty brown bags to stack on the first table. Lastly, we pull an empty table from another room and place it at the end.

The crowd returns and once they're gathered, I climb onto the chair once more.

"Okay, we sorted the food by type. Let's form a line. Grab a bag from the first table, then place two items from each table into it. You'll end up with two proteins, two fruits, two veggies, and two dry goods when you're done." I'm met with more blank stares, but some people are nodding in approval, which gives me the courage to go on.

"Place your filled bag on the empty table at the end and get back in line to do it again, okay? We need one volunteer behind each table and when you run out of food, you'll go to the kitchen and get more. The person behind the table at the end will fold the filled bags closed and move them to the floor so we can box them up later. Does that sound okay?" More nods this time.

I climb down from the chair and soon, a line forms. People take positions behind the tables. The line starts to move, bags are being filled...and it's working.

The women are laughing, chatting, and enjoying themselves as they go through the motions. Soon, an hour has passed and we're running out of food.

"You did it, boss," GiGi says.

"Hmm. Just needed to find that moxie," Mama replies with a wink and another pinch.

"Mama, those nails...*really!*"

On the way home, Mama calls.

"What are y'all doing for dinner? I made a casserole I can bring if you have something to go with it." Mama's voice is exceptionally loud through the audio speakers.

"What kind of casserole?" GiGi asks.

"A hash brown casserole thing with ham and cheese. It's pretty good."

GiGi looks at me and shrugs her shoulders.

"Sounds good to me," I tell her.

"Yeah, sounds good. See you in a bit," GiGi says as she ends the call.

Minutes later, we're home and clicking on lamps to account for the lack of light from the early-setting sun. I flip the switch to turn on the gas fireplace, then run upstairs to put on pajamas before Mama arrives. When I return, the smell of coffee is in the air.

"How can you sleep having coffee this late in the afternoon?" I lean against the counter and zip my hoodie.

"Doesn't even phase me anymore. I don't sleep much these days anyway—another perk of getting old."

"I can't imagine a day when I'd ever not be able to sleep."

"Well, just you wait. Better find yourself a hobby before then, though."

"What's your hobby?"

"I watch a lot of late-night television. Those *City Wives* are somethin', aren't they?"

An exuberant burst of laughter escapes before I can rein it in. "GiGi, you do not watch that trash."

"Oh heavens, yes, I do. You don't? No wonder you're depressed about your life. You don't have any good TV drama to compare it to."

Smiling, I shake my head and open the refrigerator, looking for a drink. I pull a sparkling water from the back as Mama opens the front door.

"Hey, I've got food," she says as she bumps the front door closed with her hip and enters the kitchen. "Needs to heat in the oven a few minutes, though." She turns on the oven, places the dish inside, then opens the refrigerator. "Do you have salad fixins, Mama?"

"Whatever you can find in there. I'm sure there's something we can throw together," GiGi says.

Mama digs through the fridge and pulls out baby spinach, grape tomatoes, a cucumber, a bag of shredded cheese, and ranch dressing. "That'll do," she says.

"Mama—"

"Hmm?" she asks as she sets to washing the vegetables in the sink.

"I really am sorry I didn't let you know when I got here. Or call more often. It's just—hard. Talking to people in a real way is hard for me, even on a good day, and talking with people about feelings—"

"I know, Jenna. This is not something new to me. You've always been reserved, and I learned how to wait it out a long time ago—just like you learned how to coax things out of me a long time ago, too. You coax because it's what I need. I wait, because it's what you need. We all have our issues here, okay?" She smiles at me for the first time today.

I set to chopping the cucumber. Mama and GiGi discuss church business.

Standing in the kitchen with the two of them, it doesn't take long for my mind to wander. If the kids were here, we'd have four generations in the very kitchen where Mama grew up and I formed some of my greatest childhood memories. How much longer do we have to do that? GiGi's healthy and stays active, but no one lives forever.

"Jenna, you about finished?" Mama asks.

"Huh?"

"Those cucumbers can't get much smaller, hon."

"Oh, yeah, here." I slide the cutting board toward them and they each grab a handful for their bowls. Then we move to the table and dig in.

"Good job at the church today," Mama says as she takes a ranch-soaked bite.

"Well, we're not still there working on it, so yeah, I'd say it turned out all right."

"Yup. I knew you still had it in you. It's hard to remember who we are after having kids, but you are a doer. A fixer. A leader. You always have been. Imagine if you remembered that when your kids are trying to run all over you. Imagine the power you could take back in your life."

The room goes silent as we eat, and I think on her words. Is she right? Do I still have it in me? Most days, it feels like I'm at the mercy of three human beings who aren't even old enough to brush their teeth unsupervised. They rule the roost. What would "taking back my power" even look like?

A few minutes later, GiGi scoots her chair out from the table, breaking the silence. She places her bowl in the sink and pulls three more from the cabinet. Removing the casserole from the oven, and not waiting for it to cool, she dishes it out.

"All that food will be enough for the folks who stop in at the shelter over the next week or so. Meals on Wheels will take some too. Asher's not very big, but the need is great." GiGi sets two bowls on the table and goes back for the third.

"We're very fortunate," Mama says.

"That we are," GiGi agrees.

I can't recall a time in my life when I worried about where my next meal came from. GiGi, Mama, Aunt Kitty, or the other women in the neighborhood always kept our bellies full. If there was no food, they brought it or invited us over for dinner. Even through college, I worked and kept myself well fed—too well fed, probably. So, once again I think, what in the world do I have to be so sad about?

"Does that bother you?" Mama asks. "Talking about the less fortunate? I guess it's not very good dinner conversation."

"No, it doesn't, but it does make me feel grateful for what I have."

As if reading my mind, GiGi says, "That doesn't mean you don't still get to have feelings, you know. Money or no money, food or no food, home or no home. We're all human and have the right to feelings."

Mama looks at GiGi, then at me, confused. She doesn't comprehend GiGi's words at first. Then, understanding comes upon her and she takes my hand in hers.

"I think it's time you knew about Pensacola."

"About our vacations there in the summer?" I ask as I scoop a bite onto my fork.

"No, about the time I moved there when you were three."

The fork slips and clangs against my plate. "We never lived in Pensacola—"

"You never lived there, sweetheart, but I sure did."

14

MAMA

GiGi walks to the stove again and returns with the saltshaker. She generously pours on the seasoning, giving Mama a squinty-faced look while she does it.

"Mama, you know I left it unsalted for a reason. What *are* you doing?" She takes the shaker from GiGi and moves it out of her reach.

"Bah!" GiGi replies.

"Anyhow, you know your daddy and I never had the healthiest of relationships, right?" Mama asks as she turns back to me.

"Yeah, I know."

"There had always been rumors about him having affairs, but I mostly ignored them. Then one day in June, just before you turned three, I was driving home with the windows down, enjoying the warm breeze on my face. It had been a pretty good day at work, but I skipped my lunch break and was starving. I was anxious for dinner and a walk with you before bedtime. It was our favorite thing to do together when you were little, remember?"

I nod my head, wondering where this story is heading.

"As I turned onto our street, 'Here I Go Again' came on the radio. I loved that song and cranked it up real loud, just as that drum intro played. You know the one, don't you?"

"Whitesnake?" I say with a laugh.

"Hey, that is an amazing song. Don't tell me you don't love it." She shakes her fork at me, daring me to claim otherwise. "Anyway, I pulled into the driveway, and I saw her."

"Who?"

"I don't know her name, but she just sat there next to him on the porch swing, like she owned the place. Like she carried a right to wave at my neighbors from the front stoop. Like she *belonged* there. She sat sideways in the swing, with one leg draped up over him and the other one dangling and wrapped around his, barefoot. And he just—stared at me through the windshield and flicked the ash of his Marlboro red into my potted zinnias.

"I thought for sure they would separate, make up some excuse for being there together. But, no, they stayed there for the entire neighborhood to see. All I could think was, 'What just happened in my house?' and 'Dear Lord, where's Jenna?'" She wipes a tear from her eye.

"I climbed out of the car and up the steps. I wanted to say something, but the words wouldn't come. I wanted to beat them both to death with a crowbar, but I couldn't find the courage—or a crowbar. So, I stood there like an idiot while she chewed her bubblegum and twirled her hair. Then, from the car, which I'd left running, I heard the chorus of that song, telling me to make up my mind; to just stop wasting my time!

"I realized I couldn't ignore it or play dumb anymore. He'd gone too far. So, I walked right past them, as he put his cigarette out in my zinnias. I went inside and found you watching TV in the living room. I packed a small duffel bag for each of us and when we walked out that door, they were still sitting there; hadn't even budged. I looked at that man and all I felt was disgust and rage.

"I plucked the cigarette butt out of the zinnias, tossed it at his feet, and scooped up the pot with my free hand. 'Keep your damn cigarettes out of my plants' is all I could say. Then, I put you—and my plant—in the car and we drove away. I looked back at them once in the rear-view mirror and they were like statues...still hadn't moved. Still didn't give a damn."

"Wow. I don't remember any of that."

"Well, I'm glad you don't. I took you to Mama's. I knew you could stay, even with Uncle Bo's family there, but there was no room for me. Mama tried to convince me there was, but I felt powerless and humiliated. I needed to find a way forward on my own—that damn song was just stuck in my head, playing over and over again. So, you stayed with Mama, and I hit the road. I stopped at the bank and cleaned out our joint checking and savings accounts. It wasn't much, but it was something.

"I wasn't sure where to go at first, but as I drove down the highway, I passed the sign for the road leading to the coast. Then, all images of him and that woman were wiped clean from my mind. All I could see was you: sand-covered, sun-kissed, with wild hair blowing in the wind, laughing—"

"So, you left."

"Yes. But I didn't leave you. I left *for* you. I hope you understand that."

I'm not sure what I understand or don't at this point. I have questions, but I don't want to ask them. I'm proud that she was brave and walked away—but why couldn't she take me with her? I'm sad at how she must have felt—but why hasn't she told me any of this before?

Not waiting for an answer, Mama goes on. "When I got to Pensacola, I checked into a cheap hotel and the next morning I went door-to-door, filling out applications everywhere I could. I ate once a day and that was the free continental breakfast at the hotel. I saved all my money for gas and newspapers to hunt for a job. It was summer and it seemed everything was already taken by the high school and college kids out for summer break.

"And right when I came to accept that I was going to have to head back home to Mama, I was offered a cashier job at a grocery store. Even with the pay, though, I wasn't making enough to continue staying in the hotel or to get my own place, so I moved in with a co-worker and we split the bills.

"It was far from anything I'd ever experienced before. It was hard and depressing and I missed you so much. Those were the darkest days of my life, being away from you. Not knowing how I was ever going to afford a place of my own and be able to bring you down with me. I felt hopeless. I didn't want to get out of bed in the morning. All day, every day my thoughts cycled between two extremes: that I missed you so much, couldn't live without you, and needed to do everything I could to get you back...and that you were better off in Asher without me, and I should leave you there and give up. I was a mess."

I gasp, unable to speak.

"Don't judge me, please. I thought you would be better for it. I really did." She removes her broad-framed glasses from her face and sets them down on the table.

I still don't speak, because I don't know what to say. I'm unable to fathom my own mother has held the same horrible feelings and thoughts that I have.

"Long story made short, it didn't work out. I ended up living in the car, it turned cold, and I got sick. I didn't have insurance or money to see a doctor, so when it got too bad, I gave up and came home. Mama took one look at me when I showed up and drove me straight to the hospital."

"She had walking pneumonia, was dehydrated, malnourished—but all she kept asking about was you. I told her we needed to get her taken care of before you saw her or she would scare you half to death, looking the way she did," GiGi says.

"And you were right, as usual." Mama looks at GiGi with a little half-smile, then turns back to me. "Being with you again was like receiving new life. The whole time I was away, I was working so hard to make a home for us, but I couldn't do it. I felt defeated—until I saw your face. Then, it didn't matter anymore. All that mattered was we were together, no matter how it needed to be done."

"How did you do it?" I ask her.

"Well, we went home," Mama answers.

"Back to Daddy."

"Yup. It was that or stay with Mama and Bo and that wasn't going to work long-term. I was uneducated—beyond high school, anyway—and possessed no actual job skills, so we went home. I made sure things were different for us, though."

"How?"

"Well, the night I walked back in that door, he was sitting on the sofa with a TV dinner. Trash and dirty clothes were strewn all over the house. He said, 'Catherine, you're back?' I said, 'You bet I'm back, and if you bring one more woman onto that front porch, I'll take you for this house and everything in it.' I told him I'd cook, clean, do the laundry and the shopping, but he was sleepin' on the couch. I got my job back at the store and saved every bit of my paychecks in an account that only held my name. That money put me through school. It's how we were fine on our own after he left. It gave us everything I tried so hard for in Pensacola, but couldn't find the way."

"But you were trapped for almost a decade to get to that point," I say.

"Oh, it wasn't all that bad. He was gone more than he was home. I did all the day-to-day things I would have done anyway, with or without him around. But he kept the lights on, and we never went hungry. We had everything we needed. And by the time he left, I could do it all for us myself.

"Jenna, things aren't always as they seem. Like Mama said before, you can appear to have everything—a nice house, a sweet family, and not want for anything in the world—but still be fighting demons nobody knows about. For me, my demon started as simply a man and transformed into something much worse—dark feelings of ineptitude and unworthiness that were nearly impossible to shake. And those feelings can come from anywhere and sometimes from nowhere at all."

I nod my head. She's right. Those feelings can come from nowhere at all, and I know them too well.

"And what I learned from all I went through was that things aren't always black and white. Sometimes the wins don't always look like a win on paper or in the view of other people, but you know it's a win because it feels like the right thing to do. Coming back to you, not letting myself die in my car in Pensacola, standing my ground with that man, and choosing to live my life the way I did to give you the best I could, was the right thing to do."

I wipe away a tear and stand from my seat. I cross the kitchen and take another water from the refrigerator. Then I squeeze Mama's shoulders as I turn toward the stairs.

"Hey, are you okay? Are you upset with me?" Mama stands and starts to follow, but GiGi grabs her by the hand.

I stop and consider ignoring her question and continuing up the stairs, but I can't.

"I am upset. Actually, I'm *pissed*. But not because you went to Pensacola or because you stayed with him. I'm pissed because this is the stuff that would have been worth knowing. I've struggled for years with those same feelings of ineptitude and unworthiness. I've been crippled by the fear of failing my children. I've never thought I was good enough for them or that I deserved to be their mother. I have failed as a parent every single day since the day Audrey was born! And I have felt it all so deeply, to the point I thought I couldn't take another minute of that unbearable pain. And what made it all a thousand times worse was thinking I was all alone—that there was something wrong with me because I felt that way. That nobody else I have ever known has struggled the way I have."

"Honey, I didn't know you were struggling. You've never said anything—"

"Because I thought I was a monster!"

"No, you're not a monster," she says.

"I see that now! But why didn't you ever tell me? Why didn't Aunt Kitty or Michelle or someone like Gloria ever tell me?" I can't hold in the tears anymore. I feel small, like a blubbering teenager fighting with her mom because she broke curfew.

"Jenna—" Mama takes a step forward and I step back. GiGi grabs hold of her hand again.

"God, I'm so—I can't—I can't even think straight anymore. And I suppose you have a story to tell also?" I'm looking at GiGi, pleading for it to not be true.

"Well, we all do, Jenna. I think that's the whole point here," she answers.

"Great. Well, I've heard enough for one day, thank you." I turn to walk up the stairs and as I climb the creaky steps, picture-framed faces of beloved grandmothers, cousins, and aunts seem to scream for me to stop and listen to their tales of heartbreak, too. And I feel wholly and brutally betrayed by every single one of them as I leave them all behind.

I close the door behind me and collapse onto the bed. My heart aches. How much of what I've felt and gone through could have been avoided if someone had told me I wasn't alone? How much of what Mama or Gloria felt could have been avoided if someone would've told them their story? Why do we do this to ourselves? Why don't we just talk to each other?

And then it hits me. My heart is racing, and I feel six feet underground with no air to breathe—I've never talked with anyone about it either. How many people have I failed to save?

I pull the journal from the nightstand and flip to a new page. I write "Mama" at the top in stick letters. I'm not sure how I feel about this page yet, so I start by scribbling what comes to mind from our afternoon at the church.

"It's hard to remember who we are after having kids..."
"You are a doer. A fixer. A leader. Always have been."
"I knew you could do it. Just needed to find that moxie."
"Imagine the power you could take back in your life."
Then I move on to all I learned at dinner.
Shock. Deception. Humiliation...powerlessness.
Search for a new start.
"Fighting demons nobody knows about...ineptitude, unworthiness."
Defeat.
Home.
Courage. Sacrifice...happiness.
"Things aren't always as they seem; aren't always black and white."
"All that mattered was that we were together, no matter how it needed to be done."

I fill the margins of Mama's page with sketches of music notes. Then I continue with a cigarette butt sticking out of a potted plant (which may or may not be zinnias), a porch swing, two duffel bags, and a road sign showing the way to Pensacola. Next comes the beach with waves, a giant radiant sun, a car with the outline of a house around it, and the Alabama state welcome sign.

As I stare at Mama's story on paper, the similarities between her feelings and mine strike me once again. But I also can't help but to see that while we both ran, we did it for two different reasons. She ran to make our life better. I ran to escape mine.

See? You are that monster, after all.

That crushing feeling is back again. I can't breathe. My heart feels as if it's grown arms and is clawing with all its might to escape from my chest. I'm sweating and freezing all at the same time. I'm shaking and I cannot stop. Horrible, angry words are crashing into each other in my head, and all I want to do is scream to let them out. For a split second, I'm an eight-year-old girl again, running to seek Mama's shelter from a bad dream. But this time, my hand never makes it to the door.

Instead, I turn to the bedroom window, throw it open, and shove out the screen. It tumbles to the ground below and I push my upper body through the window frame and take a long, deep breath of the cold night air. Then another. And another. And another.

I turn my face upward to the full moon, close my eyes, and imagine its healing light pouring into my hollow body through my nose, ears, and parted lips. In my mind, I see it filling my toes, my feet, then up to my ankles, calves, and knees. It fills me entirely like the empty gasoline tank of a car that's stranded with no way to go. My breathing slows. The heaviness in my chest lifts. My angry, scattered thoughts take a back seat as I focus on the rising of that imaginary fill-line and all the peace lying beneath it.

Leaving the window open, I crawl into bed and slip beneath the thick, warm covers. The curtains dance in the night breeze and I'm salvaged by the comfort of that brilliant full moon.

15

KRISTA

I wake again to a knock on the door.

"I'm not walking today. Your mama was here until late and I'm tired. Keys are on the kitchen counter if you still want to go," she says, before shutting the door again.

Do I want to go? I'm spent; emotionally raw. I'm not sure I can handle more people—more talking—today. But the run calls to me, and that's not something I can ignore. With that thought, I'm up and out the door in no time.

As I pull into the parking lot at the park, I don't see Kitty's car or Gloria's but there's a yellow, mud-covered Jeep Wrangler parked in the front row. I pull up next to it and see Krista sitting behind the wheel.

I park and get out of the car and Krista does the same.

"Where's everyone else?" I ask her.

"Your grandma sort of leads the pack. If she doesn't come, they don't either. I figured you might still show up, though."

"Yeah, thanks," I say, as we make our way to the trail.

We start at a slow jog, but before long, I'm struggling to keep up. Still, I refuse to ask her to slow down this time and I'm not sure I'd be able to get the words out, even if I wanted to.

Eventually, we round the bend, and our starting point is distant, but in sight. Krista jerks her head to the side, toward the direction of the parking lot, to ask if I'm ready to bring it in. I give an enthusiastic nod, and as we make our way back to the picnic table, we slow and come to a stop. I double over with my hands on my knees and fight for every breath.

"I think you're trying to kill me," I manage to say, gasping for air.

Krista laughs, coughs, and spits into the dry, dead grass. "If it makes you feel any better, that was a stretch for me, too." She pulls her long brown hair down from its ponytail, then re-ties it back up into a bun at the top of her head.

"Yeah, no. Doesn't make me feel better. A 'stretch' is nowhere near what I'm feeling."

After a few more minutes and several trips back and forth down the sidewalk to cool off, I'm beginning to feel like I can breathe again. "How old are you, anyway?" I wipe my face with the bottom half of my shirt. "You make me feel prehistoric."

She laughs. "Twenty-eight, but I've been a competitive runner since I was ten. I still work with a coach five days a week. So, I'd say you're doing pretty damn good."

"Holy hell—you could've warned me!"

"No way. I wanted to see what you could do. I'm impressed. Did you ever compete?"

"Cross country in high school and college. I did all right."

"Ah, that makes sense. Do you want to grab something to eat or do you need to head back?"

"Food. Food is always good. But only if we go in your car—so much cooler than GiGi's sedan."

"Deal."

We choose Waffle House for breakfast and over our eggs and bacon, yogurt, and toast, I learn Krista is Kitty's great-niece; the granddaughter of Kitty's sister, Lois. I also learn she's never been married and has no children, but has both a bachelor's and master's degree in kinesiology.

"Wow. So, what do you do? I mean, for work?" I ask.

"I'm an assistant athletic trainer at the community college, but I'm considering going for a doctorate in physical therapy. I should make up my mind about that soon." She scoops another bite of yogurt.

"Well, that's awesome. I've gotta admit, I'm a little jealous," I say, hoping she won't ask why.

"Really? I'm jealous of you. I was engaged once. We were together for four years and I just knew he was the one. Yeah, not so much."

"What happened?"

"Short of the long: He found someone else," she answers.

"Oh, I'm sorry. What a bastard."

Krista laughs so hard she chokes a bit on her coffee. "Yeah, what a bastard!"

"So, tell me about that Jeep. Is it yours? Did you put that mud on the tires?"

"Well yeah, who else? I told you I don't have a man." She leans across the table and—almost in a whisper, as if she's suggesting something scandalous—says, "Wanna go find a hole?"

"Are you serious? Yes! God, I haven't done that in—I don't even know—ten years?"

"Geez, how old *are* you?" she asks with a smile.

We finish up, pay for our food, and thirty minutes later, we're deep in the woods by the lake and searching for a bit of mud to fling.

"I don't know if we'll find anything. It's all pretty dry by now. What's on the Jeep is from a couple of weeks ago. She doesn't get washed much."

"Better than crackers and dry cereal smashed into your carpet," I reply.

"Yeah, I'll take the mud."

"Good choice."

Krista spots a trail off to the right of the main path we're on. "Oh, I know there'll be something that way. It takes you closer to the waterline and there are a few creeks running through." She whips the steering wheel to the right, and we make a sharp turn onto the much smaller road—if you can even call it a road at all.

"Lord, this thing can pretty much go anywhere! Andrew's old truck would've never made it down a path this small."

"She's tiny but tough. Aunt Kitty says it suits me and she couldn't ever imagine me driving anything else. I think she's right."

We come through a final row of trees and find a large, open area at the foot of the lake, as Krista said we would. And she's right. There's mud for days and tire tracks going every which way through it.

"I guess we're not the first ones here," I say.

"Nah, but we're the only ones here and that's all that matters." She puts the Jeep in neutral, then moves the four-wheel-drive shifter into 4-high. Then, we head straight for the thick of it.

I'm slightly terrified as I imagine giant boulders or twenty-foot sinkholes hiding beneath the surface, but Krista's face is bright, excited, and confident. So I take a deep breath, trust, and let go.

We don't creep into the mud—we dive into it. My first instinct is to grip the dash and shove my foot into the floorboard, to cram on my non-existent brake pedal. But Krista accelerates, flinging mud up on both sides, then whips the steering wheel to the left. The back end of the Jeep swings 'round and mud flies up and over the top.

I let out a loud squeal as the mud falls and Krista casts a quick glance my way to make sure I'm okay. Then, she downshifts and pushes hard on the gas pedal. The tires spin for a second before catching hold and lurching us forward again. I grab the handlebar on the dash and let out another squeal as she pushes the wheel to the left again, and we come full circle in the mud. I'm giggling like a child, with bursts of laughter each time she pushes us in any unexpected direction.

"You're such a girl!" she says with a laugh.

"Nah, I'm just old, remember? It's been a while!"

She laughs again, we climb back out to solid ground, and she drives us around to the other side—pointing the nose of the Jeep dead-center of the pit, at its deepest part.

"Oh, no..."

"What? It's fine," she says. And before I can protest, we're off again.

I let out a shrill, "Eeek!" as we accelerate into the mud, and Krista thinks it's pretty damn funny. She laughs, whips the jeep this way and that, and turns the wipers on to clean the windshield when it becomes impossible to see through. Then, it happens.

We hit a rut beneath the surface. My side of the Jeep sinks lower than the driver's side and we slow. Krista tries to give a little gas to crawl our way out, but the Jeep struggles and a few seconds later, we stop. She tries a second time, but we're not budging.

"Oh, no..." I say again.

"Well, we're screwed," she says.

"What? Are you serious? We're stuck?"

She laughs, puts the shifter in reverse, and says, "Of course not. I don't get stuck." She attempts to move us backward to firmer ground, but to no avail. Then she shifts to 4-low and tries forward again. Backward again. We're not going anywhere.

"I guess it's time to get dirty. You coming?" She opens her door and jumps out into the mud. I hesitate for a second, then hop out after her.

Krista trudges around to the back, swings open the rear cargo door, and pulls out a small shovel. "Can you grab the floor mat from the front?"

I do as she says and stand there with it, awkwardly, as she sets to work shoveling mud away from the entrenched tire.

"All right, that should do it." She tosses the muddy shovel back into the Jeep, then walks back around to the passenger side. She holds her hand out for the floor mat and I give it over, feeling pretty useless, but totally in awe. "We'll put this here in front to give the tire something to grip on to. You'll want to get back in. Sometimes these things can launch pretty far when the tire spins."

We both climb back inside, Krista puts it in gear, and tries the gas pedal one more time. The tires spin in place for a second, then catch fast and we're once again moving forward.

"Told you I don't get stuck!" she yells as she navigates us right out of the pit.

"That was amazing! How do you even know how to do that?"

"I've been muddin' since I was a kid...first with my dad and then my older brothers. I've done that more times than I can count." She turns the Jeep around and takes us back to where we started from before.

"Seriously? You're going in there again?"

"Well, yeah. It's just mud—and I've gotta get my floor mat back for next time."

Back at the park, Krista hands me a towel from the back seat.

"Here. You'll want to put this on the floorboard, so Laurel doesn't freak out about the mud," she says.

I take the towel because she's right. Mud in GiGi's car might just be the end of me yet. "Geez, is there anything you don't have in here?"

"Not much. See you in the morning?"

"Yeah, I'll be here. Thanks for all the terrifying fun."

"No problem." She laughs, and we go our separate ways.

Before I leave the park, I shoot a text message to Michelle.

"Hey. I may have promised GiGi I'd head home on Sunday and I'm not sure I can do that. Pretty sure she's going to kick me out. Can I come back to your place?"

Before I can even put the car in drive, she replies.

"Well yeah, duh. Maybe we can go to The Tavern." There are about a dozen laughing emojis at the end of that message.

"Yeah, let's skip that part this time."

***

"Good Lord, what happened to you?" GiGi asks as I kick my shoes off on the front porch.

"Krista took me for a ride. I survived, I think."

"I'm gonna have to spray you off with the hose!"

"Don't you dare, woman. It's cold out here!"

"Well, at least take off your breeches, or hike 'em up, or somethin'."

"Take off my pants? On the front porch?"

"Well, I'll get you a towel or you can come around the back. What did you expect? You know I'm not about to let you in my house like that."

"GiGi, what do you want me to do? I'm freezing!"

"Just—hold on." She shuts the door behind her, leaving me on the front porch steps. When she returns, she hands me a thin, old towel straight out of the 70's.

"You couldn't find anything a little less *transparent*?" I say, sticking my fingers through a hole.

"My good towels? No. You get what you get."

I wrap the towel around my body and secure it at my waist. Then I peel off the sticky, mud-covered leggings and hold them up toward GiGi.

"Well, I don't want 'em. Throw them out into the yard, get yourself cleaned up, then come spray them off before you put them in my washer, please. What a mess. Did you have fun, at least?"

"Oh yeah, lots of fun."

"Good. Take your butt upstairs, clean up, and come tell me about it."

I do as she says, and we spend the late morning and early afternoon in the kitchen, making and eating lunch, while I tell her all about my morning with Krista.

"Wow, I didn't know that girl was such a tomboy. I mean, the running is one thing, but wow."

"GiGi, seriously? Is there even such a thing as a 'tomboy' these days? Pretty sure women are free to do as they choose, for the most part, and have been driving and running for a really long time."

"Oh, you know what I mean. Don't go getting all sensitive on me now," she replies, standing to fetch herself a cup of coffee. "And so you know, your mama's coming back by for dinner tonight. She feels pretty bad about yesterday."

"Okay."

"You need to make things right with her before you go."

"I know. I will." I give GiGi a peck on the cheek and head up to my room.

I shut the door, plop down onto the bed, and pull the journal from the nightstand. I write "Krista" across the top in bold block letters.

Independence, perseverance...no fear.

"Tiny but tough."

"I don't get stuck."

"It's just mud."

Learn the skills, claw your way out, then try again.

I draw the grill of a Jeep Wrangler in the white space at the top, a pair of running shoes, and a stack of textbooks on either side of it. What I've learned from Krista doesn't take up much of the page, but it's meaningful to me, nonetheless.

As I stare at the last line I've written, I remember the book Michelle was so excited to give me. I pull it from the Walmart bag on the floor and crack the cover.

16

GIGI

Seven chapters and a short nap later, GiGi's at the door again.

"Your mama's on her way. Stir-fry for dinner tonight sound okay?"

"Yeah, sounds good. I'll be down in a minute."

But I'm completely sucked into the book, which is anything but the tedious read I thought it was going to be. I don't make it down before Mama arrives. She enters the room with a soft knock and a push on the door, carrying a shoebox in her hands.

"Hi. Can we talk?" she asks.

"Yeah, but I go first." I sit up and place the book on the bed next to me.

Mama sits at the foot of the bed, places the box down beside her, and swings her legs back and forth, staring at the toes of her sneakers.

"Mama, I'm sorry."

"What do—"

"No, I am. I shouldn't have yelled at you. I should have thanked you for being brave enough to tell me."

"Jenna—"

I hold up my finger to pause her words. "I realized after you left, I have no right to be angry at you, or anyone else, for not telling me your stories sooner. I mean, it would have been helpful to know I wasn't crazy or alone, but it's hard. I know. I've never told anyone about my struggles before all this, either. I was being a total hypocrite. I see that now."

"Yeah, I guess you kind of were," she says with a playful smile.

I toss a pillow, which lands in her lap. "But not anymore. The one thing I've learned from all this is we all struggle, in one way or another, and it's time we stopped hiding from it and hiding it from everyone else. I never want to make anyone feel as alone as I've felt all these years."

"Well, don't be too hard on yourself, either. You're a good person, sweetheart. And smart. You'll get this all figured out."

"Thanks, Mama."

"I do want you to promise me something, though."

"What?"

"When you get back home, I want you to find someone to talk to. You can do all the reading in the world—" She picks up the book on the bed and examines the front cover. "—but that's just words going in. You've got to get the words out, too. They're both important. Find yourself a good therapist and go."

"Ugh—"

"I know you don't want to. You're proud. But do it for your mama."

"Okay." I pick up the shoebox and give it a shake. "What do you have in here?"

"Old Polaroids. Thought you might like to see them." She pulls the lid from the box.

I remove a few photos and see images of myself as a baby, as a small child at the beach, and even a few from my camera-shy teenage years—some with Michelle.

"Wow, I haven't seen these in ages." I keep digging and find a photo of Uncle Bo, reading a newspaper and one of GiGi standing at the kitchen sink, before her hair started going gray.

"What are these?" I ask as I pull several images of flowers in jars, sitting on window ledges and tabletops.

"The flowers you would pick for me on our walks. Flowers can't last a lifetime, but a picture can," Mama says.

My eyes fill with tears at the thought of how fleeting this all really is. I wipe my face, place the lid back on the box and hold it out to give back to Mama.

"Thank you," I say.

"You're welcome. And you keep them. Take them home with you."

"Mama, I can't do that."

"Sure, you can. I took pictures of all of them with my phone. I'll still have them. They're your memories, too. Take them."

I stand from the bed, hold my hands out for hers, and pull her up with me. Then she wraps me in a warm, tight hug.

"Okay, let's go eat," she says, and we make our way downstairs.

Mama brought the groceries we need for dinner, but it still has to be made. She starts with cutting the chicken breast into strips and GiGi and I work on slicing the bell peppers, onions, mushrooms, and carrots for the stir-fry. We chat as we cook; about Andrew, work, the kids, and when I'm going to bring them for a visit.

"So, you're going to Michelle's tomorrow morning after your run, right?" GiGi asks.

"Yes, ma'am."

"And you're staying the night there and leaving the next morning?"

"Um—I'm not sure yet."

"What do you mean? You told Andrew you'd be home on Sunday, didn't you?"

"Yes, I did, and I've learned a lot here—from all of you—but I still don't know if I'm ready to go home."

"Jenna—" she says.

"GiGi, you don't seem to grasp how ready I was to just give up before I came here. That's not nothing."

Mama lets out a little squeak and tears spring to her eyes.

"No, it's not," GiGi says. "Well, you're going to have to figure that out, and I'm not sure how much more help I can be. It's good you're going to Michelle's." She takes the bowl of sauce from my hands and walks to the stove.

She's disappointed in me. Nothing hurts worse than disappointing GiGi.

"But I do think you need to hear me tell my tale before you go," she says.

A knot forms in the pit of my stomach. I'm not sure how much more I can handle on one trip to Asher or how much good it can do, for that matter.

GiGi reaches for the sesame oil and pours it into the hot wok. It sizzles and pops as white smoke rises from the too-hot pan. She turns the burner down a touch, lifts the pan from the fire for a few seconds, and turns on the vent hood over the stove. Not until she puts it back down onto the fire, adds the chicken, and gives a nod of approval for how it's cooking, does she go on.

"Well, my story is not as dramatic as some you've heard, and you already know most of it." She waves the spatula in my direction and oil flings across the kitchen, landing on the tile floor.

I bend down to wipe it up.

"Don't worry about it, child. I'll get it when we're done," she says, as she stirs the chicken around in the pan. "Well, you know your Grandpa Philip died young, and I was young, and your mama and Uncle Bo, too. Hell, we were all babies."

I glance over at Mama. She removes her glasses, wipes her tears, and pulls herself upright to face the brunt of GiGi's story.

"Well, I kind of had the exact opposite reaction than Kitty did when she lost her baby, and it wasn't necessarily a good thing. Rather than lock myself away, begging for the Lord to take me too, I was panic-stricken he *would* take me, and my poor children would be left with no one. I spent my days praying for protection, and the anxiety I felt from it all about drove me out of my mind."

Mama nods her head as she dumps the vegetables into the wok with the chicken.

"Well, in the middle of all the fear and worry, I refused to let myself grieve. I've never been one for wallowing or self-pity and I thought that's what grieving was. I wouldn't allow it. Instead, I threw myself head-first into doing all the things Philip used to do around here: the yard work, fixing all the broken things around the house, taking the car for oil changes. I was trying to prove to myself—and to you kids—we were going to be okay."

"But you were not okay," Mama says.

"No, I wasn't. I ran myself ragged trying to do it all myself. And between that and the anxiety—which has a name these days, but didn't back then, by the way—I hit a breaking point. I picked up the phone, called Kitty, and said, 'Kitty, I could use a little help.' She was at our house in minutes—the fastest she'd ever gotten here. She later told me she was scared I'd slit my wrists or something because I'd never asked her for help before. She bawled the whole way here because she didn't know what she was going to find when she got here.

"But when she arrived, the kids were sitting at the kitchen table having dinner, and I was folding laundry on the sofa. She walked in and said, 'Laurel, what the hell? I thought you were dying.' I looked up at her with a face full of tears and she said, 'Oh, you *are*. You poor thing.' She pulled me up off the sofa and took me to my room. Then, she held me like a baby on the bed and let me cry. Months had gone by since I lost him, but it was the first time I cried. It was like, all at once, I realized all my hopes and dreams for our future no longer existed and you kids would never get to know the Philip I knew. I was so sad, shattered, and broken."

Mama wipes her tears with her apron again and sniffs, pulling GiGi from her storytelling trance.

"Anyhow, after that, Kitty and Charlie were here more than they weren't. We all ate dinner together as a family almost every night. She forced her way into my kitchen to help with the cooking. If I grabbed a cleaning rag, she grabbed one too. Charlie did the yard work and all the work on the car. They helped me shuttle you guys to and from school, work, and all your sports and club events. She even helped with the grocery shopping and trips to the cleaners. It was like we gained a parent in this house instead of losing one. Of course, I would have much rather have had Philip to share that part of my life with, but given the circumstances, I couldn't have asked for anything more.

"I never suffered from thoughts of suicide or felt like I couldn't go on. I was in a high-functioning state of depression, too focused on keeping things 'normal' for the kids to allow those kinds of thoughts. If I didn't have them to worry about, or if I didn't have Kitty and Charlie here, I'm sure my story would have ended up quite different.

"So, I guess the moral of my story is, you aren't expected to do everything on your own. It's okay to ask for help and sometimes you should. Also, like I've told you already, it's okay to have feelings. I wouldn't let myself have feelings about your grandfather's passing for a long time and it was a bitch to process them all once I did. When the feelings come, let them in. Figure out how to work through them. Then let them go."

"I can't imagine what it would be like to lose Andrew in that way," I say. "You're a stronger woman than me, GiGi."

"No, child. Our strengths only look different is all. Find yours, learn to embrace it, but don't let it make you hard. Then, never forget it's there. That strength is your superpower and with it you can do—and survive—anything."

We eat our dinner with sparse conversation, which is mostly contained to Mama and GiGi reminiscing on old times, with a bit of town gossip thrown in for good measure. Then Mama and I say our tearful goodbyes, not knowing if this is a final goodbye before I return home, or if we'll soon see each other again.

But I hug her like I'm never going to see her again, wrapping my fingers around her dark, soft auburn hair and breathing in that fresh jasmine scent. Hers is a scent I know so well, I often catch a whiff of it in my dreams.

Still standing on the cold front porch after watching Mama drive away, GiGi wraps her arm around my shoulder and says, "It's all right, child. It's all right," then gives a soft kiss on the back of my hand before guiding me back into the warmth of the house.

"GiGi, how do you do it?"

"Hmm?" she asks as she clears the table.

"How do you lose Grandpa Philip, lose Uncle Charlie, deal with your babies growing up and moving away, then live with knowing you've got grandbabies and great-grandbabies living their lives somewhere else, without you? How do you not crumble and die from the heartache? I feel like I'm going to be sick, just watching

Mama drive herself home. I want to be with her. I want to be with you. I want my kids to know you both—I want it all."

"Ah, there it is." GiGi stops what she's doing and turns to face me.

"What?"

"You want to know how I know you're going to be okay?"

I can't bring myself to conjure an answer.

"Because those words tell me so. You have so much love in your heart for everyone around you, which is what's going to get you through."

"But how—"

"And as for your question, I think the most important thing to understand—and force yourself to accept—is your kids don't belong to you. They're yours for such a brief moment in time and it's gone in the blink of an eye. It's terrifying and heartbreaking, yes, but the sooner you come to accept it, the more right you can do by them. The more you'll focus on guiding them to become the best person they can be, and the less you'll focus on the small things like shoes on the wrong feet, not picking up toys, or fighting like cats and dogs. And later, purple hair and eyeliner."

"So, you're telling me to 'enjoy every minute, because it goes by so fast,' like the little old ladies in the grocery store do?"

"Well, yeah, but with a dose of reality because I know from experience that poop on the walls is not at all enjoyable."

I give a little smile because I know it's what she wants to see. "But does it ever get any easier? Or will my heart feel incomplete forever?"

"The answer to that is different for everyone, but I don't think you're ever completely whole again after becoming a mother. When they're little, you lose a part of yourself. After they're gone, you get some of it back, but you're missing *them*. I feel at peace with where I'm at though—even if it took a while to get here."

At this, I collapse into a chair and bury my head in my hands. My head hurts, my heart aches, and the tears won't stop.

"Don't cry now, child. No sense in taking yourself off to sleep that way. Go on up and get some rest."

We give one final hug and each head to our rooms. I pull the journal from the drawer, flip to a blank page, and write "GiGi" across the top. I stare at the white paper and its thin blue lines for a long while. GiGi's words stretch all the way back to the jailbreak, which feels like an eternity ago. The details are fuzzy already, but as I replay everything in my mind, it all comes back.

"Women—mothers—have gone through what you're going through since the beginning of time."

"Your kids don't belong to you...the sooner you accept that, the more right you can do by them."

"It's okay to ask for help and sometimes you should."

"Find your sisters...you need to find yourself a shrink too."

"Money or no money, food or no food, home or no home...we all have the right to feelings."

"When the feelings come, let them in. Work through them. Then let them go."

"Find your strength...learn to embrace it, but don't let it make you hard."

"You have so much love in your heart for everyone around you, which is what's going to get you through."

Sisterhood, strength, wisdom...GRACE.

17

REVELATION

I reach for my phone on the nightstand and send it crashing to the floor with a solid *thud*. After fishing it out from under the edge of the bed, I text Krista.

"Can we meet at 9:00 this morning? I'd like to have breakfast with GiGi first."

I lay the phone on my chest and drift in and out of sleep while I wait for her reply. A few minutes later, I receive a text: "Sure. See you then."

I force myself out from under the warm blankets, slip on my socks, and tiptoe to the kitchen. GiGi skipped her walk again today, and I'm hoping not to wake her. I pull eggs and bacon from the fridge, fry up some breakfast, and as the coffee begins to drip into the pot, hear her footsteps on the stairs.

"No run this morning?" she asks, tightening her velvety purple robe around her waist.

"I thought we could have breakfast first. I'm meeting Krista at 9:00."

"Sure smells good." She sits, I pour a hot cup of coffee, and set it in front of her on the table.

"Thanks, hon. Need any help?"

"No, it's only bacon and eggs, but I can cut up some fruit, too, if you want."

"Bacon and eggs are fine," she replies with a wave of her hand.

I bring our plates and silverware to the table, and we eat in near silence. Further words, beyond what's already been said, aren't necessary. I know how she feels and she's intelligent enough to know there's no sense in beating a dead horse. This is the part where I'm meant to do the soul searching and application of all she's told me, in order to make the best choice. I thought I left this part of my life behind in my teenage years, but I guess I was wrong.

When we've finished, I stand and place our plates in the sink. I rinse and load them into the dishwasher, and she brings the frying pan over for washing. Once all the work is done, I dry my hands on the dish towel and hear a tiny sniffle.

"GiGi, what's the matter?"

Her chin quivers. "I just want what's best for you, is all."

"GiGi—" I wrap my arms around her, and we share a long hug, filled with tears on both ends. "Dammit, woman. Why'd you have to go and cry? I do enough of that on my own, thank you." I step back and dry my face.

"Trust me, I didn't mean to." She pops me on the hip with her towel. "Don't forget, your pants and shoes are in the laundry room."

"Yeah, thanks." I retrieve my leggings and running shoes and return to the kitchen. "I guess I'm going to get dressed and pack my things."

"Okay. I'm going to have another cup."

I refill her coffee, grab the newspaper off the front porch, and set both in front of her seat at the table. Then, I head upstairs to prepare myself for leaving GiGi's home, knowing full-well I've failed her more than she's willing to admit.

My run with Krista is a long, slow one. The coffee and greasy breakfast sit heavy in my stomach and the somber mood of the morning seems to call for a more relaxed pace anyway. It's also a quiet one, providing the perfect opportunity for reflecting on the week's events, if I'd only allow myself to do so. But instead, I choose to focus on breathing in the fresh morning air, on the soft thud of our feet on the pavement, and on the pounding sensation of the quick beating heart within my chest. It's enough to self-hypnotize into a meditative state if I can calm my thoughts and emotions long enough to reach it, and this morning, I do.

Thirty minutes later, as we finish and stretch in the cold, wet grass, I am suddenly hyper-aware of how much I need this in my life. One thing is for certain, regardless of where it occurs: Running is not negotiable.

"Wow, that was a good run," Krista says when we stand to leave.

"Yeah, thanks for meeting me a bit later this morning."

"No problem. I appreciated the chance to doze a little longer."

We've reached the parking lot and given the uncertainty of everything before me, I'm not sure if goodbyes are in order or not. And if they are—is it a hug, a handshake, or something in between? A high-five, maybe?

"Well, it was fun meeting you again, now that we're grown and can remember meeting this time," Krista says, opening her car door.

"Yeah. It was." I kick a rock under GiGi's car with the toe of my shoe. I don't know what I'm supposed to say, but I have to say something.

"Look, you know I wasn't in a great place when I got here—and to be honest, I'm still not sure that I am now—but I'm thankful for you taking the time to run with me. And maybe for reminding me how much fun it can be to pee your pants in the woods every once in a while, too."

Krista tosses her head back with a laugh, which is hearty and genuine. "Really? You're that old?"

"Hey, now—" I shoot her a playful look of warning, open the car door, and grab my water bottle for a drink. "Seriously though, thanks."

"Well, I didn't do much, but you're welcome. Make sure you bring your shoes next time you visit. Maybe you'll be able to beat me by then."

I don't want to bore or tire her with the details of my indecision regarding this trip home everybody expects me to take, so I take her lead and end things on a light note, despite everything within me screaming to the contrary.

"Oh, it is so on, sister," I tell her.

"Looking forward to it," she replies with a smile and a wave, then hops up into her dirty yellow Jeep and drives away.

When I make it back to GiGi's, I find her sitting on the sofa with her chin tucked to her chest, asleep, while the local morning news airs on the TV. I head upstairs to shower and then come back down to load my things into the car. She wakes as I walk back through the front door.

I sit next to her on the sofa and lay my head on her soft, round shoulder. "I think I've got everything ready to go. Can you drop me off at Michelle's?"

She leans her head onto mine for a second, then holds my head in her hand and plants a long kiss into my hair. "Yeah, okay. You sure you got everything?"

"Yes, ma'am. I've double checked already."

"All right then. Let's do it."

The drive to Michelle's is even quieter than breakfast. I'm not good at goodbyes—even if they're only potential ones. Flying past my husband with blinders on, so I didn't have to see his face as I ran away is proof of that.

"You'll call me? Let me know what you decide?" she asks.

"Yes."

She takes a deep breath. "Jenna, I mean this with so much love—"

I meet her eyes and see the tears there again.

"—But I don't want to see you again anytime soon. You need to go home."

"I hear you. And I love you," I say with a smile.

Only GiGi can pull off that delivery, with full impact.

"I love you too, child."

I give her a hug and a kiss, grab my things from the floorboard, and wave one last time as the car door closes. She honks twice as she pulls away and I watch until she turns onto Main Street and disappears from sight.

There's that feeling again...the same torturous heartbreak and longing I felt watching Mama's bumper sticker fade into the distance. My stomach twists into a knot and my heart jumps into my throat. For a moment, I have to remind myself how to breathe.

"You gonna stand out here all day?" Michelle says, opening the door and stepping out onto the porch.

"Not if you'll have me."

"Get your butt in here." She grabs my free hand as I climb the steps and leads me inside.

"It's so quiet. I guess the boys are at school?"

"Yup. I'll have to leave about 2:30 to go pick them up. How was GiGi's?"

"Girl, it's been one hell of a week."

"Oh yeah? What happened?" She retrieves two cans of Coke from the fridge, sets them on the dining table, and pulls out two chairs.

"A lot. I don't even know where to start."

I begin by telling her all about what happened with Tyler at The Tavern. Then I fill her in on all the nonsensical details of being arrested by JD and spending the night in jail. From there, I go day by day chronicling every event, telling every story.

Somewhere in the middle of summarizing my run with Krista this morning, I take both our cans to toss into the recycle bin. When I turn around, Michelle is staring up at me with tears in her eyes.

"What in the world? Why are you crying?"

"Jenna, don't you see? These women—they've rallied around you in a way that's nothing short of incredible. Most women would take those stories to their graves."

"Yeah, I know—"

"It's amazing, the gift they've given you. How do you feel? Do you *feel* like the same person you were when I found you in a heap on my front porch a week ago?"

"I, uh—"

"Those poor women—" She rests her chin in her hand and stares off into the distance. Then she sits straight up in her chair and looks at me again. "So, what are you going to do?"

"I still have no idea."

Michelle takes a deep breath, then pulls out the dining chair, prompting me to retake my seat.

"Okay, look—you know you're welcome to stay here as long as you need to—always. But if what's holding you back is fear, I don't think you have much to worry about. You've learned so much. You have the tools now, Jenna."

"Do you think so?"

"I do."

"That book you gave me is great. I do think I'll try to sign up for a class, if I can find one."

"Oh, you'll love it. I'd take it a second time if it were offered here again," Michelle says.

"And I promised Mama I'd find a therapist."

"That's unexpected."

"Yeah. I'm obviously long overdue." I laugh at my attempt at a joke, even if the truth of it hurts a bit more than I care to admit.

"And I need to see Bonnie. I was drowning on dry land before I met her and didn't even know it. Her kindness—her letting me rest when I couldn't do it anymore—is what made me realize how badly I *needed* to rest. As guilty as I've felt about running away, I don't know where I'd be a year from now if I didn't. I think she—and you, all of you—may have saved my life."

"Oh, sweetie—" Michelle drops from her chair to her knees, puts her arms around my shoulders, and squeezes them tight. "I'm so happy for you. I don't know what I'd do without you, ya' know. Although I wish I could have more to offer in this life-changing experience of yours than 'Come As You Are'."

I pop her on the head, and she laughs at her own joke. "Don't be ridiculous."

She giggles and climbs back into her seat.

"Well, there's one last thing I need to do," I say.

"What?"

"Call Andrew."

"Do you think he's angry?"

"How could he not be? We haven't talked but once since I've been here. It would just be nice to know what I'm going back home to, if he even lets me come home at this point. I hope I haven't done too much damage."

"I don't know, Andrew's a pretty understanding guy. I don't think you have much to worry about."

"I left him, Michelle."

"You didn't *leave* him, leave him. You just left. There's a difference."

"Well, not much of one, if there is. I guess I'll find out soon enough."

After we've picked up the kids from school, had dinner, and said our goodnights, I retreat to my room and thumb through the journal by the lamplight. I re-read everything I've written, digesting it all over again.

My God, Michelle's right. This is what GiGi was trying to tell me all along.

I do have the tools; actionable steps I can take. I have Michelle, Mama, GiGi, Aunt Kitty, and even Krista and Gloria in my corner now. I had no one—or at least it felt that way—when I left home a week ago. I have Bonnie and Maggie too, if I can bring myself to be open enough with them to let them in. I have running. I can find a therapist. Most importantly, I have Andrew—at least, I think I still have Andrew.

What it all comes down to is this: For the first time in a very long time, what I have most is *hope*.

"You awake?" I text to Andrew.

"Yeah," he replies.

I call him.

"Hey," he says.

"Hey. I'm—uh—about to go to bed and wanted to remind you I'm hitting the road tomorrow."

"Okay. Are you driving straight through?"

Tears careen down my cheeks, faster and more forceful now than ever before. *I'm going home.*

"I think I'll stop for the night near Lafayette or Beaumont, so I'll get home earlier on Sunday and can see the kids before they go to bed."

"Okay. Sounds good. Be careful."

"I will." The line is silent and if I was ever anxious before, I'm in a terrible place now. "Andrew, what should I expect when I get there? I mean, are the kids upset with me?"

"No, I told you already, they're fine."

"And you? Are you fine?" A lump forms in my throat and I hold my breath for the answer, imagining all the worst possibilities.

"Jenna, just come home. We're all just ready to have you home."

"Oh—okay."

"Get some rest and call me when you get to a hotel tomorrow," he says.

"Okay, I will. I love you, Andrew."

"Love you too. Goodnight."

He ends the call—leaving me alone with an unheard goodbye.

The next morning, I wake before anyone else. I didn't sleep much and lying in this bed is killing me. I need to get going. I need to see Andrew.

I pack up my things and leave everything Michelle let me borrow on the nightstand. Then I strip the bed and put the sheets into the washer and set it to delay start, mid-morning. After I've changed into comfortable clothes for the drive, I sneak into the kitchen and grab a yogurt from the fridge. Just as I'm finishing up, Michelle enters the kitchen.

"Wow, you're up early," Michelle says with a yawn.

"Yeah. Didn't sleep much."

"Ah—I see. Looks like you're hitting the road?"

"Yes. I'm going home."

"Good. You're going to need lots of this for the drive, then." She picks up a bag of ground coffee and places heaping scoop upon scoop into the coffeepot. "Where will you stay tonight?"

"I'm not sure. I was planning to stop for the night somewhere along the Louisiana/Texas border, but I don't know—things don't feel right with Andrew at all. It's driving me crazy. I think I might drive straight through."

"Huh—that's not terrifying or anything."

"Right? Like I said, I didn't sleep much."

"Well, do you want me to make you a proper breakfast before you go?" She gestures towards my empty yogurt cup.

"Nah, I'm good. I think I'm pretty much ready. How long before the boys will be up?" I glance at the clock on the microwave—6:42.

"Any time now. They don't ever sleep in, unfortunately." She pours herself a cup of coffee, tops mine off, then says, "Oh, I almost forgot!"

She picks up her phone and a few seconds later, mine buzzes. I pick it up off the table and unlock the screen.

"Aw, Shelly, did you AirDrop me a mix tape?" I ask, holding the phone to my chest.

"Hell yeah, I did. And there's some good stuff on there too. You're gonna keep that thing *for-eva*."

"Only you would do such a thing, you know." I smile, but the reality of leaving Michelle—and everyone else—behind is starting to set in. Smiling isn't an easy task. "Thank you. I'll treasure it always."

"You're welcome. Let's get those boys up so you can say goodbye and get out of here before you make me cry."

"Okay, but really, thank you. For everything."

"Yeah, yeah...okay. Stop talkin' and start walkin'."

We wake the boys with tickles and screams and lots of giggles. I wrestle with them on the floor for a bit, then we break the news.

"You guys remember Auntie Jenna has to go home today, right?" Michelle asks them.

"Can we come too?" Alex asks as he climbs into my crisscrossed legs to sit.

"I don't think so. Not this time. We'll be back this fall, though, and maybe you guys can come visit us in Texas this summer." I look at Michelle, hoping she'll say yes.

"Yeah, I think we can do that."

"Yay!" The boys are back up and running around the room, celebrating the good news.

"Okay. Can y'all help me carry my stuff to the car?"

In a flash, they're up and running to the living room to find my things. Michelle heads to the kitchen and comes back with a travel mug of coffee and an umbrella for the boys to share.

"I'm going to miss you, ya know," she says with a hug.

"Yeah—I know." There's no stopping the tears at this point. The emotions of the past week rush in on me all at once, reminding me just how much I need Michelle in my life.

The screen door slams, then the boys yell, "Auntie Jenna, it's cold out here. Hurry up!" They're both bouncing up and down in the rain, Jasper holding the umbrella over both their heads.

"I'm coming, I'm coming—sheesh!"

Three minutes later, I pull out of the driveway and wave goodbye through the windshield as they're huddled together on the covered porch. Maybe someday I'll learn to handle goodbyes with a bit of grace, but today is not the day.

I turn onto Main Street so that I'm out of sight, then pull off to the side of the road and let go. I cry not only for this goodbye, but also for all the others. I cry over their stories, my story, and even for those of women I don't know and will never meet. I cry for the universal unfairness of it all—and with a heart which desires nothing more than to let every single person in the world know *they're not alone*.

Then I remember the playlist. I find it, hit play, and the angsty, melodic dopamine of Kurt Cobain erupts.

I laugh, cry, then laugh some more. I crank it way up and shoot a quick text message to Michelle.

"Thanks for that."

"Yeah, man. Enjoy. There's a lot more where that came from."

18

HOME

Several hours later, I receive a text from Andrew. "How's it going? The kids are excited to see you."

A look at the gas gauge tells me it's a good time to take a break, so I take the next exit and search for a place to fuel up. Spotting a gas station with a Taco Bell, I stop, and reply to his message. "Going good now that the rain's let up. Stopped for lunch and gas, coming into Lafayette. I'm excited to see y'all too. Might drive straight through."

"Okay, be careful. Let me know when you stop next."

"K. Love you."

After filling the tank, I move the car to a spot in front of the store and go inside for a restroom break and food. As I'm waiting for my order, I receive another text, this time from Bonnie.

"Hi, love. Wondering if I'll see you this week. I hope you are well. XO."

"I'm on my way back. We'll see you on Tuesday," I reply.

"Great. I can't wait. I could use a little company myself. See you soon."

I get a sinking feeling in the pit of my stomach. Bonnie's never even hinted at needing anything before. So, I text back, "Everything okay?"

An eternity later, she responds and "Yes, love. See you soon," is all I receive in reply. Something isn't right.

The loud, ticking clock on the wall tells me it's 1:40 in the afternoon. Maybe I will drive straight through, after all. I finish my tacos in a hurry, grab a refill on my soda to go, and get back on the road.

Long drives are a heck of a lot easier without kids, that's for sure. I cross the Texas state line and come into Beaumont with the sun still high in the sky. It seems strange to quit for the night when there's still several hours of daylight left, so I set Houston as my next stop.

As I drive past the last exit for Beaumont, my mind reels with all the possible "what if" scenarios of my homecoming and I'm filled with both excitement and full-on dread. How Andrew will respond when he sees me is still unknown. Will he be cold? Distant? Angry? He has to be angry. He'll try to hide it from the kids, but what happens after they go to bed? Will he let it show then? Am I ready for that?

Maybe I should stop for the night. At least then, I won't be so tired when I get in and maybe I'll be better able to handle the full brunt of his wrath. But does Andrew even have wrath? I've never seen it if he does.

And something still doesn't feel right about Bonnie. Maybe she's moving? A move to Houston to see Megan more often wouldn't be too surprising. I can't think about losing Bonnie, though. Not now.

I feel warm tears slide down my cheeks and the road before me is lost in a blur. I can't see my way forward—can't see to navigate the twists and turns which lie ahead.

I roll down the windows to feel the brisk air on my face.

"One...two...three...four."

By the time I get to seventeen, my heart has settled back into place and the answer is clear. I can't put it off any longer. I need to get home.

"Driving straight through. See you in a few hours," I text to Andrew.

Then, I crank up the volume on the radio and hit play on Michelle's playlist.

"Oh my God," I say with a smile, as Green Day's "Basket Case" hits me right in the face. "Oh, Michelle. How do you do it?"

I stop once more. It's 7:30, and the sky is dark. The kids are probably getting ready for bed. I'll make it home just as Andrew's tucking them in.

The palms of my hands are sweaty on the wheel and it feels like butterflies are performing fantastic feats of acrobatics in my gut.

"No time for that now," I tell myself as I focus on the road ahead and count the yellow lines as they pass, knowing each one brings me closer to my biggest fear—and greatest hope—all at the same time.

Forty minutes later, as I enter our neighborhood and navigate the turns I know so well, I'm surprised at what I feel: The same sense of belonging and nostalgia which came upon me as I rode through GiGi's neighborhood, has also found me here. This is home too—much more than I've ever realized.

With a deep breath, I make the turn into our driveway and stop. There, shielding his eyes from the bright white headlights, is Andrew sitting on the front porch step. Audrey spots me next and waves, screams, and flings herself off the porch. She sprints across the yard with her long hair trailing wildly behind her. Her brothers are hot on her heels and Andrew follows, scoops Noah up in his arms, and waits—a lighthouse in the storm, guiding me home.

Oh, my babies—*oh my heart.*

As she flies, Audrey's legs tangle themselves in her nightgown and she trips, jumps back up, and keeps running. Every instinct within me is pushing to leave this car right here and run to her with open arms. Somehow it feels like that way, the distance between us will close faster and I can hold her sooner.

But I push forward to meet her halfway down the drive. I stop, force the car into park, open the door and explode from its confines, sobbing like a child. I'm nearly bowled over by her little body, then squeezed tight by her tiny arms. Seconds later, Ryan charges at me from the other side. I drop to my knees and secure my arms around them both, convinced I can never, ever let them go.

As my sobs inch ever closer to hysterics—and when I think I've reached my end—Andrew appears. He pulls me up with one hand and sets Noah at my feet with the other. Then he wraps his heavy arms around my convulsive body, and I am enveloped in his warmth. He moves one hand to the back of my head and pushes my tear-soaked cheek into his hard chest. At the sound of his heartbeat, I crumble.

"Andrew—" I gasp for air. "I'm—" And gasp again. "So—"

"Shh." He hugs me tighter.

I take a deep breath, set it free again, and all my tired, tight muscles soften. And all at once, my soul is both shattered—and made whole.

When Andrew lets me go, all three kids are hanging on my legs, pulling at my shirt, begging for their turn.

"I made the mistake of telling them you were coming home tonight. There was no getting them into bed after that," Andrew says.

"Well, I sure am glad you guys didn't go to bed. I've missed you like crazy!"

"I've missed you too, Mama. Come see what I made for you!" Audrey takes my hand and points toward the house.

Andrew gives me a peck on the cheek then jogs up to where the van sits, still running, in the driveway. He backs it into its regular spot in front of the garage as the kids lead me through the front door. At the end of the hallway, I see a colorful, Fiesta-like banner made of sparkly construction paper cutouts. "Welcome Home" is written across its front, one bubbly letter on each pennant. Homemade streamers hang from each end, where the garland is tacked into the wall.

"Audrey, you made this?"

"Yup. The boys helped, but I designed it and did most of the cutting," she answers, beaming with pride.

"Wow, it's beautiful! Y'all did a great job. Thank you." I hug them all again and the sweet smell of shampoo rises from their still-wet hair.

"All right, it's time for bed, you guys." Andrew shuts the front door behind him.

"Aww, but she just got here!" Ryan cries.

"Yeah, and she'll be here in the morning, too. Mama's tired. Give her some hugs and run on up. I'll come tuck you in in a bit."

They protest, but do as he says.

Andrew's right, I am tired, but I also want to hold them all until my arms can't physically hold them anymore. My heart sinks a little to see them climb the stairs and disappear so soon after I've just gotten them back.

"They'll be here tomorrow too, you know," Andrew says. "I figured you'd be tired and want to get washed up and settled in."

"Yeah—you're right. I am. It's been a long week, though. I've missed them."

"Well, why don't you go tuck them in then? I could use the break, anyway. And maybe a drink."

"Okay, fine. If you're gonna make me." I bound up the stairs and see Noah playing on the floor in the playroom. "Hey, sweet boy."

He looks up from his trucks, stands, and runs over to me. I scoop him up and he lays his soft head on my shoulder. "Love you, Mama," he says in a tiny, sleepy voice.

"Oh, I love you too, baby. Let's go read some stories, okay?"

"Yeah, okay."

An hour later, I return downstairs. All three kids are settled in and Andrew's in his favorite chair with a glass of wine.

"There's one for you on the counter," he says, looking up from his magazine.

"Okay, thanks." I head to the kitchen, find the glass, and stare at the small, sticky fingerprints on the white cabinets as I take a sip. Suddenly and silently, I feel Andrew's arms slide around my waist. He crosses them in front of me and presses his body against mine.

"I have missed you so much." His breath tickles my ear and before I can respond, he spins me around, places his hands on each side of my face, and tilts my head up toward his. He leans forward and pauses, his lips hovering just over mine. Then he runs his fingers through my hair, brushing it back and away from my face.

"Andrew—"

"Hmm?"

"I don't understand. Aren't you angry?" I lean back enough to see his eyes.

"Huh?"

"You have to be mad about what I did. You sure sounded mad on the phone."

He scoots his feet a few inches back and drops his hands to the counter; one on either side of my hips. "Do you want me to be mad? Why do I have to be mad?"

"Well, I don't guess you have to be, but it would make a lot more sense if you were."

"Well, I'm not."

"But I left you—I ran away! I left our kids!"

Andrew turns, crosses the kitchen, and picks up his wine glass. Leaning against the counter opposite of me, he says, "I've felt a lot of things since you went away, Jenna."

"Then I need you to walk me through it. We can't pretend like this didn't happen and if you're angry with me, I need to know."

He lets out a sigh. "Well, if we're going to do this, we should do it outside." He stands upright and walks into the living room, through the patio doors, and to the back porch.

I follow, but my stomach is in my throat. This is it. And I'm terrified.

He chooses to sit in a rocker, so I take the one next to him. And wait.

"Yes, I was angry, but not at first." He pauses for a sip of his wine then swirls the glass, squinting in the moonlight to see how much remains. "When you passed by me in the driveway, I was confused. At first, I thought you were taking the kids to pick up takeout for dinner. But when you didn't slow down to talk to me—when you didn't even look my way—I knew something wasn't right."

All I can do is stare at my feet. Hearing his version of this story brings the guilt all over again.

"Then I went inside, and the place was a mess. Things you were doing in the kitchen were left undone. And the kids...when I realized you'd left the kids, well, that's when the confusion slipped away, and I was terrified.

"I knew you would never leave the kids, not for anything in the world, and that was the scary part. I thought you'd left so you could do it without them seeing it, you know? So, they wouldn't be the ones to...find you. I grabbed my keys and started to run out the door to catch up to you—to follow you—but I couldn't. I couldn't leave them alone and I couldn't take them with me. I was stuck; powerless."

He sniffs, and I realize I've brought tears to my perfect husband's beautiful face.

"Can you imagine that feeling? That panic and dread? All I could do was call, and call, and call. Then text and text. And when you didn't respond, God, Jenna, I was so scared. I wanted to scream for you and hope somehow it would carry across the wind and you'd be forced to hear my voice! That maybe you'd pause, think, and turn around. But I needed to keep my cool, for their sake.

"Then, you texted that you were going home to Alabama and finally, I could breathe. There was a destination; a goal. I knew if there was a goal to reach, you'd do it. You always do. I just tried to have faith you'd make it.

"Then you got there, and I knew you were safe with Michelle. It was when I went so long without hearing from you that the anger came."

He's quiet and I wonder if he's done talking. He can't be done. I need to know the rest.

"I was so mad, Jenna. I was pissed that you'd ever abandon us. I was terrified you weren't coming back; that I'd never hold you again. That I'd have to explain to the kids why Mama doesn't live here anymore—why she ran away and left them behind. I was furious. The angriest I've ever been about anything in my life...but it didn't last long."

"Why?" I ask, sensing this moment has been the safest one yet in which to interject.

"I saw the novel you bought at the book festival last year. It was sitting on a shelf in the corner of your closet and was dog-eared where you'd last left off—on page twenty-three. Then, I saw a pair of your running shoes on the floor. One of them was turned upside down and there wasn't a speck of dirt on it. The more I walked around this house, the more I saw little signs of the person you once were, but couldn't be anymore."

His voice catches in his throat and he takes another sip before continuing.

"That's when I became angry with myself for not having noticed it sooner; for needing something so drastic to catch my attention. That's when I realized how much I've let you down. That I haven't been much of a husband to you at all. I mean, I knew you were de-pressed—especially around the holidays—but I guess I didn't realize what it was truly all about...or the role I played in all of it."

"Andrew, you didn't—"

"And then those kids! Holy hell, our kids are nuts."

I laugh at his attempt at deflection—and the sheer truth in it, too.

"That they are."

"No—seriously. By day two of having them all to myself, I was ready to call in reinforcements. I was googling babysitters and drop-in day cares, and supernannies. I was losing my mind! And then all I felt was guilt, knowing this is what you deal with every single day. Well, there was some panic mixed in there too...that you'd never come back, and I'd have to do this alone for the next sixteen years."

"So, what you're saying is you're glad to have me back so you can save all that money from the supernanny."

"Well, yeah—why else?" He nudges me with his elbow. "Cheers," he says, holding up his glass.

"To—"

"To surviving parenthood—together. We're highly unlikely to come out in one piece in the end, but at least it will be the end."

"Andrew! I'm not toasting to that. They're crazies, but they're our crazies."

"All right then, to parenthood. And I'll embellish in my mind how I see fit."

"Fine. Cheers—to parenthood," I say, as our glasses clank together. "But you might want to clear out the garage, so my car fits in there from now on."

"Ah—good thinking. Put that road to freedom out of sight, out of mind, right?"

"Exactly."

"You got it, babe. Tomorrow."

19

NEWS

Over the next two days, Andrew and I steal away whenever we can. I tell him bits and pieces of what I learned in Asher. We talk about therapy, parenting classes, weekly calls and more frequent trips back home, and booking a babysitter at least once a month for date night, among other things.

By Tuesday, I'm feeling optimistic and excited to see Bonnie.

"Do you want to ring the bell?" I ask Noah as I unbuckle his seat.

"Yeah, ring bell!"

I half expect Bonnie to open the door before he even has a chance to, but we make it out of the car, up to the porch, and ring twice, with no answer. I knock on the door and we wait. I knock harder and we wait. Noah rings the bell once more and I pull my phone from the diaper bag to make sure it's Tuesday.

Finally, the door opens, and Bonnie greets us with her usual sweet smile.

"Hello! Oh, it's so good to see you two." Bonnie bends down low to hug Noah, then stands and takes my hands in hers. "Especially good to see you, love." She leans forward and gives a soft touch, cheek to cheek.

She's in her lounge clothes again, donning a plum-colored velour track suit with a blush pink tee-shirt underneath. Her hair is down, touching her shoulders, and she looks tired, worried, or sick.

Noah and I follow her inside and into the kitchen. I look to see what help she needs with setting the table, but there's nothing here; no pastries, no treats for Noah, and no tea.

"Would you like me to put on the kettle?" I ask for the first time ever, pretending as if it's not abnormal at all.

"Oh yes, that would be fine," she says, pulling out a chair at the dining room table. She takes a seat and lifts Noah onto her lap. "And there's a box of doughnut holes in the refrigerator. You didn't think I'd have you over empty-handed, did you?" She pinches Noah's chubby cheek and gives a little kiss on the top of his head.

I fill the kettle with water, get it going on the stove, and take the box of doughnuts from the refrigerator. Then, I pull a sippy cup from the diaper bag and fill it with milk from the fridge as well. I take both to Noah and sit across from the two of them at the table.

"Well, how was your trip?" she asks.

"It was...crazy. But helpful, I think."

"Yeah, how so?" She and Noah are playing the slap game with her free hand, but she's looking at me.

"I don't know. It gave me time to think, I guess. It's hard to think in our house. I needed that break."

"Mm-hm," she says, waiting for more.

"And I saw my best friend and Mama and GiGi—who I hear you've introduced yourself to, by the way."

"Oh, yes. Sorry about that," she answers with a grin.

"It's okay. I'm glad you did. Made for one heck of a jail break story."

"*Jail*?" She lifts an eyebrow and, for the first time since I sat at the table, her hand is still.

"Yup. It's not as exciting as it sounds, though, I promise."

I tell her about my night in the county jail and the dramatic rescue by GiGi the following morning. Bonnie laughs and says, "I knew I liked her. She's got spunk."

"That is a true statement." I can't help but to laugh at how much of an understatement it actually is.

The kettle whistles on the stove, so I stand and return to it, turning off the fire. I place a few bags of Bonnie's favorite Earl Grey into the bottom of the empty teapot and pour the piping hot water over the top. Then I round up the usual fixins and carry it all to the table on the tray.

"You've sure learned your way around here, haven't you?" Bonnie says with a smile.

"Oh, I'm sorry. I didn't mean to be rude." I feel my cheeks grow hot.

"Oh, it's not a bad thing, love. I like that you feel comfortable here. It's been a long time since I've enjoyed that in my house."

"You mean since your daughter moved away? Why did she go to Houston, anyway?"

"Work, of course...or so she says. I think, really, it was to get a break from me." Noah grows antsy, so she sets him down and releases him to play.

"Oh, surely not."

"Well, I wasn't always the person you know, love. I made my mistakes with Megan and I've regretted them greatly. Maybe sometime we can talk about that, but I'd prefer to save it for another day." She uses her spoon to pull the tea bags from the pot and places them on the saucer. "I don't have the energy for it today."

I pour the milk and sugar into her cup, stopping when she raises her hand. She pours the tea, and we sip in silence. The flames bounce in the fireplace behind Bonnie's head and for a while, I am lost as they entangle themselves in a wild, erratic dance with my thoughts.

What is it she wants to tell me? It can't be any crazier than what I've already heard. I consider pressing her to talk, but the thought doesn't last long. Her story is her story and she'll tell it when she's ready.

"So, what else did you do on your little getaway?" Bonnie breaks the silence.

"I listened. I did a lot of listening, actually. I heard stories that have been kept for decades. Why do we do that? Why are we so afraid to tell our stories?"

"Oh, I'm sure the answer to that is different for everyone," she says. "Shame. Denial. Fear. Plus, talking about it makes it real again...and who wants that?" She picks up a doughnut hole, gives it a sniff, then puts it back. "Why haven't you told yours?"

"What? My story?"

She nods.

"I guess I didn't realize I even have one. I didn't realize it was something that needed to be told."

I hear Noah bonk his head on something in the spare bedroom, most likely the corner of the dresser. He's done it a thousand times. He whines for a second, then goes back to playing.

"And to be honest, I was afraid of what people would think of me. I thought I was a monster—a crazy person who should be locked away somewhere. Thought that all the things I've done and felt were somehow unique."

"And now?"

"Now I know better."

She nods her head again. "Good. Now, how about we go sit by the fire and warm up a bit? I'm freezing in this cold kitchen."

We stand and move into the next room. Bonnie takes her spot on the sofa and I take mine. There's an assortment of magazines on the coffee table and she leans forward to choose one, borrowing my usual way to convey that she doesn't feel like talking any more today.

I choose one as well, grab a blanket from the back of the sofa, and get comfortable. I flip through the pages while sneaking glances at Bonnie over the top of the paper. She's tired—and not the kind of tired felt from getting a poor night's sleep. She's bone-tired; the kind of weary that comes from something more. And as much as I want to know, I can't ask. For countless hours over so many weeks, Bonnie and I sat on this sofa and she knew I was struggling, but she let me work through it in my own time. She let me come to her when I was ready to share. And now, all I can do is wait...and hope she'll do the same.

The following Tuesday, I preempt the awkwardness of a potential lack of snacks by stopping for kolaches on the way to Bonnie's house. She answers the door in gray plaid pants and a white, fuzzy sweater—a wardrobe choice that may or may not still be pajamas. It's hard to tell.

"Good morning, Bonnie. We brought kolaches," I say, holding the box up for her to see.

"Oh, yum. Come on in."

We enter through the doorway and make our way to the kitchen. The tea kettle is on the stove and somewhere out of sight there's a vanilla candle burning, throwing its smooth scent into the air.

"How's everybody doing this morning?" she asks.

"We're okay. The older two have been battling a bit of a bug the past week or so, but so far, this little guy's been spared. How are you?" I make sure to stop and look at her when I ask that question. She's lost weight.

"Oh, could be better, I guess. Getting old's a bitch. Don't ever let anyone tell you any different." She plops into a kitchen chair with a huff.

"Is there anything I can do? Do you have any laundry, or cooking, or anything I can help with?" I look around to find something I can do to help, but the place is sparkling clean.

"Ah, no, love. I have help for that. She comes a couple times a week and makes sure I'm all taken care of, but thank you." Bonnie stands from her seat, steadying herself with the table. Then, she moves to the stove to check on the kettle.

She busies herself with placing everything on the tray and as she crosses the kitchen with it, I realize this is not the same woman who carried this tray back in October. This woman is frail and in pain.

I stand and help her guide it down and onto the table. We sit, prepare our tea to our liking, and talk until Noah runs in, searching for his kolache.

"Here, love. Ms. Bonnie's got your treat." She fumbles with the lid on the box, pulls one out, and attempts to hand it to Noah. Only her reach is a bit short. She lets go too soon, and it falls to the floor. "Oh, dear. Sorry about that." She tries to stand to retrieve the fallen snack, but lets out a little yelp and sits back in her seat.

"No problem, he's got it. See?" I say, as Noah scoops it up off the floor and heads back into the other room to play.

"He's going to eat that thing off the dirty floor?"

"You said you have someone clean for you twice a week. Your floors are a whole lot cleaner than mine, for sure." I snag a kolache from the box and take a bite.

"Still—"

"Bonnie, I don't want to intrude, but is everything okay? Are you feeling okay?"

She takes a sip from her cup and I wait for an answer.

"No, I'm not okay," she replies. "I went to the doctor a few weeks back because I wasn't feeling too good and he, of course, sent me for scans. I haven't told you this, but I've battled cancer twice in my life, so I'm sent for scans pretty much anytime I sneeze. Usually it's nothing, but this time—"

"It's not nothing."

"No, it's not nothing."

"Oh, Bonnie—" I lean over the table and try to take her hands in mine, but she folds them in front of her instead.

"Don't 'oh, Bonnie' me. I've kicked its butt before, and I'll kick it again."

"Okay. But you have to tell me how I can help. You don't need a cleaning lady, but does she prepare meals for you, too?"

"Yes, she's got that covered. All I need from you is a weekly visit. Come see me, is all. And promise me you won't stop bringing that baby. He lights up my world, at least for a few hours every Tuesday."

"All right. We'll press on as usual then, but you're not making or buying snacks or tea anymore. I'll take care of that."

"Okay," she says without a fight.

It's quiet again. The popping fire and what we can hear of Noah's conversation with himself in the other room are the only sounds.

"Have you told Megan?"

"No, not yet. I'll tell her if I need to." Her words are hard and final.

"Okay then. Wanna turn on an old movie?"

"Oh, they don't make 'em like that anymore, do they?" she says with a glimmer in her eye.

"No, they don't. Let's go see what we can find."

We choose *Breakfast at Tiffany's*, but Bonnie's snoozing on the sofa before Holly Golightly even saunters into Sing Sing. I cover her with a blanket, turn the sound down low, and join Noah in the other room.

My mind tumbles with the most basic of questions. What does she mean she's had cancer twice before? What kind of cancer? How did she survive it? How old was she then? What about her church family—do they know?

Then the emotions come. She must feel so lonely dealing with this with no family nearby. Am I all she has? Will I be enough for her? Will I be able to give her all that she needs? And I know it's selfish to even ponder, but what if I lose her? What would I do without her? I'm supposed to be building a community here, people I can lean on, and who can lean on me—my sisterhood. Bonnie's such a huge part of that for me. I need Bonnie.

I play with Noah a while as the questions bounce around my brain like a ping pong ball, with no reason for existence other than to keep bouncing, infinitely, in its confined space. There's no reprieve. Not here, with Bonnie's gentle snores carrying from my usual resting place on the sofa, down the hall to this room.

I gather up our things and we sneak out the front door, leaving Bonnie to her dreams.

⸺ ◆ ⸺

After the kids have gone to bed, Andrew pulls me onto the sofa next to him.

"Everything okay?" he asks.

The words catch in my throat, afraid to be spoken; afraid to be made real.

"No, everything is not okay." I've held myself together by a thread all day, determined to not cry in front of the kids or to let my emotions dictate how I've treated them. I can't do it anymore. "Bonnie's sick, Andrew." I wipe my face with the back of my hand.

"What kind of sick?"

"The cancer kind."

"Oh, I'm so sorry, Jenna." He squeezes my knee. "Is she going to be okay? Will she need chemo or what?"

"I don't know—I think so? She said she's survived cancer twice already and she can beat it again, so I guess that means some sort of treatment, right?"

"Yeah, sounds like it. Do you think you'll keep going to see her through that?"

"Of course I will! Why wouldn't I?"

"Okay, okay...was just a question. Sorry." He pulls his hands back and holds them up in the air to show me he meant no offense. "Have you called and scheduled an appointment with that therapist yet?"

"Yes, I go on Friday. I'm going to have to find a sitter."

"Okay. Do you want to talk about it though...about Bonnie, I mean?"

"No, I don't think so. I just want to go to bed." I stand, and he follows.

"Me too." Taking my hand, Andrew leads me to our room, clicking off the living room lamps as we go.

We go about our normal bedtime routine—washing faces, brushing teeth, and setting out clothes for the next day. When we crawl beneath the covers, I turn onto my side and Andrew throws his heavy arm over me and pulls me in close. It's not until I've cried myself to sleep and woken up again two hours later in a fit of panic that I realize he's let go.

How sick *is* she, though? Cancer has stages, right? And certain cancers are worse than others? Maybe she's not all *that* sick.

I cringe at the stupidity of the thought. Cancer is cancer—of course she's sick. So, what does that mean? Should I visit more often? Less often? Should I find a sitter for Noah when I go, so he doesn't bother her—or have to see her in pain? How will I explain it to him?

Stupid, selfish thoughts.

I refocus. What can I do to help? What is it she'll need? It's almost two in the morning, but I pick up my phone and search, "how to support a loved one with cancer." I read through several articles, traveling down the link-spam rabbit hole until I land on a one titled, "A Cancer Patient's Final Days of Life–What to Expect." I'm not even through the first paragraph and I'm silently bawling, fighting hard to not let the sound erupt. I'm sweaty and I can't breathe.

I stand, place my phone on the nightstand, and move to the living room, where I'm free to cry without fear of waking anyone. My mind spins, and I feel lost and useless, but at least without that devil of a search bar my thoughts are my own—and not those of some expert attempting to pummel sound advice into my brain, whether I'm ready to receive it or not.

And I'm not. I'm not ready to hear the practicalities of what this is going to be like. I don't want sound advice. I don't want truth. Right now, I want to wallow in the shock and sadness—and somehow, across the miles, I hear GiGi's voice.

"Well, then you go right ahead, child. You are allowed to have feelings, remember?"

I remember, and I allow them to come. I allow them to stay. And once I'm completely undone and have nothing more to offer them, I sleep.

I've woken up on the sofa more mornings than not since last week and today, Tuesday has come, yet again. Today I'm supposed to visit Bonnie—and I'm terrified.

As Noah and I turn into Bonnie's neighborhood, I notice for the first time that the courtyard fountain is dry. The bright, beautiful flowers that surrounded it in early fall are long gone, and only the lifeless brown sticks and stems of their skeletons remain. Nobody's gardening, or out for a morning stroll, and it's hauntingly quiet and still. It's colder than usual this morning and blankets of glistening frost cover the windows of parked cars left behind as we move onward to Willow Lane.

We don't ring this time. Instead, I give a light knock and enter when I hear Bonnie's invitation through the heavy wooden door. She's sitting on the sofa in the living room with a burgundy knitted afghan blanket hanging over her legs. There's no candle burning, but the smell of firewood hangs heavy in the air and Dean Martin's "Sway" emanates from the Bluetooth speaker in the kitchen.

"Morning! We're not too early, are we? Ryan was surprisingly easy to part with at drop-off this morning."

"No, no, you're fine. Come here and give Ms. Bonnie a hug, love." She beckons for Noah and he runs to her, throws his arms around her neck, then climbs up onto the sofa beside her, eager to show her his new toy truck. "Oh, that's very nice," she says.

"Mama bought it," he says, driving the truck across Bonnie's legs.

"Oh—I see. Well, you're a very lucky boy. Your mama must really love you, right?"

"Mm-hmm," he answers, before climbing down off the sofa and sitting in front of the fireplace to play.

"I love this song," I say to Bonnie as I fill the kettle and place it on the stove.

"I do too, but I never was a big fan of Dino. I was more into The Mama's and The Papa's, The Doors, that sort of thing."

"Ah—you truly were a hippie."

"Oh, but a cool one, dear."

I laugh and place tea bags in the bottom of the teapot, waiting in the kitchen for the blue-hot flames to force the kettle to sing. I notice Bonnie watching Noah and a sadness comes over me. How much longer will we have together? She's in her seventies, for sure, and should still have many great years to come. But the cancer...how many times can one person win that fight? When does fate eventually say *enough*? The water begins to roll in the kettle. It won't be long now.

"Snack, Mama?" Noah asks.

"Yeah, sweetie. Come get it." I pick a few pieces of cheddar cheese and slices of strawberry from the small tray I prepared at the house and place them on a plate.

Noah runs into the kitchen, takes the plate, and sets it on the table. He pops a piece of cheese into his mouth, then runs back into the living room to play.

"Bonnie, would you like any cheese or fruit? I've got cheddar, pepper jack, berries, and pineapple."

"Sure, I'll take a little. Not too much, though."

As I'm making her plate, the kettle whistles, so I turn off the burner and pour the water into the teapot. I prepare the tray of snacks and tea and place it on the coffee table in front of Bonnie. She scoots herself forward to the edge of the sofa so she can reach, and I'm pretty sure I catch a lightning-quick grimace on her face as she does.

I help her pour and prepare her tea and hold it for her as she scoots back on the sofa. Once she's settled, I hand it over with what I hope is a nonchalant, "How are you feeling today?"

"Okay, considering," she replies, then blows on her tea.

"I hope it's okay to ask this, but have you started treatment? Or is that coming soon?" I look down at my cup, afraid I've intruded too much. "I mean, I don't know how it all works."

"No, not yet. I go in on Friday to have part of it removed. The doctor said it's too risky to try to take it all this time. Chemo will start after that."

"Oh—wow. Do you need anything? A ride home, or someone here to help you get settled in afterward, to bring you food?"

"No, love. It's all taken care of."

"Okay. Maybe I can visit at the hospital. We can watch a movie or read, whatever you want."

"That's very sweet of you, but I'll just need to rest."

"Okay, but you'll text if you change your mind, right?"

"Of course, love."

Friday morning, as Noah and Ryan sit at the kitchen table eating cereal for breakfast, I sip my coffee on the back deck and watch the sun rise. Brilliant beams of orange, pink, and lavender peek above the hilltops and climb to penetrate wispy, fast-moving clouds. A few short minutes later, the sun takes its place in the sky, the clouds move on, and the pastel tapestry fades into a rather ordinary hue of azure blue.

Yesterday was Valentine's Day, but I was in no mood for celebration. My mind has been on Bonnie all week. I've called and texted her more since Tuesday than I think I have the entire time we've known each other—checking to make sure she's okay. I've offered to bring food or to come help around the house, but she's a proud woman and refuses every offer I make.

Staring at the still brightening blue sky, I wonder if she witnessed the spectacular cotton candy sunrise this morning too? Or did she wake instead to this ordinary sight? And if it were me going into the ring to fight my third round with the devil, which would I prefer to be greeted with while slipping on the gloves—distinctively breathtaking? Or dependably familiar?

I pick up my phone to check the time—7:23. It's too early to call or message her, so I stand and go inside to check on the boys.

"You guys about finished up? I have to leave for an appointment soon, and I want you dressed before the sitter gets here."

"Almost!" Ryan replies.

An hour later, our neighbor's daughter has arrived to watch the kids and I'm sitting in the car. I pick up my phone and type, "Morning, Bonnie. Thinking of you today. Please let me know how everything goes and if I can do anything to help. I'll come visit as soon as you're up for it. Hugs."

Then, I search for the address of the therapist's office on my GPS and put the car in drive. I take a moment to calm the butterflies in my stomach, then allow the car to move forward—ready as I'll ever be to start this day.

20

SLIPPING

Charlene, the therapist, is maybe ten years older than me with short, brown, curly hair, and tiny glasses. She seems nice enough, but there couldn't have been a worse day to meet her. I'm worried about Bonnie and as we're making our way through the introductory questions, my eyes frequently shift to the clock, which doesn't go unnoticed.

"Is there a reason you're watching the clock?" she asks.

"Uh—yeah. A good friend of mine is having surgery this morning. I'm a little anxious about it."

"I see. Is it serious?"

"She has cancer. They're removing part of it so she can start treatment." I look at the clock again, then down at my hands.

"I'm sorry to hear that. Why don't you tell me about her?" She crosses her ankles, puts an elbow up on the arm of her chair, and supports her chin with her hand, waiting.

"Well, she's a fairly new friend. We met last fall. She reminds me a lot of my grandmother. She's patient, wise, a great listener. Witty, with some spunk to her. She's the least judgmental person I've ever met." I reach for a tissue on the table and wad it into a ball in my hand.

"This—"

"Bonnie," I answer.

"Bonnie sounds like a wonderful friend."

"She is."

"What do you and Bonnie do when you spend time together?" Charlene asks.

"Usually, we eat. And drink tea. Sometimes we play games or read or talk. There's been many times when we simply sit, even sleep. Or I sleep, I guess."

"That sounds nice."

I nod. "When I met her, I was...going through the motions of my life, digging myself deeper and deeper into a hole as I went. And I think I would have kept going—but she allowed me to stop. To be still."

"And how did that help you?"

"Well, I think if I wouldn't have spent that time with Bonnie, I may not have felt the instinct to run when I couldn't take any more. I think there's a real possibility I wouldn't be here today—as dramatic as that sounds. Before I met Bonnie, there was no concept of how far down the hole I was. It was when she allowed me to rest that I realized how much I *needed* the rest."

The clock ticks, catching my attention once again.

"Sitting in that car, fighting with myself over whether I should stay or go—and deciding to run—I didn't know it then, but I was saving myself. And I never would have done it if I never realized, on some level, that I need to be saved—if I never met Bonnie."

A short, nearly imperceptible vibration sound comes from the watch on Charlene's wrist. Our time is up.

"Well, I'm looking forward to hearing more about Bonnie," she says with a smile.

We both stand, shake hands, and I schedule my next appointment with the receptionist at the front desk on my way out. As I walk through the parking lot toward my car, all I can think is, it's just not fair.

Then I remember the unfairness of Aunt Kitty's story, and Mama's, and GiGi's too…and wonder again, how any of them survived. But maybe it's not about fairness at all. Fairness implies order, but in this moment, when up feels down and left feels right and I'm walking the earth with my insides on the outside, order is nothing more than a pipe dream: an eternally hopeful impossibility.

February slips away in a tangle of doctor visits, new meds, therapy sessions, and solemn visits with Bonnie. Her surgery was unsuccessful. The cancer has twisted and turned and wrapped itself throughout her abdomen, digging deep and leaving nothing untouched. Chemotherapy, radiation, and medication are her lifelines now.

Pacing the kitchen, I wait for the babysitter to arrive. Noah has a cold, and I can't risk passing it on to Bonnie by taking him with me. As I pour myself another cup of coffee, the doorbell rings. I give the usual instructions, hug Noah goodbye, and drive to Bonnie's.

Once there, I give a light knock on the door and push it open. I cross into the living room and find her sitting on the couch, with a book in-hand.

"Good morning," I say, as I give a little peck on her cheek.

"Good morning." She dog-ears her page, sets the book on the cushion next to her, and places her reading glasses on top.

"How are you feeling? Up for a game of dominoes?" I ask.

"No, not today. You didn't bring the baby?"

"No, he has a cold, so I left him with the sitter. Would you like tea?" With all the treatments and medications she's taking, her appetite has all but disappeared, and the nausea is in full force.

"Water's fine, but I have a cup here." She hands me the lidded cup from the end table next to her and I turn to the kitchen to refill it.

"Do you want anything else while I'm in here?"

"No, thank you. I'm fine."

I bring the fresh cup of water and sit next to her on the sofa. As I sit, I see a hairbrush on the coffee table. Looking at her now, it's easy to see she's combed one side of her hair straight, but the other remains twisted and tangled. I lean forward and pick up the brush.

"May I?"

She nods.

I pull up my leg and turn sideways on the sofa to brush her fine, delicate hair. A tear rolls down her left cheek.

"There, that's better." I smooth the last of the staticky, fly-away strands with my hand.

"Thank you." She puts on her glasses and picks up her book.

I stand and pull a few logs from the rack to place in the fireplace.

"You're going to need kindling; some of those smaller ones there." She points to a small basket of sticks and twigs. "And there's some old newspaper, too."

I follow her instructions and build the first real fire I've ever built in my life. "Wow, I didn't know I could do that."

"Not so hard, is it?" she asks, before returning to her book.

"No, I guess it isn't." I sit back down on the sofa and take a magazine from the table.

She's right. Building the fire wasn't hard at all, but knowing she doesn't have the strength to do it on her own anymore certainly is.

For weeks, our visits are mostly non-verbal. I sit next to Bonnie on the sofa, snuggled into her side, while we watch movies, read, or stare into the fire. Well into March, the weather is warm and sunny, but Bonnie lives with a chill in her bones she can't quite shake, and the fire seems to help.

By April, I'm visiting each day Ryan's at preschool. I often arrive while Bonnie's at her chemo appointment, so I make her bed, do her laundry, and light the fire while she's away. She spends the day in her room after treatments, but having the fire lit when she gets home and an orderly bed to climb into comforts her.

Today, as Noah plays and watches TV in the other room, I sit at her bedside, helping her to take small sips of water through a straw.

"So, I think it's time I told you that last week was my final round of treatment."

"What does that mean? Is the cancer gone?"

"No, love, it isn't gone." She takes my hand and I stare, trying to make sense of her words.

"It's not working, Jenna. It's moving too fast. There's nothing more to be done."

"What do you mean, there's nothing more to be done? Can't they switch to a different kind of chemo or something? Immunotherapy?"

"We've tried it all, love." She lays her head back on her pillow and closes her eyes. "It's time to call Megan."

I fall forward, my forehead resting on our entwined hands, afraid to look up. I don't want her to see me cry. I want to be brave.

"Hey—it's going to be okay. Even an old stubborn broad like me can't live forever, right?" She squeezes my hand.

I look up at her but have no words.

"The doctors want to do a surgery to remove my stomach and run a tube to the bowel. It would ease the pain, but given the aggressiveness of the cancer, won't buy me much time."

"Are you going to do it?"

"No, I don't think so. There are other alternatives to ease the pain."

"I'm so sorry, Bonnie. Do you—know how long?" I hate to ask, but need to know the answer.

"A few weeks—months, maybe. Okay, how about a pain pill and a phone so I can call my daughter while I have the nerve to do it?"

I reach for the medication bottle on the nightstand, open it, and help with her water as she swallows the pill. Then I pick up her cell phone. "Do you want me to dial it for you?"

"No, I can do it. And the nurse will be here soon. You don't have to stay."

Bonnie rarely asks me to leave and when she does, I don't argue.

"Okay. Need anything else before we go?"

"No, I'm all set."

I squeeze her hand one more time, kiss her forehead and leave the room, closing the door behind me. In the hallway, I lean against the wall, slump to the floor, and bury my face in my hands.

Through the door I hear, "Megan, it's Mom," and Bonnie's soft, gasping breaths as she fights to hold back her tears.

"The dark days are here again." Sitting cross-legged on Charlene's sofa, I focus on my fingernails, pushing the cuticles back, so I don't have to look her in the face. "And I'm not sure this time if it's because of Bonnie or if they would have come, anyway. It doesn't feel any different. Well, maybe more sad than angry or numb. I thought I was better, but I feel like nothing's changed, like I'm back to square one."

"It could be a little of both. You're going to have a response to what Bonnie's going through. It's not uncommon to grieve the loss of a loved one before they're even gone." Charlene scribbles something on her notepad. "But, also, positive mental health isn't a light switch that, once flipped on, stays that way. We have to retrain our brains how to react to the triggers, form new habits, and practice them."

I nod my head to show I understand. "So, what do I do?"

"Well, is there anything at all that makes you feel better when you're having a bad day?"

"I don't know—running, I guess? But it's hard to find the time between three kids and being at Bonnie's so much. And I don't want to cut into the time I spend with her."

"But it's critical you take care of yourself first. You can't take care of anyone else—not well, anyway—if you don't take care of yourself."

That is something I now know to be true and as I think on Charlene's words, my mind turns back to running with Krista in Asher. I remember the stiff wind on my face and the feeling of my heart pumping wildly in my chest. I unfold my legs and the right one bounces up and down, as I grow impatient at the mere memory of it.

"Well, I think that's about all the time we have for today. See you next week?"

"Okay."

Leaving the medical building and emerging into the sunlight, I realize how beautiful of a day it is. There's still a slight chill to the air—that short-lived, small window of Texas weather perfection before spring melts into the scalding summer.

Running. I haven't even thought about running since I came back from Asher. It's such an obvious thing. How did I miss it?

I can't get home fast enough and when I do, I burst through the front door to find the sitter playing on the floor with Noah. She goes to stand.

"Nope. I'm not here...changing clothes, then heading out for a run. I'll be back in thirty minutes. Can you stay until after I shower?"

"Sure. No problem."

———◆———

Thirty-three minutes later, after what may have been the most intense run of my life, I'm back home, stretching my legs in the driveway and willing the relief of the stretch to travel through to the rest of my tense body. I do a few quick yoga poses, imagining all my muscles softening and releasing their energy through the skin. In my mind, I'm steaming, like a pool of molten lava, venting through the surface to prevent implosion. Sliding my feet to the right, I find the soft grass, lower, and fold myself forward into child's pose.

As I rest and fight to keep my mind clear, I hear birds. Somewhere nearby there are hungry nestlings calling out for their mama and also a hawk, squawking from the sky. Do hawks eat baby birds? No, surely not...mice, rats, and rabbits maybe, but not birds, right? But don't they eat chickens?

Even in yoga, I worry.

"Mrs. Cartwright, are you okay?" The sitter has poked her head through the front door to check on the crazy lady laying, face-down, in the front yard.

I lift my head from the ground and wipe a few blades of grass from my forehead. "Yeah, fine...just stretching. I'll shower quick so you can go."

Minutes later, as the hot water runs over my skin, all I can see is fire being thrown onto the lava pool. I reach forward and turn the water to cool.

Megan's in town. She came right away after getting that call from Bonnie. I've kept my distance since she arrived. I know they deserve their time together, uninterrupted, but I can't help but to feel envious. I don't know how much longer Bonnie has and I hate that I'm missing it.

I sit on the shower bench, lower my head into my hands, let the water run down my back, and make a decision. It's time to meet Megan.

21

BONNIE

The following Tuesday, Noah and I stop for coffee on the way to Bonnie's. I order an extra one for Megan. I have a feeling she may need it.

I can't imagine watching Mama die—watching her slip away before my eyes. How would I explain it to the kids? At least, with Bonnie being in her seventies, that must mean Megan's kids are probably older—better able to understand. And how tragic is that? That as we age, our innocence is ripped from our being and something as devastating as death becomes understandable—acceptable even. Commonplace.

I round the corner onto Bonnie's street, make my way to her driveway, and park behind a white Tesla with fancy wheels and low-profile tires. Moments later, we're standing at the door and Noah rings the bell.

The door swings open and standing before me is a much younger version of Bonnie, right down to the beautiful, thin-lipped smile.

"Hi. You must be Jenna and Noah?" she asks.

"Yes, that's us. And you're Megan?"

"Yup. Y'all come on in. Mom's resting in her room, but will be up soon." She steps back, opening the door further, and motions for us to enter.

I'm surprised she's so young; probably about my age. And I've never seen a woman look so much like her mother.

"You look—"

"Exactly like her, I know," she says with a roll of her eyes. "You're surprised by my age, too, right? Most people are when they first meet me."

I guide Noah to the kitchen and set the coffee cups on the table, pushing one toward Megan as we both take a seat. "Yeah, I guess I am."

She picks up the cup and holds it up as if to toast with mine. "Thanks for this. I've yet to find any decent coffee in this town. Maybe a local's pick will be the one." She takes a sip. "Hmm, not bad!" Her words say one thing, but her face says another.

I give a little smile and then her sing-songy laughter fills the room and seems to bounce off the walls. I look down the hallway toward Bonnie's room, wondering if we've woken her.

"Oh, don't worry about her. She sleeps through anything these days. And as for my age, well, Mama was a bit of a free spirit. I was a 'whoops' baby, though she refers to me as an 'unexpected gift'." She laughs again. "She was forty when she had me."

"Wow, I didn't know. So you're..."

"Thirty-three," she interrupts. "And no, I'm not married. I don't have any kids either."

"And no brothers or sisters?"

"No. It's only me and Mom." She looks down at the lid of her coffee cup and runs her finger around the rim.

"All of this must be very hard for you, then."

"It is, but I'm not sure there's been enough time to process it all," she says. "Stubborn woman waited until the very end to call me—sorry if that's crass—but damn her for that." She shakes her head, then takes a sip of her coffee. "In all fairness, Mom and I have never been close. Our relationship is a bit—off-beat."

"How so? I mean, you don't have to answer that if you don't want to."

"No, it's fine. I don't mind," she says as she stands and moves to the paper towel roll near the kitchen sink, tearing off two. She wipes the outside of her coffee cup with one of the paper towels, and peers out the window into the backyard for a moment before she continues.

"Well, I mentioned she was forty when I was born, right?" She turns back to me, leans against the sink, and folds her arms across her chest. "Mom has never been married. She's never even been in a serious relationship that lasted more than a couple of years, that I'm aware of. She never wanted to be married. Never wanted to be a mother. She enjoyed her freedom and the fact her life was all her own. It doesn't make her selfish in my mind, and it's never bothered me she felt that way. She simply knew who she was—and who she wasn't."

I nod to show I'm listening, but I'm having a hard time believing that the Bonnie I know could ever have been such a person. She's so wonderful with Noah and so much like a grandmother to me that it all seems impossible.

Megan returns to her seat at the table and hands me the second paper towel. I fold it in half and place it under my cup.

"But, to her surprise, she became pregnant with me at thirty-nine and her whole world changed. I don't know how much you know about Mom, but her most treasured memories involve a starry sky, a campfire, and lots and lots of substances and sordid behavior." She sniggers, then shakes her head once more. "A true hippie, if there ever was one."

"So, what was it like then? Your childhood, I mean."

"It was fine. No trauma to report here. Mom comes from old money, which she always refused to accept until I was born. Then, I guess she justified it by claiming the money was for me, rather than for her. There were nannies, a cook, and a housekeeper. I was never left alone or neglected. Mom was around, but she wasn't involved as much as mothers are these days." She looks over at Noah, playing with toys on the rug, and smiles. "She's mellowed—softened—with age, and I think she may regret that somewhat now."

"It's hard to imagine her as the hippie she—and you—claim her to be." I say, gesturing to the fine furnishings all around us.

"Oh, this all belonged to her parents. When they passed away, they left her their fortune, as well as their entire estate. I think she felt guilty about not being the daughter they wanted her to be, so she put it all in storage, then brought some of it here when she bought this house. The art, a lot of the books, the chandeliers—this table." She runs her hand along the worn wood of the dining room table. "I think it's her homage to them. And it makes it feel like home for her, even though they're gone."

Megan points to the portrait of the woman over the fireplace. "That's my grandmother, there on the mantel."

I have never examined the portrait closely or bothered to ask Bonnie who it was. The family resemblance isn't there as much as it is with Bonnie and Megan, but looking again, I can see a bit of familiarity in the eyes.

"So, when did you move to Houston?" I ask her.

"Shortly after my twenty-first birthday. I had no intention of moving there. I went to visit a friend for her bachelorette party, but I met someone. Then the restaurant I was working at opened a location in Houston a few months later. I took it as a sign and put in for the transfer."

"And that didn't work out?"

"The job? Yes, I manage several of their Houston locations now. The relationship? Eh—it did, and it didn't. We were together for eight years. When gay marriage was legalized nation-wide, Allison wanted to be one of the first in line. I wasn't ready, though. And Mom was going through cancer then, too—it just wasn't a good time.

"Allison thought I was ashamed of her—of us. She didn't understand why I didn't talk with Mom about our relationship more often or why I didn't come home for the holidays and bring her with me. No matter how many times I tried to explain that we had never had a close relationship, that we'd never been ones to talk on the phone every day or spend every holiday together, she didn't believe me. She just couldn't wrap her head around the idea that some women are not best friends with their mother. I mean, she and her mother were close, so I guess I understand why she would think that, but there was just no convincing her that my lack of a relationship with *mine* didn't have anything to do with shame or embarrassment of *her*."

"So, why haven't you been close with Bonnie then?"

"I honestly don't know. We just never bonded in that way. I had nannies growing up, and I moved away pretty young, so it's never felt odd to me that we don't have the typical mother-daughter relationship. We love each other, of course, but if we go a couple of months without being in touch, there's nothing strange or offensive about that for us. That's hard for some people to understand."

The sound of a television coming to life from Bonnie's room catches both of our attention.

"I guess Sleeping Beauty has awakened. Let me go check to see if she needs anything and if she's up for company." Megan stands and moves down the hallway to Bonnie's room. She gives a light tap on the door before pushing it open.

A moment later, she returns.

"She's asking for you," she tells me. "But don't be alarmed if she drifts off to sleep again. She's on a lot of meds and has a hard time staying awake."

Nodding my head in understanding, I rise, straighten my shirt, and start on my way to Bonnie's room.

Bonnie is sitting upright in her bed, leaning against the headboard. The TV remote lies in her lap and she has a cup of water in her left hand.

"Jenna, it is so good to see you," she says. "Come. Sit with me." She points to the chair at the side of the bed and I walk over, give her a peck on the cheek, and sit, as she requests. "Well, tell me, what have those little angels been doing to keep you on your toes since we last spoke?"

"Well, Audrey has made the honor roll at school again."

"Mm-hmm." She nods.

"But still never seems to bring that model behavior home with her in the afternoons."

"No, of course not. She's comfortable at home. You better get used to that." Bonnie takes a sip from her water cup.

"And Ryan has a newfound love of snakes." I grimace to show my displeasure.

"Oh, goodness. So long as he's not bringing them into the house, right?"

"Exactly." I shudder at the thought. "And Noah, well, he's Noah. Adorable and ornery as always."

"Aw, is he here? I'd like to see him," she says.

"Yes, he's here. Playing in the living room. I imagine Megan is keeping him company."

"So?"

"So, what?"

"What do you think of Megan?"

"Um, she seems very nice. Very smart," I answer.

"That she is." Bonnie smiles. "Have you two talked?"

"Yes, a little, before you woke."

"Okay, I must confess. I know you did. I may have overheard bits and pieces of your conversation in the kitchen."

"Bonnie! You were eavesdropping?" I ask with a laugh.

"Only a little." She gestures with her thumb and forefinger to emphasize *little*. "It's not my fault your voices carry under the door. And she's right. But that's not all of it, love."

"What do you mean?"

"I mean, there's more to the story that I assume she didn't want to share with you because she didn't feel it was her place."

"Oh?"

"Yes. It wasn't that I never wanted to have children or to become a wife." She purses her lips together a bit and takes a deep breath, as if steadying herself to go on. "My upbringing was rather sterile. My parents were even more aloof than I was with Megan.

"I was raised by the help, and I rebelled against it from an early age...all of it. I was desperate for my parents' love and attention and determined to gain it, one way or another. I was a rather mischievous child from the start, and as I grew to be, oh, I don't know—eleven or twelve years old—I started to notice boys. Then, everything got worse.

"I was sneaking them into the house after dark, sneaking out to meet them in the woods behind the house, skipping school to be with them. You name it. I was learning things I shouldn't have learned, at way too early of an age."

Her face is sad as she takes a moment of silence, then continues.

"It was when I was fourteen that I was taken advantage of for the first time."

I feel my mouth open in horror and disbelief.

"Then again at fifteen, and many more times after that."

"Bonnie, you were—"

"Yes, love. But I told no one, because nearly every time it happened, I was drinking or partaking in some substance I shouldn't have, or placed myself in a location or situation in which I never should have been. I blamed myself. I know now, I shouldn't have. I should've told someone—asked for help. I know it wasn't my fault. But it was a different time then. So many things were still taboo; enveloped in shame. So many things still brought dishonor upon a family and that was not something I could do.

"As I grew to be an older teenager, around seventeen, I became angrier than ever at my parents. How could they not see what was happening to me? Why did they not help? Why didn't they care? So, that was when I decided I didn't want to be shackled. Not to them, not to anyone. I left home and never returned."

"You were seventeen?"

"Eighteen by the time I left," she clarifies. "At such a young age, I saw and experienced so much, and I knew the only way I could ever survive was if I maintained full control. I was smart enough by then to know how to handle myself in…certain situations…so I never found myself abused again in the way I was when I was younger. But to me, betrothing myself to someone was out of the question. I would never let anyone have that power over me again. So, I never married. I always thought maybe if I met the right person, I would feel differently, and I did meet the right person—a couple of times. Megan's father being one. But I could never bring myself to do it."

"So, when I found myself pregnant with Megan, I was scared. I didn't know how to parent a child in a way that differed from my own upbringing, and I didn't want her to become damaged, like I was. I loved—love—her more than anything. So, I hired nannies and housekeepers who I knew could offer her so much more than I ever could. Women who could offer more than my nannies ever did for me. I surrounded her with smart, educated women. Strong women. Women who were kind, caring mothers to their own children. I wanted her to have the best, always, and I was smart enough to know that wasn't me. I was more involved than my parents ever were, but I wasn't the mother I should have been."

"Oh, Bonnie."

"What have I told you about that 'oh, Bonnie' nonsense? I don't need it. I'm not asking for it. I've done what I've done, and I accept it. No need for pity or sympathy. Just a bit of understanding would be fine."

"I do understand." I understand better than she probably thinks I do. So many times, I've held those same feelings of not being good enough for my own children. If I had the means—and the guts—to hire someone to take over for me in raising them, I would have done it too. For my sanity, but most importantly, for their benefit.

"But how do you feel about it now? Motherhood—and having Megan nearby?"

"Like I've missed out on so much." She turns her head to look out the window. "She is an amazing human being, despite my lack of ability to take credit for it."

"She loves you, Bonnie. She doesn't blame you for anything or harbor any bad feelings. She told me so."

"I know. Like I said, she's an amazing person." Bonnie sighs and tilts her head back to lean against the headboard. "I'm tired, love. Might we talk more later?"

"Yes, of course. You get some rest." I squeeze her hand, take the water cup, and place it on the nightstand before heading back to the kitchen.

Noah and I visit with Megan a while longer, then take our leave. I'm eager to get home, put him down for a nap, and crack open my journal while Bonnie's words are still fresh in my mind.

Settled onto our bed and staring at the blank page before me, snippets of our conversation find their way to the page.

"I was learning things I shouldn't have learned, at way too early of an age."

"I blamed myself."

"The only way I could ever survive was if I maintained full control."

"I would never let anyone have that power over me again."

"I was scared...I didn't want her to become damaged, like I was."

"I've missed out on so much."

"I love her more than anything."

I write "Bonnie" at the top of the page. I doodle in the margins to show a campfire under the stars, a bouquet of tears, and what I perceive to be a young child all alone and fearful in the woods.

Bonnie's story may be the most heartbreaking of all. Aside from Mama's, hers is the only one I've heard that is permeated with pure ill intention. Even Mama's story of wrongdoings by my father doesn't compare with the evil Bonnie experienced at such a young age.

And that guilt and fear you're never going to be good enough—that your own children would be better off if left in someone else's hands—well, that's something I know all too well. Not to mention the regret she feels, when she was only doing what she felt was best.

It's all too much.

I close the journal, lie back, and stare at the ceiling, watching the fan blades cast shadows across the room as they move. Suddenly, an overwhelming feeling of urgency strikes me at my core. I sit up and move to the edge of the bed, feet planted on the ground, and stare across the hills lying outside the bedroom window.

This is important. All of it.

These stories need to be told beyond my ears and beyond this journal. We need to know we are not alone. GiGi, Aunt Kitty, and Gloria were not alone. Mama was not alone. Bonnie was not alone. Michelle, Maggie, and I are not alone.

It's a tale as old as time. Mothers bearing the weight of the world, with feelings of loneliness, anger, and inadequacy always bubbling beneath the surface. From decades ago, to decades in the future, it will persist.

How many will not survive it? How many will come as close as I did to a fateful meeting with a power pole or other tantalizing form of perceived instant release?

No, these stories need to be told, and it looks like I must be the one to tell them.

22

GONE

"Bonnie's not doing well," I tell Charlene several weeks later. "I visit her often, but I can't remember the last time she was awake when I was there. I miss our talks, the tea, watching old movies, listening to music—" I pick at a loose thread on the corner of the chair. "I just miss her."

"I'm sorry to hear that. How are you taking care of yourself when you're feeling sad or overwhelmed by all of this?"

"Well, having Megan here is nice. I hate to admit it, but at first, I felt like having her here would interfere with my time with Bonnie. I didn't want to share the special thing we have with someone else, which was selfish, I know."

"And now?"

"Now, I'm glad she's here. I'm glad she's had a chance to spend time with Bonnie and they've had time to talk things through. Their relationship has never been close, but now, I think it's changed. And Megan has been so kind to me. I think if I were in her shoes, I would be upset that another woman had grown so close to my mother when I was never close to her myself. But, she's just so...understanding about it all. And I can see so much of Bonnie in her, too. It's just—nice to have her around."

"I see. And how are things at home?" Charlene asks.

"Things at home are better. Still crazy as ever, but I think Andrew's more perceptive to when I need a break than he was before. But there are still days when I just can't do it. I don't want to do it. I can't handle the noise, or the fighting, and I just want to be alone."

"Well, what do you do on those days?"

"I don't hide in my car anymore, if that's what you mean." I laugh nervously at this, knowing how ridiculous it must sound. "And I've read the book Michelle gave me and learned a lot from that. So, I think I handle it better now, but that all feels like a change in what's visible on the outside. On the inside, I'm still screaming—praying for relief; a chance to get away from it all. That's what visits with Bonnie always were for me—a chance to get away. I don't know what I'll do without her." Tears careen down my cheeks and I reach for a tissue on the coffee table.

"Jenna, have you reached out to Maggie? Or any other friends you have nearby?"

When was the last time I talked to Maggie? I texted her in Asher, and then again the week after I got back, but I haven't seen or heard from her since. "No, I haven't," I reply.

"Well, maybe that would be a good start."

"Okay, I hear you. I'll call Maggie."

<hr>

Sitting on the deck, sipping my morning coffee before the kids wake, I open my laptop and pick up where I left off two days ago. Chronicling the stories of the women in my life has taken more of a toll on me than I ever imagined it would. Their stories are heartbreaking and typing them out only makes me re-live hearing them all over again.

I want to give up. I don't want to do this anymore, but something continues to drive me forward, urging me to get these stories out into the world so others can hear them, too. If they saved me, who am I to not bring them to life when they could potentially save someone else?

The patio door opens and Audrey steps outside with a bowl of cereal in her hand.

"Mama, can I have my breakfast out here with you?" The look on her face tells me she doesn't know what to expect. Will I be angry she's interrupting my time alone, spout ugly words to make her feel bad about it, then send her back inside? Or will I smile and draw her near? That look breaks my heart.

"Of course, honey. Pull up a seat," I say with an open arm, to let her know I want a hug.

One thing I've learned through all of this is that I'm presented with dozens of choices every day with these three, and I don't always do the right thing. I'm much more capable now of recognizing the choices when they're presented to me, and I've come a long way. Still though, there are times when I choose anger or frustration as a response. But I can only take it one choice at a time, and in this moment, with my oldest child at my side, I choose love.

We've been knocking at Bonnie's door for several minutes, but with no response. Finding it unlocked, I crack it open a few inches. "Megan, it's Jenna and Noah. Can we come in?" Still no reply.

"Come on, honey. Let's make sure everything's all right." I take Noah by the hand and we enter through Bonnie's front door. I check the sitting room, living room, patio, and kitchen, but Megan is nowhere to be found. Turning toward the hallway, we head toward Bonnie's bedroom. The door is ajar, and I see Megan sleeping in the chair next to Bonnie's bed. She's covered with the afghan blanket from the living room and her head is leaned over to one shoulder. Her breathing is slow, steady, and in-sync with Bonnie's—as if she were once again an infant, finding cadence with her mother's own breath.

I turn to lead Noah back down the hallway, but Megan stirs and catches my eye through the crack in the door. She stands, lays the blanket over the arm of the chair, then joins us in the hall.

"Hey, sorry I didn't hear you ring the bell," she says with a yawn.

"Yeah, no worries. How are you? How is she?" I ask, pointing at Bonnie's bedroom door.

"Uh—I'm exhausted. She's still Sleeping Beauty." Megan scratches her head. "I have a hard time shutting down my brain. Overthinking doesn't lead to much sleep."

"Don't I know it. Come on, let's put on some tea and a movie. We'll just zone out and all three take a nap today."

I head to the kitchen and put on the kettle. Megan turns on the TV, gives up on selecting a movie, and puts on cartoons for Noah instead. Before either of us has finished a single cup of tea, we're dozing on opposite ends of the sofa, with Noah entertaining himself quietly on the living room rug.

Driving to Bonnie's house again today, I think of how much all our roles have changed. Before, Bonnie was my rock. She let me read, sleep, talk, and cry all I needed to and passed no judgment for it at all. Now, she's the one sleeping and I'm the one assisting with not only her needs but also for those of a daughter who is now feeling the full weight of grief, even while her mother still breathes.

I pull into the driveway and park behind Megan's car. I take a deep, steady breath, then walk to the door. Megan asked me not to ring or knock anymore, so I open the door and walk to the kitchen.

She's sleeping on the sofa again. I don't think she's slept in the guest room for at least a week.

"Megan," I say, nudging her shoulder.

"Hmm?" she asks, half awake.

"Why don't you go to bed?"

"Can't. Hospice nurse will be here soon," she replies.

"And I can handle it. I know how to open a door. Megan, go to bed." I nudge her a little harder.

"Okay, if you insist," she replies.

"I do. And I don't want to see you again before 3:00. I know you're not sleeping at night. You need the rest."

She gives a thumbs up over her right shoulder, as she walks down the hallway to the guest room—to her room. I walk down the hall at the opposite end of the house to check on Bonnie. Surprisingly, she's awake.

"Well, hey there, pretty lady. Good morning," I say with a peck on her forehead.

"Jenna, where have you been?" she asks me.

"Where have *I* been? I've been here, with you, like always. You're the one on permanent vacation in Dreamland." I smile and hold her hand.

"Yes, I suppose you're right. Where's Megan?"

"Just sent her to bed. She was crashed out on the couch when I got here."

"And Noah?" Bonnie asks with a hopeful expression.

"Oh, I left him with the sitter today. I needed a break, too."

"Oh." She visibly deflates.

"Well, I'll bring him tomorrow. How's that? At this same time, so maybe we can catch you awake again."

"Okay," she says, without the sound of much hope.

"Jenna, how is Megan? I fear this is all too much for her."

"She's struggling a bit, yes, but I'm here for her, Bonnie. Here for her, just as you've always been here for me. We're all just taking care of each other now."

"Good. As it should be." Bonnie leans her head to the right and peers through the open curtains. Then she sleeps once again.

———◇———

It's been two weeks since the last time I saw Bonnie awake. Megan has been blessed with a few conversations with her since that day, which is why she doesn't sleep. She never knows when Bonnie will wake and she doesn't want to miss the opportunity to talk with her, love on her, *be* with her while she can.

As Bonnie continues to drift farther and farther from us, Megan seems to chase her, hoping somehow to bring her back. She sits at her bedside, holds her hand, reads passages from Bonnie's favorite books, and tells her stories from her life—some are childhood stories which Bonnie may remember and find comforting, and others are adventures she's had in her adult life, without Bonnie. She brushes her hair, massages her arms and legs, and tries every trick she can think of to get Bonnie to sip water or tiny bits of a protein shake through a straw.

Now, though, it's only a matter of time, and we all know that time is fleeting.

I've taken up the role of house manager: ordering groceries, scheduling hospice visits, coordinating with Bonnie's assistant for what days are best for cleaning and which meals to prepare for Megan.

Now, as I comb through the mail, tossing out the junk and placing anything that could be important in a pile for Megan's review, my eyes land on the back of her head as she sips coffee at the dining room table.

Her shoulders rise with a sharp inhale, then I see them bounce along with her silent sobs. Pulling out the chair next to her, I join her at the table. She wipes her face with both hands.

"It's okay to cry, you know. You are allowed to have feelings." I give her a sideways hug around the shoulders. "Nobody expects you not to. And if you're afraid you need to be brave for her, you don't.

She loves you—and she can't see you out here, anyway. It's okay to cry."

"I just—I can't—" Her words are lost as she fights for breath. "I just wish things—would've been different."

"I know. I'm sorry." I hug her again. Her head drops onto my shoulder, and she lets go.

So much pain and regret. Is this how my children will feel when I'm nearing the end? When I'm gone? Will they wish things would've been different? That I would've let them in just a bit more?

They're only yours for such a brief moment in time and it's gone in the blink of an eye. God, how is GiGi always so right about everything?

Megan pulls herself upright. "Excuse me," she says before heading down the hallway to the bathroom. A few moments later, she returns with a tissue box in one hand. Her eyes are puffy, but dry.

"Do we have anything to drink around here? Or does the old bitty keep nothing stronger than that damn tea?" she asks.

"I'll go get something. Pick your poison."

"Wine. And beer. And vodka. Hell, just buy the whole store."

She is truly a clone of her mother.

"You got it. Be back in twenty."

"All right, I have supplies," I announce upon walking back through the front door. I move to the kitchen and unpack bottles of red and white wine, three different kinds of beer (a light, an amber, and a dark), a plain bottle of vodka, and a fruit infused vodka, too. Plus, several kinds of juices and mineral water for mixers, a bag of ice, and burgers I picked up through the Whataburger drive through.

"I know you try to take it easy on the meat, but who can say no to Whataburger?" I ask her.

"Not me." Megan tears open the packaging on a cheeseburger and goes in for a big bite. "What's with all the variety, though? Dang."

"Wasn't sure what you prefer, so I went for a range. Too much?"

"Maybe a little, but desperate times—" Megan shrugs and picks up each type of beer, eyeing the label. She settles on the amber, which is the only cold six-pack of the three.

I pull my phone from my back pocket and text Andrew.

"If it's okay with you, I'd like to stay here with Megan for a while."

"Of course. Will you be home for dinner then?" he texts back.

"I don't think so. You guys can order in or eat the pasta leftovers, whatever's easiest."

"Okay, we'll figure it out."

"Thanks, Andrew."

"Sending love letters?" Megan asks with a smile.

"Ha—no, letting him know I'm off the hook for dinner tonight."

"Well played," she says.

"Yeah, well, you learn the tricks over time." I crack open a beer for myself and put the rest in the fridge.

I stay with Megan into the early hours of the morning, listening to her tell stories of Bonnie's colorful past and a few of her own too.

When I crawl into bed somewhere around 4:30 in the morning, I realize we had four beers between the two of us, over all that time. I guess it wasn't so much the alcohol Megan craved, but the company.

I'll visit her more often. Even if Bonnie's rarely awake, I'll do it for Megan. And I think when I call GiGi this Sunday, I'll ask her for advice. What was it she needed most after losing Grandpa Philip? How can I help Megan the way Aunt Kitty helped her?

And then another thought comes—who's going to help *me* when I lose *my* friend?

Oh, Bonnie—don't go just yet. We still need you. I need time to figure this out. I cannot make a mess of everything again. I need to find a path—a way forward.

Sweet Bonnie, please hold on.

"Morning," Megan says as I walk through Bonnie's front door a few days later.

"Good morning. How's she doing today?" I ask her.

"Um—I think it could be any day now. The hospice nurse talked with me this morning about what signs to expect as she's getting closer, and well, we're there." Megan refills her coffee mug.

"Oh, no."

"Yeah," Megan says.

"Wow—I don't even know what to say. I just—I want to cry."

"You and me both," she says.

"Has she been awake at all?"

"No, not in the last two days."

"Okay, well—what do we do?" I ask.

"We sit with her. And we wait."

"Do you need a break? A nap? I'll wake you if I need to," I tell her.

"No, I'm okay. I want to be with her."

I squeeze Megan's hand and we walk down the hall to Bonnie's room. Megan takes a deep breath before pushing the door open and entering. She takes a seat in the chair next to Bonnie's bed and I sit on the dining room chair we've brought in for the days when we're both in here together.

"Should I turn on the TV?" Megan asks.

"Sure."

Megan clicks it on and scans the channels.

"Wait, go back," I say.

She flips back a couple of channels and there it is: *City Wives* of—Houston? Seattle? I don't even know.

"Stop. Let's try it." I laugh.

"Really?"

"Yes! GiGi told me it's her guilty pleasure. I'd like to see what I've been missing out on all these years."

"I'd venture to say, not much." She leaves it on the channel.

A few minutes later, we hear, "Oh, my—what is *this?*"

Megan and I both turn our heads in disbelief.

"Mom!" Megan cries.

"Oh, Bonnie, it's so good to see you awake!" I say to her.

"Well, if there's anything that can wake the dead, it's probably this." Bonnie gestures toward the TV.

"I'll be sure to let GiGi know you disapprove," I say with a smile. "Bonnie, is it okay if I call Andrew and ask him to bring the kids by? Noah's been asking for you. And I'd like you to meet Ryan and Audrey, too."

Megan looks at me, concerned.

"Only if you both approve—" I tell her.

"I would give anything to see that baby," Bonnie replies.

Megan gives a little nod. "Okay, Mom, if you're up for it."

Bonnie nods.

I excuse myself and text Andrew.

"Bonnie's awake. Bring the kids. And hurry!"

"Are you sure?" Andrew asks upon entering Bonnie's sitting room with all three kids.

"Yes, Andrew. I'm sure. I'll take them in one at a time."

They take turns, each getting about ten minutes with Bonnie, and Andrew gets to meet her too. Then, she asks for water and a few minutes alone with Megan.

"Thank you, Jenna," Andrew says to me as we sit at the table on the back patio, letting the kids play in the yard.

"For what?"

"For thinking of us. For inviting us here to meet your friend, too."

"I should have done it sooner," I reply. "I think I was in denial. Or maybe I was just being selfish."

"You have every right to be selfish about Bonnie. God knows, there's not much else in your life you get to be selfish about."

Just then, a cool breeze blows through the yard—an odd occurrence for the Fourth of July in Texas. One of Bonnie's pink flamingos spins on its stake. Its face now appears to be keeping watch over the patio and the kids in the yard, while its rotating wings spin fast, as if trying to take flight. Andrew gives me a look that says, "that's weird," which is what I'm thinking, too.

A few moments later, Megan appears, with tears running down her cheeks and a look which tells us all we need to know. Bonnie is gone.

23

TEMPTATION

Andrew and I load the kids back into the car, then I return inside the house to check on Megan.

"Hey, do you want me to stay?" I ask her.

"No, go home. I've called the hospice agency and the funeral home already. They're on their way."

"But I can stay. You shouldn't have to go through this alone."

"I can't ask you to do that, Jenna."

"You're not asking me. I'm insisting."

She falls to the sofa in tears.

"Okay, let me tell Andrew he can go on without me. I'll be right back."

I jog toward the front door and up to the driver's side of Andrew's truck. He rolls down the window.

"You guys go. I'm going to stay with Megan."

"Do you want me to call the sitter and come back?"

"No, that's okay. I just don't want her to be alone. I'll see you guys later, okay?" I blow kisses to the kids in the back seat and Andrew pulls my head through the window and gives me a kiss, too.

"Call me if you need anything," he says.

"Okay."

I return to the house and Megan hasn't moved from the sofa. She's staring at the wall, with a faraway look, focused on nothing at all.

"What can I do? What do you need?" I ask her.

"My mother. I need my mother." Her voice cracks and she begins to sob.

"Megan, I'm so sorry." I sit next to her on the sofa and wrap my arm around her shoulders.

"I can't believe she's gone. We didn't have enough time. We wasted so much of our time. I never should have moved to Houston—"

"You were living your life. You did nothing wrong. You can't be blamed for that."

"How could I not see? I should've known better. She was already forty when I was born. I should have realized what that meant—that our time together would be short. I should have known not to waste it!"

"Megan—"

There's a soft knock at the door. I stand, squeeze her shoulder, and walk over to open it.

"Hello. I'm Gerald, with Abrams Funeral Home. Are you Megan Thompson?" The man at the door is probably in his sixties, with a bald head and kind eyes.

"No, but she's here. Come in." I stand aside and open the door wider for him to enter as Megan appears by my side.

"I'm Megan," she says.

"I'm so sorry for your loss. Can we sit down to talk, just for a moment?" he asks her.

Megan moves to the kitchen and takes a seat at the table. He takes the one across from her and I'm not sure if I should join them or give them their privacy. Megan pulls out the chair next to her and gestures for me to take a seat.

"Your mother was in contact with us a couple of months back," Gerald says as he opens a leather-bound folder with paperwork inside. "She left very specific instructions for how she wanted everything to be handled. She did not want you to be left with any decisions."

Megan nods her head. "That sounds about right."

"We will take care of everything. If there's anything that comes up that requires your assistance, we'll be in touch. You should hear from our office tomorrow regarding setting a time and date for the service."

Megan nods again.

"Do you have any questions for me now?" he asks her.

"I don't think so," she replies.

"Okay. Can you take me to her now or would you like more time?"

I look over at Megan and she's lost in space. I'm not even sure she heard his question.

"I can take you," I answer.

We both stand from the table, and I walk toward the hallway leading to Bonnie's room.

"Wait—" Megan says. "What am I supposed to do? I mean, you leave with her...and she's just gone? What do I do after you take her and it's just me in this house? In her house?"

"Do you have family you can call?" Gerald asks her.

Megan turns her head, closes her eyes, and brings her hand to her forehead, massaging the brow bone with thumb and forefinger. Then she pinches her tear ducts and her chin quivers.

"I'm her family. I'll stay with her," I answer.

There's another knock at the door and I open it to find a doctor from the hospice service. I show both him and Gerald to Bonnie's room, where she is officially pronounced dead and removed from our lives forever.

I stay with Megan for hours. We don't talk or eat or even move from our spots on the sofa. Yet somehow, just being in each other's presence is comforting. Around 11:30, Megan insists I go home to my family. We're both cried out, for now, and tired from the emotional weight of the day.

"I need sleep, I think," she says to me when I voice concerns about leaving her alone. "And there's no reason for you to be here if I'm just going to sleep."

"Okay, but I'll be back first thing in the morning. And you can call me if you need anything—at any time."

"I know. Thank you." She gives me a hug and walks me to the door.

"I'm really sorry, Megan." I tell her. "But she knew how much you loved her. I can promise you that."

Megan nods her head and wipes away her tears. I give her one more hug before turning to leave.

In the car, I sit for a moment, alone.

She's gone. She's really gone.

My heart is heavy and broken. *She saved my life.*

Did she know how thankful I was? *Did I tell her enough?*

The movement of one of Bonnie's spinning pinwheels catches my eye, startling me. The air is heavy with the smell of burned paper and smoke from the evening's fireworks and somewhere, a few blocks over, one screams and shoots up into the sky. It explodes into a giant flower of sparkling gold and crackles as it falls back to the earth.

I can't do this. I can't bury her. I can't be strong for Megan. I can't lose my friend.

But she's already gone.

Panic comes upon me. I start the car, eager to get away from this house; to be anywhere but here. I back out of the driveway, find my way out of the neighborhood, and drive the ten minutes from Bonnie's to the highway intersection which splits the town in half. The light turns red, and I stop.

Our house is straight ahead, on the other side of the city, past the highway. I can see the turn that will take me to our neighborhood. But I can also see the sign pointing me to the right, toward the highway on-ramp. The urge to make that right turn is real and strong, but where would I go? Not back to Asher this time, that's for sure.

No, this time, I would need to disappear. I would need to go someplace where I know no one. Somewhere I wouldn't have to try so damn hard to never again hurt anyone I love with my temper, my words, my rage. Somewhere I would never again be hurt by losing someone I love.

I make the right turn and accelerate onto the on-ramp. It's like déjà vu, as I once again attempt to outrun all the horrible things I'm dying to leave behind.

If I just drive far enough, fast enough, get enough distance from this town—*I won't feel the pain.*

One hundred and eight miles per hour is as fast as this van will let me go. I count the mile markers as they're reflected in the headlights—twelve, thirteen, fourteen.

Then, my phone rings. I glance over at it in the passenger seat. It's Andrew.

I can't breathe. *What am I doing?*

I can't do this again. That would mean it's all been for nothing; that I learned nothing. That GiGi's story, and Mama's, and everyone else's doesn't matter at all. It would mean that none of it was enough to save me—*to convince me to save myself.*

I pull over onto the shoulder of the highway and wail and scream at the top of my lungs.

God, why is it so hard?

I pound the steering wheel with my fists and scream until my throat is sore.

Go home, Jenna.

It's my thought, but I hear it in GiGi's voice.

Then I see Andrew, Audrey, Ryan, and Noah; a figment of my imagination, but they're there. Is that what they will become if I continue down this road? Figments of my imagination? Would I someday wonder if they ever even existed at all?

No. I refuse to give in. I refuse to lose. I refuse to die.

I merge back onto the highway and search for the next exit, to turn around and go home. I'll call Andrew back, tell him I'm on my way, and push on. I know now, I have no other choice.

No, I know now, that's what I choose.

The phone rings again as I continue to drive, looking for a place to turn around. I reach for it, but it's slid to just beyond my fingertips. I lean further over to reach it and then—the horrific sound of crunching metal, the feeling of having hit a wall, the world a spinning blur, and a scream I don't recognize as my own.

As the van comes to a stop, I squint over the half-inflated airbag, trying to make sense of it all—but can see nothing but a kaleidoscope of shattered glass and deep red blood.

I wake to sirens and flashing lights. Then again, all is dark.

I wake a second time in the back of an ambulance, with people poking and prodding me from either side of where I lay. The lights are bright, and the voices seem *so loud*. The siren screeches and my head pounds.

What have I done? I take it all back. I don't want to die—I can't leave my kids.

Please don't take me from them now.

I try to sit up, but my neck, arms, and legs are strapped tight. I can't move, and I'm confused.

"Ma'am, please, be calm. You've been in a car accident and we're on the way to the hospital now."

"My husband—call—my husband," I say.

"We will, ma'am. Please try to stay calm."

Then it all comes back.

Bonnie's dead. Megan's alone. Andrew's waiting.

I feel the vomit rising and cough. Just as it reaches my lips and begins to spew, the paramedic shoves a hissing tube into my mouth, stabbing into the back of my throat.

I gag and vomit in cycles, as the tube sucks it all away. The putrid smell, the warm, claustrophobic confines, the strangers trying to keep me calm—it all feels like a terrifying, lucid dream.

When I come-to a third time, I can't open my eyes, but I hear Andrew's muffled voice, along with someone else's.

"It was a deer. The airbag only partially deployed. She's lucky she wasn't traveling any faster than she was, or her injuries would have been much worse."

"So, what *are* her injuries, then?" Andrew asks.

"We have more tests to run, but right now, there's bruising, a broken pelvis, and a pretty severe concussion."

"A broken hip? From a deer?"

"It's our understanding she over-corrected, the car spun, and there was an impact with a guardrail on the driver's side. The injury to her pelvis is consistent with that type of collision."

"Okay. When will you know more?"

"In a few hours. She's sedated and not likely to wake until morning. You should get some rest."

"Okay, thank you."

And all goes quiet once again.

In my dream, I live in a world with Bonnie, Megan, GiGi, Mama, and Michelle. We play dominoes, sip sweet tea, and watch all our kids run and play in the sprinkler on a hot summer day. We chat about neighborhood gossip while Andrew and Thomas cook on the grill. We roast marshmallows and play cards after the kids have gone to bed. In my dream, we're a real family; together, enjoying *life*.

I feel someone massaging between my pointer finger and thumb on my right hand and could swear I hear Bonnie humming a song. When I open my eyes though, it's not Bonnie at all—it's Andrew, sitting at my bedside.

"Hey there, gorgeous," he says to me.

"Hey," I say with a crackling voice before being thrown into a coughing fit, which sends pain through my ribs and pelvis.

"Whoa, take it easy. Here, sip some water." He holds a plastic cup up to my lips and I sip through the straw. "You have a broken hip and two broken ribs—as well as a concussion—but you're going to be okay." He sets the cup back on the table. "Where were you going, Jenna?"

I close my eyes and tears escape from their corners and roll down my cheeks.

"Yeah, that's what I thought." He leans back into his chair and folds his hands in his lap.

I open my eyes and look at his, which so clearly show all the hurt he's desperately trying to hide. "I was turning around. I was going to go home. The phone rang, and I couldn't reach it, and—"

"Shh. It's okay. We'll talk about it later. You should rest."

I nod. "Megan—someone needs to check on Megan in the morning."

"Well, it is morning, babe. I'll check on her, though. Anything else?"

I shake my head and drift off to sleep.

———◆———

This time, when I dream, I hear their voices so clearly it's almost painful because it feels so real.

"When do you think she'll wake up?" Mama asks.

"I don't know. They're keeping her on pain meds through the IV and she wakes every now and again, then falls back to sleep. They said tomorrow should be better," Andrew replies.

I open my eyes, expecting to see Andrew in the chair next to me, as he's been every other time. Only now, he stands by the window and it's Mama at my side. *Am I still dreaming?*

"Mama?"

"Oh, honey. You scared us, you know." She takes my hand.

"How did you—Did you drive all this way by yourself?"

"No, we all came. The others went out to get food, but they're here."

I'm so tired and overwhelmed and thankful to have Mama here that all I can do is cry.

"Shh, it's okay. You're going to be okay."

"I don't know what happened, Mama. I just—Bonnie died," I say between sobs.

"I know. I'm so sorry." She strokes my hair with one hand and places the other one heavily on my chest, like she used to do when I was a child. "We're going to get through this, okay? *You're* going to get through this. We'll make sure of it."

The door opens and I hear talking and a "Shh!" from GiGi. She and Aunt Kitty enter, with Michelle filing in last. Michelle carries a stack of pizza boxes to the table next to the fold-out sofa.

"Oh, the princess has awakened!" GiGi says, as she approaches the bed to stand next to Mama.

"Hi, GiGi."

"Hello, child. Boy, do you have some 'splainin to do." She says it in her Ricky Ricardo voice, which always makes me laugh, but not today.

Aunt Kitty and Michelle stand on the other side of the bed and Andrew is pushed into the corner to make room for them all.

"I'm going to run home and check on the kids and the sitter—make sure they haven't run her off yet. Is there anything you want me to bring back for you?" he asks.

"Maybe my earbuds and my journal?"

"You got it. See you in a bit." He squeezes my toes and leaves me to the women.

"I can't believe you guys came all this way. I feel like such an idiot," I say, looking straight ahead at my feet.

"Stop it. You know better than that," Mama says.

"Yeah, it got me away from the kids for a bit, so I ain't mad about it," Michelle chimes in with a smile.

"I'm sorry to hear about Bonnie," Aunt Kitty says. "I know she meant a lot to you."

The tears come again, and I can't speak, even if I could find the words.

"Well, where's the TV remote? Maybe we can find something worth watchin'," GiGi says.

Michelle hands it to her from the table on her side of the bed. GiGi clicks it on, and we all watch the programming guide scroll across the bottom half of the screen.

I look around the room at all these women who care so much about me—and for whom I care so much—and for a moment, I almost forget the circumstances which brought them here. For a moment, I feel whole again.

GiGi clicks the remote and the channel changes. *City Wives of Chicago* appears on the screen and there's a communal groan, which echoes around the sterile room.

"What? You got a problem with what I pick? Too bad—I'm gonna watch my show and you're gonna like it. You'll see." GiGi shoos Mama from the chair next to me and makes herself comfortable.

"Laurel, really—" Aunt Kitty protests.

"Shh—it's about to get *real* good."

Michelle folds out the sleeper sofa and she, Mama, and Aunt Kitty cram onto it like best friends at a slumber party.

"Pass the pizza," Aunt Kitty says.

"Yes, ma'am." Michelle grabs the box from the table, snags herself a piece, then passes it on down the line.

24

FAMILY

It's sunny and stifling hot, even so early in the morning. I could say I can't believe Bonnie passed away on the Fourth of July, but the fact is, I can totally believe it. She was such a force; so much so that only fireworks would suffice in marking the occasion.

"Are you ready?" Andrew squeezes my hand as he asks this one unanswerable question.

"I suppose." I wipe my face with a handkerchief I've pulled from my handbag. "I miss her Andrew. I think I will always miss her."

"I'm sure you will. You loved her."

I take a moment to center and prepare myself for goodbye. "Okay, let's go."

He steps out of the rental car, pulls the wheelchair from the back, and makes his way to my door. He helps me into its seat, then we travel up the sidewalk to meet GiGi, Mama, Aunt Kitty and Michelle. I spot Megan, standing with what must be a few friends from Bonnie's church, at the other end of the walk.

"Andrew, can we go say hello to Megan?"

"Of course." He turns my chair toward her, and she smiles as we approach.

"Hey," she bends down to give me a hug.

"Hey," I reply. "Is there anything we can do for you? Anything you need?"

"No, not really. Everything's handled and all arrangements have been put into place. There's a moving company at Mom's house, taking away things I set aside to be sent to Houston—things I'd like to keep. But, how are you?"

"Feeling better. Glad to be out of the hospital and thankful for all those crazy ol' bats." I nod toward my family and smile. Megan gives a little smile, too, but there's pain in her eyes.

"Would you like us to stand with you?" I ask.

"I would, thank you. I don't know any of these people." She wraps her arms around her chest and glances around at the strangers who've gathered to pay their respects to her mother.

I gesture to Michelle and she, as well as all the other women I hold most dear in my life, make their way over to join us.

"This is Megan," I say to them. "She's Bonnie's daughter."

I expect to hear the typical, "I'm so sorry for your loss" line from each of them in turn, but Mama lifts her sunglasses to her head and leans in for a hug. She squeezes Megan tight, taking her by surprise. Then Michelle does the same and Megan lets out a tiny, almost imperceptible little yelp as the emotions become too much. By the time Aunt Kitty has taken her turn, Megan's red in the face from trying so hard to hold back the tears.

Then GiGi steps forward. "It's wonderful to meet you, Megan. You live in Houston, right?"

"Yes, ma'am," she replies.

"Do you have family there?"

"No. Mom was my only family."

"Well, I've heard you and our Jenna have gotten close over the last few weeks. I hope the two of you stay in touch. And maybe for Thanksgiving, you can tag along with her to visit us in Asher."

"I would love that. Thank you," Megan replies.

"Of course. We all need our sisters." She leans in to wrap her arms around Megan and as Megan's chin rests on GiGi's shoulders, tears fall down her face. GiGi takes her hand.

"Shall we?" she says, with a look in my direction.

I nod and we all go together, as a family, to say our goodbyes.

The service was beautiful, with a plethora of pastel pink, purple, and green flowers covering Bonnie's walnut wood casket and surrounding us on all sides. There was a slight breeze to keep us all comfortable, birds singing as a chorus in the distance, and words I recognized from some of Bonnie's favorite books, interspersed with the words and prayers of the minister.

Those same sweetly scented flowers cover every surface of the reception room, except for one table displaying photos from Bonnie's unique and story-filled life, and a guest book laid out for us all to sign. Servers dressed to the nines are mingling amongst the crowd, passing hors d'oeuvres and champagne.

Most of the people here are from Bonnie's church. They're gathered in groups, wiping tears, and telling their favorite stories of their dear old friend.

As I'm enjoying eavesdropping on one conversation about a time when Bonnie caught a young couple canoodling behind the choir curtain, I feel a light touch on my shoulder.

"Hey, can I talk to you for a minute?" Megan asks.

"Of course."

We move to the next room, which is empty, except for a couple of servers preparing trays for their next round. Megan reaches into her handbag and retrieves an envelope, which she hands to me.

"What's this?"

"It's from Mom."

"*What*?" I hold the envelope to my chest, feeling as if I've received mail from the beyond.

"Yes. Open it."

I open the envelope and pull out two pieces of paper. The first is a letter.

Jenna, love. I hope you know how much I've enjoyed what little time we've shared together. You are a beautiful soul with such a big heart. Please accept this small gift of my appreciation for your companionship, your trust, and your love. You know I don't think much of money...never have. But as they say, you can't take it with you, and it might as well be put to good use. My one request: that you use that big heart of yours—and my gift—to do something great for yourself and for others. Not that I need to make that request known, because I know you would of your own accord, but there it is anyway. Please take care of my Megan.

Love you always, Bonnie

I flip to the second page and see an excerpt from what must be Bonnie's will. Skimming the legal-ese and looking for something I can understand, I spot a number. An awfully *big* number.

"What? This can't be right." I look up at Megan and she gives a simple smile.

"That woman, I tell ya', always full of surprises," she says.

"I—Megan, I can't accept this."

"You can. And she wouldn't have left it to you if she didn't think you'd do amazing things. She would've left it all to the animal shelter instead. Those pups got almost as much as I did, as it is."

"Wow. I—uh—I don't know what to say. Thank you."

"Don't thank me. It's Mom's money, not mine." She leans in and gives me a hug.

I say a silent prayer of thanks to God or Bonnie or whoever is listening—then Megan and I rejoin our family in the next room. Still in shock at what I hold in my hands, I search for Andrew. I've already decided exactly what needs to be done with Bonnie's gracious gift.

25

BONNIE'S PLACE

So much has happened in the two years since Bonnie died.

Today, I'm at the welcome counter of Bonnie's Place, stocking courtesy copies of my book right next to the one Michelle recommended in Asher. Just as I place the last one, the bell on the door handle jingles and a young mom walks through it—a baby boy on her hip and three more rambunctious boys in tow.

She glances up at the crystal chandelier hanging over the entry. With Megan's approval, we moved it from Bonnie's house to here, after investing her gift into this old ranch-style home and the acreage that came with it. Sweeping a flyaway strand of hair behind her ear, she says, "Hi. I'm Samantha."

"Welcome. I'm Jenna. Have you been here before?" I ask her.

"No, but my friend has, and she told me I needed to come check it out," the woman replies.

The youngest of the three ambulatory boys is holding onto the ledge of the counter, feet tucked under his butt, swinging like a monkey from a branch.

"All right. Let me show you around."

I take her to the first door on the right side of the entryway. Beside it is a half-wall with a window above, allowing us to see into the adjoining room.

"This is the rumpus room—which would be a great place to leave this little guy to play." I give the tiny monkey a high five. "Nothing in there is breakable, sharp, or in any other way dangerous and we have certified caregivers to watch over the kiddos, just to be safe." I give her a smile, then lead her and the boys down the hallway to the left of this room.

"At the end of this hall, you'll find a sensory-friendly room for little ones who may feel more comfortable without all the noise and distraction. There are quiet toys, books, puzzles, art supplies, and a caregiver in that room as well.

"About halfway down the hall is the nursing room, and this one closest to us is the library." I lead her through the doorway.

The library contains Bonnie's cream chaise sofa, as well as a second one in the same style. The two sofas face each other in the middle of the room, separated by Bonnie's coffee table with the second of her chandeliers hanging above. Bonnie's sitting room chairs live here now, too—one perched on either side of her golden, camel-back sofa tucked beneath the window. Her beautiful paintings are placed throughout, and two long walls are filled with books, many of them also Bonnie's.

"This is amazing. You mean, I can drop them off to play and come in here and...read?"

"Yup. Or scroll on your phone, whatever you choose, so long as it's quiet."

"Wow."

I lead her back out to the main part of the house where she first entered. Behind the counter is a living room, which has been converted into a game room with large, round tables. The fireplace roars with popping firewood, casting cozy shadows and warmth throughout the space, while flicks of gold glimmer in the third chandelier.

"This is our grownup game room. Lots of moms meet here to play cards, bunco, dominoes, and such. All the games are on that bookshelf, but you're welcome to bring in your own as well." There are two tables full of ladies here now, including Maggie, who looks up from her cards to give a wave.

"To the right of the game room, we have a mini theater for the older kiddos. We show a movie at the top of the even hours, and we open it up for video games in between movies."

We move to the left side of the game room and through the archway opposite the theater room. What once was the kitchen and formal dining room has been combined to create one large kitchen area with long tables down its center.

"You'll find coffee, snacks, water, and sodas in here...even microwavable lunches in the freezer. The kitchen is for everyone. Pack a lunch for your kiddos, stick them in the fridge, then go enjoy yourself. When they get hungry, you're welcome to pull up a chair and enjoy your lunch together, right here."

She's still in disbelief, as most everyone is when given the tour, but I keep moving. I lead her back into the game room and down the hallway situated along the left side of the house.

"The first two rooms on the left are our conversation rooms, where you can share private space and chat with friends. The last—down at the end—is our resident therapist Charlene's office.

She takes walk-ins until noon, scheduled appointments in the afternoon, and we have an after-hours number for emergencies as well."

"You have a therapist? Here, all the time?"

"Yes, and there's no charge. Follow me. I've got two more spaces to show you."

We head back to the game room and exit through one of the patio doors flanking either side of the fireplace.

"Here we have a playscape and in the summer we turn on the splash pad, which is everybody's favorite."

The boys get excited and run off toward the slides.

"Can they play here?" Samantha asks.

"Yes, it's fine. We'll be just around the corner." I continue to lead her to our final destination, traveling along a long walkway wrapping around the side of the house. We turn the corner and four prefab trailers come into view. All are tucked beneath the shade of a massive grove of heritage oaks. As we approach the trailer closest to us, its door swings open, and Megan steps out with a basket of linens on her hip.

"Hey, good morning," Megan says with a smile.

"Good morning! You're here early," I reply.

"Yeah, I had an appointment with Charlene today, so I figured I'd swap out the bedding while I was here."

"Thank you for doing that." I turn to Samantha. "This is Megan. She recently moved back home from Houston and volunteers with us a few hours each week."

"I'm Samantha. Nice to meet you." She moves the baby to her other hip, then reaches out her hand to shake with Megan.

"Nice to meet you. I hope you enjoy your tour." Megan moves down the path, and I grab the door to lead Samantha inside.

"And these are our zen pods." I sweep my hand around the room, showcasing my favorite piece of Bonnie's Place. "You can reserve one at any time and it is perfectly acceptable—and encouraged—for you to rest, whatever that means to you. You can sleep, borrow a book from the library to read in solitude, do a crossword puzzle, or even shower—whatever you need."

Samantha is stunned. Standing in the center of the trailer, she turns in a circle, taking it all in: the twin sized bed, the Bluetooth speaker, the white noise machine, the blackout curtains, the Keurig stocked with coffee and tea, the massage chair—all of it.

"This is incredible."

"Yes, it is. And it was all a gift."

"A gift?"

"Yup, from Megan's mother, actually. Come on, let's drop the boys off to play inside and grab a cup of coffee in the kitchen. I'll tell you all about it, if you have the time."

AVAILABLE NOW

**Looking for more from the *Women of Asher?*
Keep reading for a preview of Catherine's story!**

Two decades after divorce, high school sweethearts come together to learn how it all went wrong in the sweeping, romantic women's fiction saga, *When We're Broken.*

How many years apart are too many for a first—and only—love?

Catherine didn't just lose her father at sixteen: She lost everything. From her mother refusing to grieve, her brother distancing himself in all the worst ways, and her best friend abandoning her in her time of need, to becoming a social outcast amongst her peers—Catherine was buried beneath the rubble of her own life.

Meeting Glen—the arrogant, attention-seeking new kid from Chicago—was just the thing she didn't need, until he befriended her brother, and she was left wondering...*what if?*

From a whirlwind teenage romance to their escape into young newlywed bliss, neither foresaw how the impacts of trauma they didn't understand would lead to decades of longing: for each other, for the lives they were meant to lead, and for the people they were meant to be.

A southern, multi-generational story of love, loss, and life that asks: What happens when two people who can't be together—but also can't be apart—find each other one last time, after their scars are healed?

When We're Broken **is the second novel in the *Women of Asher* series, following Shawna Holly's debut novel, *The Stories We Keep*. Find it at all your favorite online retailers.**

PROLOGUE

The world bathes in a hazy orange glow, as the sun rises over rooftops, willow oaks, and loblolly pines. There's nothing extraordinary about this particular Alabama sunrise, other than the man I'm unexpectedly enjoying it with. It feels like it's been a lifetime since we've sat side-by-side on this rickety wooden swing. The last time I saw him, I was thirty-seven years old, and it's been twenty years...where has the time gone?

Glen places an arm around my shoulders and passes me a cup of coffee. Holding the warm mug in both hands, I push off with my bare toes, and the swing creaks as we rock back and forth, back and forth.

"So, what do we do now?" he asks, staring at slow-moving clouds.

"Aside from sleep? It's been a long time since I've pulled an all-nighter. I'm exhausted."

He smiles. "Yes, aside from that."

"First, I need to call into work. I'm too old to go in on no sleep. Then, I suppose we have to talk to Jenna. Tell her everything." The thought of it makes my stomach turn.

"She's not going to like it, Cat."

"She needs to know the truth about her parents. We've kept it from her long enough."

He sucks in a deep breath, then lets it out again. "Of course she does. I'm just sayin' she's not going to like it."

"Well, lucky for you, it's up to me to tell her." Reaching out to touch his cheek, I smile. "When I woke up yesterday, I never imagined that twenty-four-hours later, we'd be rockin' in this old swing on the front porch, watching the sunrise."

"Me neither," he says. "I honestly thought you'd throw things at me and slam the door in my face."

"No, you didn't."

"No, I didn't." He smiles again, then stands. "I'll let you rest. Call me later?"

I nod.

He kisses my forehead before descending the porch steps, two at a time, and climbing into that old truck. As he leaves, he swerves from one side of the road to the other, in pure joy—just as he used to, decades ago when we were so young and full of hope.

That afternoon, I call Jenna, telling her it's time she knew the truth about her father. Three days later, I fly to Texas, hug my grandkids goodbye as they embark on a camping trip with my son-in-law, and sit face-to-face with my daughter—wondering where I'm even supposed to begin.

I. CAFETERIA FOOD & MIDDLE FINGERS

1981

Mama lost both Daddy and John Lennon in a single week, providing my first introduction to grief. In my almost seventeen years on Earth, I'd experienced nothing like it.

There's something about witnessing a parent come undone that's disturbing to the core. Watching your life's anchor up-ended and tossed on the waves, carried away on the tide like it weighs nothing at all, brings doubts—and a primal fear—about *everything*.

Lennon was taken first. Mama sobbed on the sofa for three days. I felt her sadness in my bones, and they shook and rattled from the power of it.

Daddy went next, and she never shed a tear.

Four months passed, and I never saw her cry. My brother didn't cry either.

The tears were all mine.

———

When I sat my tray on the table, a familiar laugh traversed the cafeteria. Looking up, I saw Liza at the center of what was once my closest group of friends at that godforsaken school, in the-middle-of-nowhere Asher, Alabama.

Liza stood tall and pretty in lavender—her signature color—which perfectly complemented her golden-blonde hair and warm, peachy skin. She laughed again, and for a moment, I thought she may actually glance my way. Not daring to risk it, I cast my eyes back down, wincing at the shit-brown Led Zeppelin tee I opted for that morning and reminding myself it did my olive skin no favors.

"Hey—uh, I'm Glen." The unfamiliar voice saved me in the nick of time—just before I lost myself in the *my best friend ditched me* self-pity again.

Glancing over my shoulder, I saw a cute, but abnormally tall boy with somewhat shaggy, sand-colored curls hovering with a lunch tray. I nodded, turned back to my food, and poked a finger in the cold, rectangular cheese pizza.

"And you are?" he asked.

I let out my breath more forcefully than intended, and with a second glance, saw his shoulders drop. Realizing I'd hurt the feelings of the one person in the school who'd spoken to me in months, I replied, "Catherine."

"I'm the *new guy*, I guess. Can I sit here?"

"It's not my table. You don't have to ask permission."

He crossed to the opposite side and sat directly in my line of vision. Meeting his eyes, I noticed they were a dark shade of blue—like the deepest part of the ocean on a sunny, cloudless day. I felt my cheeks grow hot and re-focused on my tray.

"Thanks—I think?" He gave a funny look, like he'd never seen a girl be less than enthusiastic about being graced with his presence before.

God, he's one of those.

Even if I was wrong and he didn't expect every girl to swoon at his presence, I gave it till end of day for him to discover who I was and join everyone else in staying far, far away. Or worse, maybe he knew, and he'd been sent to my table as a sick, twisted joke.

I couldn't stand the thought of it. "I'm not hungry. Table's all yours." I grabbed my tray, dumped its contents into the trash, and tossed it onto the cart before exiting the cafeteria.

Liza's laugh followed me, bouncing from the walls and surrounding me, like a tornado surrounds everything lying motionless in its eye. I quickened my pace, seeking refuge from the storm.

Upon entering the musky library, I heard, "Looking for anything in particular today, Catherine?" Ms. Williams, the librarian, stared with eager eyes.

"Only a place to hide, as usual."

She looked at me with concern etched upon her bronzed, angular face. "Did you eat?"

"Lost my appetite." I blew my feathered, auburn bangs out of my eyes and looked down, noticing fluorescent pink gum stuck to the side of my clog.

"Follow me." She marched to the desk and reached for something inside a drawer. "This'll get you through." Sliding a granola bar and peanut butter crackers across the desk, she smiled, then grabbed a stack of books to re-shelve.

"Thank you."

With a nod, she headed for the romance section.

I snagged a tissue from a box and squatted, determined to handle the gum situation with discretion, before the kind librarian took notice.

Out of thin air, a pair of legs in blue denim, attached to feet in blue and white Osagas materialized. Looking up, his height, in addition to his also-blue tee shirt, brought forth childhood memories of *Gumby* on the television.

A giant, muscly Gumby. Only blue, rather than green, from head to toe.

I plucked the gum free and crinkled the tissue in my fist as I stood, knowing full-well there was no reason for that kind of boy to be in the library at lunchtime. "Are you following me, Glen?" I gripped that nasty wad of stranger-gum like my life depended upon it.

"No, but—do you *want* me to be following you, Catherine?" he asked in a mocking whisper, with a twinkle in his eyes.

Determined to provide zero ego strokes to the dimwitted oaf, I didn't answer. Instead, I dropped the tissue in the trash, grabbed the snacks, and set out to find a quiet place to be alone.

"Look, I'm not following you...and I thought you weren't hungry!"

Ms. Williams cleared her throat in warning.

"Shh! Jeez, this is a library, in case you're unaware!" I shout-whispered in his direction.

He took two long strides, stepping within normal library conversation distance. "I came because my truck's running rich and I need a book to fix it."

"I don't care enough to pretend I know what that means."

"It means the air-to-fuel ratio is—"

"I also don't care enough to *learn*." I pulled a book from a shelf and made my way to a beanbag in the corner.

He stood still, seemingly at a loss for words, which brought forth a tiny ember of guilt for not giving him the time of day. "Non-fiction's over there." I jerked my head, pointing him in the vicinity, then flipped to the first chapter of the book.

"Thanks. Nice meeting you." Then, he turned and mumbled, "I can see you're a lot of fun to hang out with," as he walked away.

Pompous ass.

And just like that, the guilt was gone.

<hr>

"Catherine, this is your stop."

I looked up to meet the bus driver's eyes in the long mirror, then out the window to the big green electrical box that was, indeed, my stop. Closing my book, I made my exit.

She shut the door behind me, then pulled away and stopped with a screaming squeal at the next corner. After tucking the book into my backpack, I started the walk home.

Traveling over dandelion-filled cracks in the sidewalk, I thought of how I used to make this walk with Bo—before Daddy died. Since then, given he was a sophomore with plenty of friends who drove, he rode with them to avoid being alone with me. I was a junior who rode the bus alone—pathetic, really.

Approaching the house, I heard the lawn mower before I saw it.

God, not again.

Mama pushed it up the incline of the yard, then pivoted and struggled to hold on as it rolled back downhill. At the bottom, she wiped her brow with a towel draped over her shoulder, looked up, and saw me standing at the bottom of the drive.

"Mama, you just cut that grass two days ago!" I yelled over the sound of the engine.

"Huh?" She cupped her ear and squinted her face. "I can't hear you! And if I shut this damn thing off, I'll never get it started again!"

I sighed and made my way into the house as she pushed that beast of a machine back up the hill.

"Why do you let her do that?" I asked Bo, who was sitting spread-eagle on the sofa watching a *Brady Bunch* re-run.

"Do what?"

"You should be mowing the yard, Bo, not her." I threw my bag on the table and pulled a grape soda from the fridge.

He shoved a handful of sunflower seeds into his mouth and changed the channel.

"Why do you think she's obsessed with the yard all of a sudden?" I asked him.

"Same reason she's obsessed with washing the car and winding the clocks, I guess. Now, shhh."

"And changing the lightbulbs, caulking the tub...She's never done those things before. Daddy always did—"

I gasped, as suddenly it all made sense.

Bo spit shells into a cup, then changed the channel again.

———◆———

"Haven't seen Liza around lately," Mama said, scooping green beans onto her plate.

"Neither have I," I replied.

"What's that about?"

"I don't know, Mama. Liza is Liza. She does what she wants."

"Have you had a falling out?" She plopped mashed potatoes next to her green beans.

I watched in horror as juice from the beans made direct contact with those heavenly potatoes. *Ruined.* "Not that I'm aware of." I focused on my plate, the wallpaper—anywhere other than the travesty of Mama's comingling of juicy and non-juicy foods.

"What she means is, Liza isn't the stick-around-after-your-best-friend's-dad-dies kind of friend," Bo piped in.

I threw my napkin at his face, honest-to-God wishing it were a coconut cream pie.

"Is that true?" Mama asked.

I cut a bite of fried pork chop and chewed slowly, hoping to choke on a piece of gristle to buy myself some time.

"Catherine, is it true?"

"Nobody knows how to stick around after something like that, Mama. It's not only Liza."

"Bo's friends still come around."

"Bo's friends are assholes who wouldn't understand tragedy if it happened directly to them, much less a friend."

Bo pointed his fork at me as the wheels spun in his head to compute a witty comeback. Instead, he shrugged his shoulders and took another bite.

"Watch your language at my dinner table, please."

"Sorry, Mama," I replied.

"We'll invite her family over for a barbecue," she said.

"And how would we do that? None of us know how to get the da—"

Mama shot a pointed glare.

"—dang grill started," I finished.

"Then I'll add that to my list of things to figure out," Mama replied. "Now, pass the salt."

The following Sunday, Liza, her younger sister, and her parents were in our back yard while Mama cussed under her breath, discarding unrecognizable carbonized chunks of meat into a garbage can she'd positioned next to the grill. She'd wait until Liza's parents weren't looking, then flip the burned portions into the can with a subtle flick of the wrist.

"Laurel, might I help?" Mrs. Mason asked Mama.

"What, you know how to—" Mama lowered her voice to a whisper. "—barbecue?"

"I know the basics. I can show you, if you'd like."

"Oh, please, Anna—show me!" Mama removed the elbow-length kitchen mitts she wore for fire defense and thrusted them toward Mrs. Mason.

Mrs. Mason held them like a dirty diaper, then set them on the beer cooler. "Your problem is your fire's too hot. See these?" She pointed to two silver dials. "When they're open, that's a lot of air getting in, and your coals are gonna get real hot. If you close them, halfway or even all the way, the temperature decreases."

"*Oh,*" Mama said. "I wondered what those doohickeys were for!"

Mrs. Mason laughed. "You'll have this down in no time."

"Catherine, fetch me another plate of patties, will ya?" Mama asked.

As I walked by, she tapped the trash can with the toe of her loafer and cleared her throat. I picked up Mama's *bin o' shame* and carried it inside and through to the garage, stopping in the kitchen on the way back.

The screen door slammed, and Liza entered. "They sent me to see if you need help."

"Sure, I guess." I pulled the bowl of seasoned beef from the refrigerator, then washed my hands at the sink.

Liza did the same, then we silently formed patties and placed them on a plate between us.

"How many do we need? Seems like a lot," she said.

"We better use it all." I grabbed another hand-full of the freezing cold mixture, rolling it into a ball.

"I'm sorry, Catherine," Liza said.

Smooshing the ball into its proper patty form, I placed it on the plate with the others.

She turned to look at me. "I've never lost anyone. I didn't know what to do—or say."

"For *four months?*" I blinked away the tears as best I could.

She hung her head and reached for another handful. "I'm sorry."

"Liza, you lead the group. When you turned your back on me, they all did. I lost my dad, my best friend, and every other friend I had—*in a night.*"

A tear rolled down her cheek, and she wiped it away with a shrug of her shoulder. "What can I do? How can I make it up to you?"

I turned toward the sink and washed my hands while she stared from behind, waiting for an answer I didn't have.

⸻

On Monday, I crept toward the cafeteria, dreading running into Liza. Mama often said I was wise beyond my years, but this wasn't something I could just forget and go right back to shopping for records and hoop earrings at the mall. Liza disappeared when I needed her most, and I didn't know how we could come back from that.

I fought my way through the hallway as people laughed and teased, complimented each other on their outfits, and coordinated after school plans. They talked about graduation and prom, their jobs, and on and on.

So much to talk about—and none of it involving a dead parent.

Eyes glued to the faded and scuffed red and white checkered floor tiles as I maneuvered around the crowd, I desperately wished to camouflage myself into the ecru cinder block walls and lockers. When I entered the cafeteria, I saw no sign of Liza. The clock ticked loudly on the wall as I gathered my tray and silverware, then waited for the line to move.

"Hi," Liza said from behind me.

I didn't answer.

"Can I sit with you?"

"Grilled cheese, please," I said to the whisker-faced lunch lady behind the glass.

"Same for me," Liza added.

Making my way down the line, I opted for fruit cocktail, corn, and chocolate milk. Liza did the same.

"Catherine, can I sit with you?" she asked again.

"Sit wherever you want."

She followed me to a table, and we sat facing the cafeteria doors. When the other girls entered, they smiled and waved at Liza, then turned to each other with whispers when their eyes landed on me.

"You see? I'm not some freak show, Liza. My dad *died*." I tore the rock-hard grilled cheese into pieces, just to have something to do with my hands.

"I know, and I'm sorry. Tell me what I can do, *please*."

I wanted to forgive her. I wanted my old friends back. I *didn't* want to be forever known as *the girl whose dad died*, and I knew it would be one long summer—and a hell of a senior year—if things didn't change. But things *had* changed, and there was no going back.

"I don't know, Liza. Not yet." I stood, noticing Glen leaning against the wall, surrounded by smiling, hair-twirling girls. After taking care of my tray, I retreated to the library—hoping Ms. Williams had more granola bars in that desk.

Exiting the bus, I again began my homeward journey alone. Just as I noticed a family of birds land on the telephone wire, an old truck in a stomach-turning hue of olive-green barreled past me. It reeked of gasoline and made such a noise, the birds and I both had an instinct to fly.

In the seconds it took to pass, a hand appeared from the passenger window, casually—but emphatically—giving me the middle finger. And I could swear that hand belonged to my brother.

I watched as the truck parked in my driveway and Bo climbed out. My stomach lurched and flipped in one lightning-quick motion when Glen exited the driver's side.

You've got to be kidding me.

When I reached the yard, I focused on the front door, hoping to avoid their attention.

"Oh, hey, *Library Girl.*" Glen popped the hood on his truck.

I trudged up the yard.

"Bo, you didn't tell me *Library Girl* was your sister," Glen said, head tucked beneath the hood. He lifted the bottom of his shirt to wipe a bead of sweat from his face and gave me a wink and a smirk as he did it.

My cheeks flushed and *hated* myself for it.

"Didn't know you'd met." Bo gave me a confused look I would've assumed was full of questions, if I thought my brother could think at all.

Entering the house to their amused laughter, I bounded upstairs to my room and flopped onto the bed. Staring at the ceiling and its layers of peeling paint—goldenrod yellow being the room's current color, then sea-foam green beneath that, then baby doll pink—I wondered what color Mama would choose next.

Why is he here?

And why did he rub me the wrong way, anyway? Was I annoyed because he expected me to fawn over him the way the other girls did? Or was I simply repulsed by him, physically?

A vision of that bare stomach flashed through my mind. *No, it certainly isn't that.*

Maybe it was being an outcast, with no one left to trust, that had me on edge—some ingrained sense of self-preservation. Every friend I had vanished when Daddy died. There's no way someone like *him* could be the one to look beyond what happened. Right?

The truck's engine revved twice, Bo and Glen exchanged *hell yeah*s, and I heard Van Halen blasting from its stereo speakers. And in that moment, I somehow knew that for better or worse, things would never be the same.

AVAILABLE NOW!

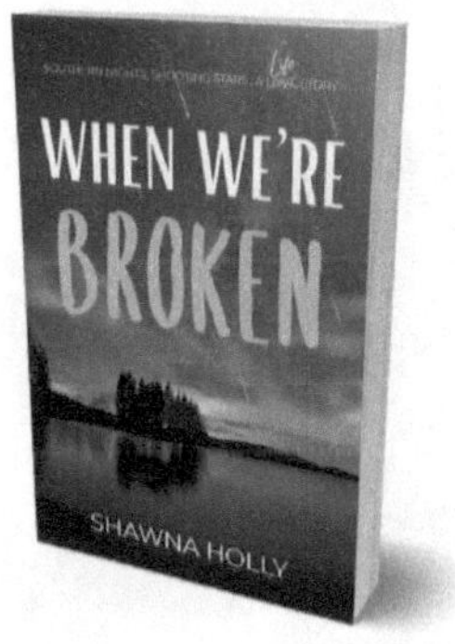

YOUR REVIEW MATTERS

The Stories We Keep is an independently published novel by a debut author. Your reviews through Amazon, Goodreads, and the retailer through which you purchased are meaningful and impactful. Please do take a moment to share your thoughts.

Thank you for supporting indie authors!

ACKNOWLEDGEMENTS

Thank you to my wonderful, encouraging husband for sticking with me through the terrifying process of learning how this writing and publishing thing goes. I couldn't have done it without you.

Thank you to my amazing beta readers, critique partners, and editors—particularly to Coco and Elisabeth. You two truly are my greatest cheerleaders and I love that you believe in this story as much as I do.

To my cover designer, Esther: You put up with so much from me and still have yet to block my email address. That's an honest testament to your level of patience and commitment to your work. Thank you for helping me to bring this story to life.

Finally, thank you to my tribe of friends and fellow mamas who provided feedback, volunteered to ARC read, and helped me find my way to the end of this story. We all need our sisterhood and I'm so lucky to call you mine.

ABOUT THE AUTHOR

Shawna Holly lives outside San Antonio, Texas, with her husband and three young kids. *The Stories We Keep* is her debut novel.

Prior to venturing into fiction writing, she served in the U.S. Air Force, worked as a government contractor, wrote a hyper-local blog focused on the beautiful Texas Hill Country, and owned a boutique web design and digital marketing firm (not all at once, of course).

When not writing, editing, publishing, or marketing, she can likely be found napping, over-caffeinating, taxiing her kids around town, procrastinating, or cheering at the baseball field.

Keep in touch at shawnaholly.com.

CONTENT WARNINGS

Direct:

— Mental Illness: Depression, Anxiety, Suicidal Thoughts

— Abandonment (though children remain with a parent and never perceive themselves as abandoned)

— Death & Grief

Mentioned Through Storytelling:

— Attempted Suicide

— Substance Abuse

— Infant Loss

— Divorce/Estrangement

— Loss of A Spouse

— Sexual Assault